ONE LITTLE MISTAKE

THE WESTBROOKS: FAMILY TIES

AVERY MAXWELL

xoxo,
Avery Maxwell

THE BEST OF US LLC

❈ Created with Vellum

This book is dedicated to The Luv Club! Thank you for being your amazingly-fantastic-selves, and thank you for believing in me.
All my Luvs,
Avery

A NOTE FROM AVERY

Lexi's story deals with the emotional toll of loss.

Having been on a similar path, this was a difficult story for me to write. I won't offer advice because I'm a firm believer that every person and every situation is different. What I will say is this: I wish I had talked about it.

When I was in the desperate despair, and heartache of it all, I wish I had opened up.

By dealing with it in private, I missed out on a wealth of support from some truly amazing people. Had I just said *I'm struggling*, I would have learned how common my journey really was.

Talk about it.

All my luvs,

Avery

"Family is what you make it, so make a good one." -Preston Westbrook

The Westbrooks: Family Ties is a spin-off of The Westbrooks: Broken Hearts Series.

The WESTBROOK FAMILY

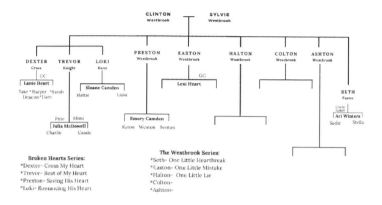

Broken Hearts Series:
*Dexter- Cross My Heart
*Trevor- Beat of My Heart
*Preston- Saving His Heart
*Loki- Romancing His Heart

The Westbrook Series:
*Seth- One Little Heartbreak
*Easton- One Little Mistake
*Halton- One Little Lie
*Colton-
*Ashton-

The Westbrook: Family Ties is a **spin-off** of The Westbrooks: Broken Hearts Series. If you're looking for Preston, Dexter, Trevor, or Loki's stories, you'll find them all in The Broken Hearts. Many people prefer to read these stories first.

Seth's story, One Little Heartbreak, is a bridge novella that connects the two series.

All books are available for free in Kindle Unlimited.

Happy Reading.

CHAPTER 1

EASTON

Eight months ago

"What?" I bark into the phone.

Caller ID tells me it's my older brother, Preston, but in truth, I would have answered the same way regardless of who it was. I'm a prick by choice; it keeps me safe. However, I acknowledge I may have taken it too far with my last assistant. It's why I arranged a hefty severance for her, even though she quit.

"Hey, sunshine. Do you always answer your phone like a Neanderthal, or is that a special greeting just for me?"

Preston is my oldest brother and has a circus happening around him right now. The fact that he's calling tells me he needs a favor.

"What do you want, Preston?" These are the times I miss having an assistant. Their job is to be my gatekeeper, even if it is my family. The only exception is my mother. No one fucks with Sylvie Westbrook.

"It's not what I want, asshole. It's what I have."

"I'm not in the mood for riddles. I'm swamped over here." My voice is flat with an edge of annoyance.

"That's what I'm calling for." Preston lets out a loud whoosh of air. "What happened to us, East? We used to be so close."

He's not wrong. Pres was my best friend growing up. Even though his three friends basically lived at our house, he never made me feel like the bothersome little brother. The five of us were a team. Then my friend betrayed me, my dad died, and it all changed. I changed. I don't know how to let them in, so I keep them all at arm's length. If my family knew the truth, they would never look at me the same. I don't want their pity, so I can't bring myself to take that step.

"It's my fault, Pres." In so many ways, he'll never understand. Feeling my neck tense, I knead it with my fingers. "I'm just trying to figure shit out."

"East? That's what I'm here for, man. Let me in so I can help."

His offer is tempting. So many times, I've wanted to come clean about what happened the day everything changed, but I'm too ashamed.

"It's just something I have to do on my own, Pres, but thanks. What is it you called for?" I ask, more gently this time.

He's silent, and I have to check the phone to make sure we didn't get disconnected. Then, finally, he sighs.

"Okay, but I'm here, brother. Whatever you need, I'm here. Don't wait so long … so long that I can't help you."

Something in his tone has me sitting up straighter. "Is everything all right, Pres?"

"Huh? Oh." He clears his throat. "Yeah, sorry. Anyway, I was calling because I have an assistant for you."

Oh fuck.

"Wh-What do you mean you have an assistant for me? If this is some ex-plaything you're trying to pawn off on me because you suddenly have a girlfriend, I don't want any part of it. My life is already a mess."

Preston surprised us last week with the news of not only a girlfriend but a live-in girlfriend. After spending his entire adult life living a bachelor, playboy lifestyle, we were all more than a little skeptical, but thankfully, Emory seems like a great girl.

"No, dickhead. It's Lexi."

It takes me a minute to place the name. Since I avoid family gatherings at all costs, it takes longer than it should. My mother sort of adopted Preston's childhood friends—Dexter, Trevor, and Loki. She hangs a stocking for them every Christmas since their childhoods were pretty fucked up. Lexi is the cousin of Dexter's new wife, Lanie. This is going to be a disaster.

"I don't know, Pres. That seems ... messy."

"No doubt. But here's the thing. Loki dropped her off here after rescuing her from her ex, Miles Black."

I let out a long, pained breath. Miles is bad news. He's part of a crime family Loki has worked for years to take down.

"How is it possible our lives are so entwined with Lexi's family? First Lanie, now Lexi?" I ask, but really it's a rhetorical question. We both know that road can only lead to Loki. And that means I can't turn this girl away.

"What's her deal?"

Preston's voice is uncharacteristically somber when he finally speaks. "I don't know all the details," he begins, "but she's in pretty rough shape. She's far too thin. She's barely eating or talking, at least to me. All I know is Loki needed to rescue her. Your guess is as good as mine as to what kind of hell Miles put her through, but she's family, East. We take care of ours."

He's right. We take care of our family, so he knows I can't say no. It's one of the first things our parents ever taught us. Family by blood and family by choice, it makes no difference. Once they're family, they're family forever.

3

Searching for my notepad, I ask, "What do I need to do?"

"She'll call you on Monday morning. Hopefully, she'll like you better than she does me."

"Wait, what? What do you mean? What the hell are you getting me into here, Preston?"

His chuckle ripples through the phone. "She seems to be the one girl I couldn't charm. We're like oil and water, and somehow, I ended up having her in a headlock about a month ago."

I sit back, stunned. Not because playboy Preston couldn't work his magic, but because apparently, she has spunk if they went head to head.

"She doesn't like you? Seems like a smart girl," I tease.

"She only thinks she doesn't like me," he says smoothly. "Honestly, we've had some kind of truce lately. But I think getting back to work would be good for her. It seems like Miles may have literally stripped her of everything. I just had my shopper bring her clothes because she showed up here with nothing. Nothing at all, East."

Preston is rarely serious, so his tone has me leaning forward.

"Are you sure she's in the right frame of mind to work? Does she know it's an executive assistant position?"

"I'm not sure, but she's extremely smart. She was the number one buyer in all of New England for a large department store until one day, everything just vanished. They blacklisted her overnight. I have EnVision Securities looking into it, but I'm willing to bet Miles was behind that, too."

Shit. "All right. Forget the call. Just tell her to be at my office by seven a.m., and I'll get her set up."

"Thanks, man. I'd hire her in my office, but I'm afraid we'll kill each other."

"And you think my sparkling personality will be a better fit? Jesus, Colton is fucking Peter Pan. His merry ass would be better suited to take care of her." I don't know if our younger brother, Colt, will ever grow up, but his heart is huge. *Unlike my blackened one.*

"I know, but Lexi is a stubborn piece of work who lets her pride run the show. Colt doesn't have any openings, and if she got one sniff of us making something up for her, she'd rip off my balls."

My bark of laughter is unexpected and has me choking on air. Finally composing myself, I try to speak. "Sounds like she might be right up my alley."

"Jesus, let's hope so. Lexi needs something to bring her back to life. Verbal sparring with me aside, she's a shell right now, and it's fucking miserable to see."

"If she can last longer than my last assistant, she'll be fine. Dealing with me isn't easy sometimes."

"No shit?" Preston remarks sarcastically.

"Whatever. I need to go. I have a shit ton to get done so I can head home for the night."

It's not a lie, but I won't go home until I'm nearly passing out. It makes walking into an empty house that much easier to handle.

CHAPTER 2

LEXI

*I*t's six a.m. I'm showered, dressed, and already on my third cup of coffee. I don't know why I let Preston talk me into this. I have only met his brother, Easton, a couple of times and never had much interaction with him. My cousin, Lanie, and her best friend, Julia, tell me he's misunderstood, but the few times I've seen him, I thought he was a grumpy asshole.

"Come on, Lex. You've dealt with much worse in the last few years. You can handle one grumpy asshat," I tell an empty room.

Peering around, I take in the apartment I've called home for the last few days. Technically, it belongs to our friend, Loki, but it's mine for now since he's out on assignment. I shudder, remembering how he could have died trying to rescue me. I don't know if the nightmares will ever end, but at least now that I have my own space I don't have to worry too much about my screams waking anyone.

My phone vibrates next to me, and I can all but guarantee it'll be one of the girls. Or both of them. Lanie, Julia, and I all grew up in the tiny town of Burke Hollow, Vermont. They, and my grandmother, GG, are the only constants in my life. Glancing down, I see I'm right.

Lanie: Kick butt today at work, chica! Luvs!

Julia: She means kick ass and take names. You've got this!

Julia: Luvs.

Their confidence in me is comforting, but it doesn't shake off my nerves.

Lexi: Thanks, guys. Luv you both.

Julia: Just throwing this out there ... East is pretty hot! (winky face emoji)

Lexi: He's also a known asshole. I named him the Westbrook Beast after the dinner at Preston's house.

Lanie: They would look so cute together, wouldn't they?

Jesus Christ.

If they knew what I've been through, they would understand. My heart isn't up for grabs, and it won't ever be again. My boyfriend finder is broken beyond repair. Or maybe it never worked to begin with, since I've only ever chosen losers.

Lexi: Don't start. That isn't an option. Not now, not ever. The last thing I need is a grumpy asshat who couldn't even fake a smile at his brother's house.

Lexi: Plus, do you not remember my choice in men almost got me killed?

Now would be the perfect time to tell them what else Miles took from me, but I can't bring myself to do it. How do you explain that a lifelong dream was physically ripped from your body, or that you can never be whole again? I'm empty. Barren. They're just starting their lives and families. I know I can't take the pity they're sure to feel for me, so I lock down my private pain. *Act tough, Lex, and eventually, you will be.*

Lanie: ...

Julia: You can't blame yourself for Miles. You couldn't

have known, but I will say this: both Lanie and I found love when we had sworn it off. You never know when it will strike.

Lexi: I do. Never. Love is a choice, and it's one I'm choosing not to make again.

Lanie: Oh, Lexi. It's cute how you think you can control it.

Lexi: Whatever. I have to get going, or I'll be late. Luvs.

Lanie: Luvs.

Julia: Kick his ass. Then maybe kiss it better! (Winky face kissing emoji) Luvs!

I don't respond because Julia has no filter. Her responses will only get worse if I encourage her. Instead, I pack up the lunch I made and head out the door, only to run face-first into a human wall.

"Leo," I grumble. Ashton, the youngest Westbrook, decided I need to have round-the-clock security. Freaking Ash. The only reason I didn't argue is I'm pretty sure he does some messed-up shit with super-spy Loki.

Leo is my day guy, and his job just got boring as hell. Realizing I never asked him what he would do all day while I sat at a desk, I stare at him.

"Something wrong, Ms. Heart?" His voice always sounds so clinical.

Tilting my head to the side, I observe him. "What are you going to do all day?"

"What I do every day, ma'am. Watch over you."

"Oh, hell to the no! Do not call me ma'am." I jab my finger into his chest as I speak. "I'm not old enough for that shit. For the last time, it's Lexi. Call me Lexi or Lex. Jesus, even 'girl' would be better than ma'am."

He doesn't answer. The only acknowledgment I get is a quick nod of his head as he steps out of the way so I can lock the door. This is going to be a long day, and I already feel a migraine coming on.

8

We climb into the car, and the driver takes off. My girls married into some rich ass families, but I begrudgingly admit they're amazing. I will never say that to Preston, though. I'm having a hard enough time separating them and their money from the wealth and cruelty I knew when I was with Miles.

Leaning back, I close my eyes, but the car pulls to a stop all too quickly, and I hear Leo exit the car.

Well, shit. The commute took less than five minutes. Leo opens my door, and I force myself to exit. I'm not sure what I expected, but the building before me emblazoned with 'The Westbrook Group' was not it. Maybe it's because Preston always presents himself as the playboy. Surely, he's doing something right if he is keeping a multi-billion dollar corperation running successfully.

Maybe I'm not giving the guy enough credit. Lanie told me Preston recently rebranded Westbrook Enterprises into The Westbrook Group to better encompass the partnership with his brothers. If they can rebrand something like that, there's no reason I can't reinvent myself to be the best damn assistant Easton Westbrook has ever seen. *Right?*

With Leo shadowing me, I make my way to the security desk and check-in.

"Welcome, Ms. Heart. You'll be on the twenty-first floor. Your badge will allow entry from the elevator." The guard is a sweet, older man whose name tag says Sam.

"Thank you, Sam."

He smiles kindly, and I'm on my way, not at all sure I'm ready to deal with the Westbrook Beast.

The elevator dings as it comes to a stop. Taking a deep breath, I exit the car and glance around, confused. The place is empty and dark. With tentative steps, I inch forward. Ever since Miles held me captive, I've struggled with dark, enclosed spaces, and I hate myself for it. I should be stronger, so I force myself forward.

9

"I'm safe. This place is safe. Leo is right behind me," I silently chant.

"Ms. Heart?" Leo's voice calls out from behind, causing my heart to stop.

With a fist on my chest, I turn. At least he appears to feel bad for startling me.

"You are safe, Ms. Heart. They locked this building down tighter than Fort Knox. I believe Mr. Westbrook's office is to the left."

"Th-Thank you, Leo."

He smiles and ushers me forward. As I round the corner, light spills out into the hallway from a single door at the end. Stealing a breath, I force myself forward, not really sure why I'm so nervous. Reaching the open door, I raise my hand to knock when a deep masculine voice cuts me off.

"Glad to see timeliness is a priority. Come in."

I can't tell if he's being an ass or genuinely complimenting me, so I keep the sass to myself. Entering the room, I realize he has yet to look up from his desk. *How the hell did he know I was here?*

"I have excellent hearing," he states, finally lifting his gaze to mine, and it knocks the air from my lungs. Fighting to keep my face neutral, I swallow, forcing the trapped air to leave. His voice softens for the briefest moment when he says, "You are always safe here, Ms. Heart."

"Thank you," is all I say. I don't need Easton Westbrook becoming some arrogant Prince Charming. Been there, done that.

He narrows his eyes as he considers me. Then, as quickly as it came, the warmth in his voice evaporates. "I expect a lot from my employees. I'm here every day at five-thirty a.m. working out in the gym because that's when I work through most of my problems. HR told me I could no longer force my employees to be here that early, but I will require you here by seven a.m. Monday through Friday. We work long hours."

The way he's glaring at me, as if I'm a charity case, makes me insane. My inner bitch is rising, and the longer I stare at his stupid, scowling face, the more I want to set her free.

"I'm not afraid of hard work, Easton." My indignation is showing, and I make no attempt to hide it.

I swear his lip twitches before he locks it down into the firm, straight line I'm thinking is forced.

"Right. I know we are in the precarious situation of having a connection outside of work, Lexi." He says my name as if testing out a new hot sauce, and it makes me smile. "But Mr. Westbrook will suffice here in the office. I have a laptop and phone for you. A desk will be here in a couple of days, but you'll sit in that general vicinity." Easton gestures across the room.

Is he fucking kidding me with the Mr. Westbrook bullshit? He might be worse than Preston. I glance behind me to where he's pointing, then back at him and take in his office for the first time. It's not what you would expect from his surly demeanor. The room is almost warm. The colors, much like the rest of Westbrook Group, are a mix of navy and gray. The furniture is a rich brown with intricate detailing that can only come from a human hand. On the bookshelf are photos of him with his family and drawings made by small children.

Seeing the drawings and paintings, presumably made by Lanie's new stepson, Tate, causes an ache deep in my chest. I tear my gaze away before I drown in my sorrow.

"Um, the furniture. They're exquisite in the craftsmanship. Were they made locally?"

Easton stares at me curiously, then sinks into his chair. He never takes his eyes off of me, and it makes me uncomfortably warm. Having reactions like this is dangerous, and I know it, so I plead with my body to cut the shit. As if he can read my thoughts, he smiles.

"They can't get much more local than this. I made them in my garage," he states proudly.

My mouth gapes open as my fingers roam absentmind-edly over the scrolling details on the armrest.

"Y-You made them?"

"I'm very good with my hands, Lexi."

I work to swallow my reaction with a new determination and vow not to let this man get to me. Men are my enemy; they have to be. He, Easton Westbrook, has to remain an enemy.

"I'm sure you are, Mr. Westbrook," I reply, barely avoiding the urge to roll my eyes. "Where is the desk for your last assistant? Surely that one's fine."

CHAPTER 3

EASTON

*F*uck!

What the hell do I say now? There's no desk since my last assistant sat in a conference room because she annoyed the hell out of me? That my reaction to you is unsettling with the need to keep you close?

How do I explain that when I heard Lexi's guard promise her she was safe, something inside of me broke? I have excellent hearing, but I overheard their hushed conversation because I was standing at the end of the hallway. Needing a moment to sit with my reaction to her, I tiptoe ran back to my desk. I've been sucking in huge gulps of air while I wait for her to arrive in a lame attempt to calm myself down.

I haven't been this tripped up since … since *her*. Almost ten years later, I still can't say her fucking name. I'm so pathetic. She really did ruin me for all things good. It reinforces my need to keep sexy Lexi far, far away. *No, dick weed, not sexy Lexi. Not sexy, Lexi.*

Glancing up, I realize I've been silent for too long. *Get a grip.*

"Ah, the last assistant preferred to work in the conference room, so I didn't have a desk for her. Obviously, that didn't work out. I need you close." The truth in those four words has the muscle in my jaw so tight I feel the veins in my neck throbbing.

Beautifully inappropriate are the two words on the tip of my tongue, but I bite them back. Staring at Lexi, I recognize the vacant, haunted look in her eyes. Forcing my gaze to move anywhere but on her, I put my asshole hat back on.

"As I said, seven a.m., not a minute later. You are not my gofer, and I don't expect you to fetch coffee. We have interns for that. However, there will be details of the job that are confidential, so I'll need you to sign an NDA with HR before you begin. I don't ask for things twice, and I expect you to learn my routine and step in to make my day easier without getting in my way."

"So, you go through assistants like underwear then?"

My head whips toward her. "Wh-What?"

"Well, Mr. Sunshine, how long are you able to retain assistants before they quit?"

Six weeks, but I'm definitely not telling her that. "I compensate my employees well for their hard work."

"Hmm, yup. Just as I thought. What's your record? Four weeks? Maybe five?"

What the fuck? I stare at her, lost for words.

"Don't worry, East. I've already been to hell and back. Whatever bullshit you throw at me will be a walk in the park. So, should I head to HR so we can get started with your precious NDA in place?"

"I … ah, d-don't you want to hear the r-rest of your duties first?" I stammer.

She rolls her eyes and I feel my lips twitch.

"Listen, I need a job. You could tell me to clean the toilets, and I'd have to do it. I'm not so proud that I can't admit that. Whatever you're going to throw at me will get handled. I'm used to hard work, and I'm a fast learner. I'm stronger than I look."

With that, she rises from her seat. "Where's HR?"

As she turns, I see what Preston was talking about. Lexi is probably one of those women who is just naturally thin. Her height gives her a statuesque quality, but she's frail. A knot forms in my gut. *Why do I hate the idea of her hurting so badly?* Because she's family adjacent? That has to be it.

Realizing I'm still staring, I clear my throat. "Ah, yes. Catherine in HR is who you'll be looking for. I asked her to come in early today, so she should be waiting for you on the seventeenth floor. It'll take a couple of hours to go through all the paperwork, and when you get back, we'll dive right in."

"Sounds good. And, Easton?" She tosses her blonde hair behind her as she squares her slender shoulders.

I know she's testing me, so I force myself to hold eye contact with her, and I nearly swallow my tongue. She's beautifully broken, and I have no right wanting to take her in.

"Yeah?" I force out.

"Thank you. I'm sure you hired me out of some misplaced obligation, but I appreciate it just the same. I've always worked hard, and I'll prove that to you. In another life, I graduated in the top two percent of my class at Northeastern, then climbed the ranks of the largest department store on the East Coast until I was the top buyer in my field. So, I'll do that here, too."

I nod because words are lodged painfully in my throat. "Just come back here when you're finished, and we'll get started."

My southern manners kick in, and I rise to walk her out. When Lexi turns to leave, her hand unconsciously runs along the detail work I spent hours perfecting on the lines of her chair. Somehow, that one small gesture seems more dangerous than the one-night stands I occasionally allow myself.

As soon as she's out the door, I flop down into my chair. What the fuck was that? And how in the hell is this going to work?

For the next hour, I attempt to get work done, but Lexi's eyes haunt me. When I finally acknowledge I'm being useless, I pick up the phone to call my youngest brother, Ashton. He runs our Cyber-Security department here at The Westbrook Group, but I know he also does some shady shit with Loki in whatever secret government agency he spies for.

"Hey, East. What's up?" Even as he speaks, I can hear the clicking of the keyboard and know he probably has four different screens running right now. Ashton is the genius in the family and has more potential than the rest of us combined. He's also a gentle soul. He's good and kind and everything I'm not.

"I need to know what happened to Lexi," I bark with no preamble.

Ashton's loud sigh has my stomach turning in uncomfortable ways. The sudden silence on the other end of the phone makes the breath I was holding catch in my lungs.

"I can't do that, East."

"Why the fuck not?"

"Loki asked me not to. Just because I can get information doesn't mean I always should. Her story is hers to tell. Miles took more from her than any of us will ever be able to understand. Why are you interested in Lexi?"

Throwing my pen across the desk, I spit, "She's working for me now."

"She's the complete opposite of Lanie," he says cryptically.

"What does that mean?"

"Neither of them have had easy lives, but where Lanie tries to keep the peace, Lexi sets the fires. I think she'll be a good addition for your grumpy ass." His laugh forces a smile to my face.

16

I roll my eyes, even though he can't see. "So what the hell am I supposed to do with her?"

"I don't know her well, but I can tell you, if you treat her any differently than you do your other employees, she'll hand you your balls for breakfast."

For some reason, that makes me chuckle.

"But, East? She's been through a lot."

"So treat her like everyone else, or like she'll break? Which is it, Ash?"

An audible intake of air has me glancing up.

"If you're talking about me, I can tell you straight up that no one will ever break me again." The frigid tone lacing Lexi's words has me hanging up on Ash without a second thought. "Listen to me very closely, Mr. Westbrook. I'm digging myself out of hell right now, there's no way around that, but my work ethic has never been up for question. All you need to concern yourself with is if I can handle your workload, not if I'm going to break. That's no one's business but mine. And, in case you're wondering, I can fucking handle anything you want to throw at me. So the next time you want to question if I'm capable of something, fucking ask me. Not Ash, not Lanie, me. I will not allow anyone to speak on my behalf ever again. Is that understood?" Flames could shoot from her ears at any moment and it wouldn't surprise me one bit. Lexi Heart is pissed off, and her ire is directed at me.

Leaning back in my chair, I don't know if I should be impressed or angry. My lack of response seems to infuriate her more, and even though it shouldn't, her anger turns me on. Quickly grabbing a folder and setting it in my lap, I glance back at her frowning face. "Is the paperwork with HR complete?"

Instead of answering, she tosses the folders she's carrying onto my desk. At this moment, I know everything between us from now on will be fire and ice. It's a battle I'm far too excited about.

Slamming my hand on the folder before it lands on the floor, I lift an eyebrow at her. Lexi stands there with her arms crossed, a defiant expression plastered on her face.

"I'll take this as a yes. Pull up a chair. For now, we'll be sharing my desk. The first thing you need to understand is I'm your boss. Family or not, I'm your superior." I try to ignore the sour taste the word family causes in my gut.

"That's not a problem, trust me." Lexi of earlier is gone. The woman standing before me is all business.

"The second thing is I don't have enough hours in the day to get all the shit I need to do done. So when my brothers call to go to lunch, I'm busy. When they pop in to waste my time, you usher them along. The only one allowed to interrupt my day is my mother. Otherwise, keep the gate closed."

She studies me for a moment but pulls up a chair just the same. Before she can sit, I stand and cross the room to where I have files and folders stacked four feet high and grab about thirty of them. As I turn, I bump into Lexi, who apparently followed me.

"What's all this?"

Handing her the stack in my hands, I say, "Torture. These are the misplaced, mislabeled, disorganized mess we need to sort through if I have any chance of securing the south block in uptown."

She glances down at the files, then to the floor. "Explain to me what you're doing and how you need the files, and I'll take care of it."

For the next twenty minutes, I explain how we're trying to acquire South Block C to revitalize the area. I show her the projects where Macombs is attempting to undercut my bid, but I don't reveal the long history between Dillon and myself.

"So, basically, there's thirty years' worth of information

that you need to be organized in a timeline so you can put together a proposal that will win over the city board and the owner?"

This woman flusters me, and I can't even hide it. I expected to waste at least three days catching her up to speed, yet she's four steps ahead of me. Realizing I'm staring like a lovesick puppy, I finally reply, "And I have until Friday at noon to hand over my proposal."

"Working with the Macombs is out of the question?" Lexi asks innocently, but I recoil as if she set me on fire.

"It's never even part of the fucking equation. The Macomb family has taken the last shot at me they're ever going to get. I don't lose, and I don't ever lose to them." My voice is deadly, but if it affects her, she doesn't flinch.

To my complete shock, I watch as she removes her shoes, rolls up her sleeves, and sinks to the floor next to the pile. "I'll need a little time to get organized," she says without looking up. When I don't move, she lifts her gaze to meet mine. The pain I see reflected in her startlingly blue eyes cuts deep, and my instinct is to reach for her. "Ah, I thought you said this was urgent?"

Swallowing thickly, I nod and turn away. "Yeah, it-it is."

"Then get to work and stop hovering."

Glancing over my shoulder, I misstep and almost crash into the chair. *Did she really just order me to get to work?*

"You're staring."

"You're a bi– bossy. You're bossy."

Lexi doesn't acknowledge me, but I swear I see her smirking behind the curtain of blonde hair.

CHAPTER 4

LEXI

*R*olling my neck from side to side, I realize I've been sitting on the floor for … Jesus, I don't even know what time it is. Carefully, I lift piles of folders off the floor in search of my phone. Easton left a while ago for a meeting, and honestly, I was thankful for the silence.

The first hour went by in a blur, both of us working on our assigned tasks, but when the office started filling up for the day, Easton went from grumpy to an all-out asshole. There wasn't a single please or thank you that left his lips all morning. God help anyone who actually entered his office.

The air shifts, and I know without seeing him Easton is back. Seconds later, he barks my name.

"Lexi? What the fuck are you doing?"

His harsh tone puts my defenses on high alert. "What does it look like I'm doing?" I snap. "And do you swear at all of your employees, or am I just the lucky bitch?" Yeah, I know he almost called me a bitch earlier. It wouldn't be the first time, and I'm sure it won't be the last. I'm better off acting the bitch than appearing weak.

East seems flustered for half a second before he's crossing the room with purpose. "It's three o'clock in the afternoon."

"What?" I search the room for a clock, but still don't know where I put my phone. "No, it's—"

Easton reaches down and hauls me to my feet. I want to yell about him manhandling me, but his powerful hands on my body are my first taste of safety I've had in months, and I swallow my words.

When he stands me up, I realize my foot has fallen asleep, and I wobble in his strong grasp. Holding me at arm's length, Easton glares at me. "Have you even moved from this spot?"

Yanking myself free, I put some space between us. "What the hell has crawled up your ass and died? You said this was a priority." I gesture toward the now neatly stacked piles. "You said you were in a time crunch, and you needed this done. It's done. All organized for his Royal Assness."

"Royal Ass ... what? What do you mean it's all done? There's no way."

"The files date back to 1972. I organized them by year, then by town, and then again by street. You didn't exactly give me much information to go on, so those were the three things most of the files had in common. It seemed like the only way to make any sense of what was in each one."

Easton blinks slowly. His nostrils flaring are the only sign that he isn't as composed as he's leading me to believe. Eventually, he breaks. Placing one hand low on his hip, he uses the other to rub his temples. "You've been sitting there on the floor for seven hours?"

"If it's three, then I guess so. Nice to see you passed second-grade math." Turning my back on him, I shift things around, still searching for my phone.

"Did you eat lunch?" His tone is accusatory, and I feel my spine tighten.

"I'm not hungry."

"Well, guess what? We're going to be here a while, so you need to eat. What do you like?"

Whipping around, I snarl in his direction. "First, I said I

wasn't hungry. Second, I brought a salad. Third, I really think you should see a proctologist and get that stick removed. It's so far up your ass, I can't figure out how you're able to bend."

Laughter I recognize fills the room. *Fucking Preston*. Now I have to deal with two rich assholes.

"Did you need something, Preston? Apparently, one of my jobs is to keep everyone away from his Royal Assness."

"You do realize that I'm your boss, right?" Easton asks. If he's expecting an answer, he'll be waiting for a long time.

"Preston?" I snap. "Did you need something?"

When Preston leans against to doorframe and smirks, I search for an escape.

"Fine, you stay and talk to your brother. I'm going to the bathroom, and then I'll find a place to eat my ..." Turning in a circle, I find Easton inspecting my Tupperware.

"What is this?"

"It's. A. Salad," I say through clenched teeth.

He pops the lid as Preston watches. "This is lettuce. Where's the rest of it?"

"I didn't realize lunch inspection was part of this job." The snark in my voice is masking my inner turmoil.

Easton walks my salad over to the garbage can and tosses the entire thing.

Preston chuckles. "I'll come back later."

"Go to the bathroom, or whatever it is you need to do, and then we're going to lunch."

I go to argue, but he cuts me off.

"Lexi, I'm starving, and I need you to talk me through the files. I'm sorry I threw your lettuce away. It was brown, slimy, and wilted. You couldn't eat it, anyway."

"You're lucky I need this job so badly, or you would have found those files in the shredder."

Easton rolls his eyes, but I don't miss the corner of his lips twitching, either.

"Are you always this difficult?"

"Are you always this bossy?" he shoots back.

"As a matter of fact, I am."

"Well, this should be interesting then because you haven't seen difficult yet, Lexi."

He places a hand on the small of my back to guide me out of the room, and I know from this one, innocent gesture he can never touch me again.

CHAPTER 5

*B*y the time we finish lunch, Lexi has given me the highlights as she could gather them, and it's after six before we leave the Italian place I love. I hate to admit I was disappointed to watch her push the food around her plate. Who doesn't love Italian food?

One comment she made keeps coming back to me.

"It's almost like the files were purposefully disorganized."

I'd come to the same conclusion on the last project I went head-to-head with Macomb on, and it's setting off all kinds of red flags. Working with Lexi will be a special kind of torture, but perhaps it's exactly what I need. She may hate me for reasons unknown, but I have no doubt she's loyal to family.

After dropping Lexi off at her apartment with Leo in tow, I head home. I'll need to talk with her sooner rather than later, but for now, I have to think, so I head to my workshop —my happy place. The one space where everything always makes sense, and I get to work on sexy Lexi's desk.

It smells of sawdust as I pull back the bay doors, and though I should, I don't bother stripping out of my suit. I can picture her so clearly—clean lines with iron accents in the warmest shade of gray. *Stoic with a touch of sadness.* The thought makes me pause. Am I describing the desk or the woman?

It takes me no time to sketch her and choose the perfect grains of wood. By the time I step back, my suit is beyond repair, but I don't give a shit. I'll need to talk to Brian at the mill for the iron detailing I have in mind, but he should be able to get it done by the week's end. I'll pay him enough that it becomes his priority.

The sense of accomplishment I achieve here in my haven isn't like anything else in my life. If things had been different, this might have been my world. I might have been happy.

~

y alarm goes off at four-thirty, just as it does every day, but I'm already awake. After tossing my suit in the garbage last night, I showered and climbed into bed around two a.m. Sleep is an elusive bitch most nights.

I toss back the covers, slip into a pair of gym shorts, grab my suit, and head down the stairs. My morning routine is the same every day. The coffee is streaming from the pre-programmed Keurig, and the muffins Alice, my housekeeper, made are wrapped in the fridge.

Thanks to my mother and a team of decorators, my house is homey, but it's not a home. No life happens here. A home is where I grew up with lots of noise, love, laughter, and support. I always thought I would have the same thing, but life had other plans. Dillon Henry had other plans, and it irrevocably changed my life.

I fucking hate thinking of my ex-best friend. It always leads to my ex-love. Having lost my appetite, I chuck the muffins back into the fridge with more force than necessary, grab my coffee, and head out the door. A few miles on the treadmill will clear my head and help me figure out how to handle the mystery that is sexy Lexi.

Entering The Westbrook Group at this ungodly hour always puts me at ease. Dad and I used to come here to work out before school. It's a hard to break habit, but truthfully, it's the one connection to him I still allow myself.

When the elevator stops on the top floor, I'm surprised to find all the lights on. I know Preston didn't come in early. That dick can't function before ten a.m. Maybe Halton?

"Hello?" I call out just as Lexi exits the woman's locker room dressed in workout gear unlike anything I've ever seen. Whoever created spandex and crop tops is both my hero and my worst fucking nightmare right now. She's gorgeous.

Stop staring, East. Suddenly, I wish I had grabbed the muffins after all. I blame my mother and her food-pushing ways for my inexplicable need to feed this girl.

With a hand on her hip, it accentuates the legs that go on for fucking miles. She's built like an athlete, even if her muscle tone has diminished. Lexi makes a show of glancing at her watch. "You're late."

"I'm ... what are you doing here?"

"You said you get your best work done here, right? You have a deadline, and I'm here to help you. It seems like the logical solution since time is running out. Plus, my grandmother is coming to visit. I need to get into shape to deal with her meddling ass. So, where do you want to start?" Her posture says, 'don't fuck with me,' but there's a vulnerability about her I can't quite figure out.

"You're going to work out with me?"

"Yes."

"As in, you want to do my workout with me?"

She taps her foot in annoyance. "Are you dense? If we're

tag-teaming the equipment, we can make the most of our time here."

"I'm running ten miles today," I tell her so she can reevaluate her plan.

"Fine. Let's go." She marches to the treadmills that face out over the ocean. Everyone thought my dad was insane wasting the top floor of this building on a gym, but this is where he did his best thinking, too.

I eye Lexi skeptically. It's not that she isn't in shape. It's that her body looks frail, and I'm nervous about her pushing herself to prove something.

"Are you sure you're up for this?" I ask, as delicately as my gruff exterior will allow.

That was the wrong thing to say. I have a feeling I'll do that a lot around her.

"Easton, I was a division one athlete. I haven't run in a few months, but I can guarantee I'm no shrinking violet. I can do anything you throw at me in here."

I don't believe her, but give her credit for trying. Stepping onto the machine to her left, I see she has her phone set to record. She's all business as her machine comes to life.

Twenty minutes in, I'm struggling to keep up with Lexi's pace. Thankfully, we're on treadmills, or she would have left me in the dust, but I refuse to slow my pace. She runs beside me with rapid-fire questions, never once losing her breath.

By the time we hit ten miles, I've caught her up to speed with every aspect of the project—everything except Macomb's involvement. As she walks to the mats, I notice a slight limp, and I feel like a dick.

"Are you okay?" I ask, nodding toward her leg that she's now stretching on the foam roller.

"Yeah, it's fine. I tore my hamstring my senior year, and it acts up sometimes."

"What did you play?" I ask, already moving toward her.

"Basketball." She lies back on the mat, and I move into position without thinking.

Dropping to my knees between her legs, I grab her ankle and knee and move them gently toward her chest. It's a stretch I know will help, but she tenses at my touch.

"Shit. Sorry," I mumble, suddenly way too aware of how inappropriate I'm being.

"It's, ah—"

"This is an injury I know well. I just ... I just thought I could help. We have a trainer that works here and has had to stretch me out more times than I want to admit. Can I ... can I help you?"

She inhales sharply, and I get the sense that accepting help, in any form, is not easy for her. Her bottom lip catches between her teeth as she nods. I shouldn't be staring at her mouth when I'm hovering above her like this, and if I don't get my shit together, she'll have a very big case for sexual harassment.

Straightening her leg, I shift so I don't embarrass either of us, and fold her knee into her chest again, holding it for a count of ten.

"You're really flexible." *What the fuck is wrong with me?*

"Yup."

Her eyes go wide and I realize I'll probably have to speak to HR about this.

Taking her leg, I place the back of her knee on my shoulder and lean into her. Whoever came up with these stretches must have been into some sort of tantric sex or something. Danny will never be able to stretch me out again without me remembering what Lexi looks like beneath me.

"Well, well, well. What do we have here?" my brother, Colton's, teasing voice comes from behind.

Lexi flinches and manages to knee me in the face in her hurry to escape my grasp.

"Fucking hell, Lex."

"Oh, shit. I'm sorry."

Colton's laughter gets louder as blood pours from my nose. *Jesus Christ.*

"I have a hamstring injury from college," Lexi explains.

"You don't owe him any explanations," I grumble while ripping my shirt over my head to hold against my nose.

"You know, we have a trainer who would be more than happy to help you with that, Lexi. And he has actually gone to school to know what he's doing," Colt ribs.

Now I have to fire Danny.

"Nah, I'm fine. I just haven't exercised in a while. I-I'm going to get cleaned up. East, your first appointment is at eight-thirty. I'll see you down there."

She runs from the gym so fast I'm surprised I don't see sparks trailing behind her.

"That was … interesting."

"Don't fucking start with me, Colt," I say, pushing away from the mat.

"The view at the gym just got a whole lot better, don't you think?"

"Cut the shit, Colt. I know what you're doing."

Leaning against the wall, he observes me. "Do you? What am I doing? I'm just making small talk. You're the one who was getting cozy with Lexi-con."

"Lexi-con? What the hell are you talking about?"

"I don't know. She seems like a force of nature that's about to knock you right on your ass."

"Fuck off. I've got shit to do." I'm so tempted to tell him about Macomb and Dillon, even when he's being an ass. Of all my brothers, Colton's the first one to have your back no matter what, but seeing his shit-eating grin pisses me off, and I storm off to the showers instead.

I'm trying to get the memory of Lexi and her long fucking

legs out of my head when I'm suddenly thrown back and I land on my ass with a thud. It takes me a minute to realize what the hell is going on. I'm covered in slimy, sticky … saran wrap?

Colton, gasping for breath, has me tearing at the shit covering my upper body so I can kill him.

"You saran wrapped the fucking door, you imbecile?"

He's doubled over laughing his ass off, so he doesn't see me charge. I drop my shoulder and barrel into him, knocking him back onto the mat. Using my knees, I pin his arms down and want to strangle the fucker.

"You're twenty-seven goddamn years old. When are you going to grow up?"

Colton bucks his hips, trying to throw me, but it's Lexi's voice that causes us both to pause.

"What the hell is going on?"

Colt and I both turn toward the sound. Her brows are lifted so high it's almost comical. In slow motion, I glance around at the shitshow she's seeing. I'm still half-covered in the saran wrap that Colton clotheslined me with, and it leaves a trail from the locker room to the stretching mats.

Shoving off Colt, I shake my head while he's laughing so hard he has tears streaming down both cheeks.

"Y-You should have seen him hit the ground, Lexi. It was the funniest thing I've seen in a long time," he gasps.

"What if one of our employees had come in here first, asshole? You know what kind of lawsuit that would have ended in?"

"No worse than one for groping an employee," Colt fires back, but his eyes gleam with mischief as he glances at Lex.

"Are you two ten years old?" she huffs.

"Colton is," I bark. "Fucking Peter Pan over here thinks he's the king of practical jokes."

"Wait until you see the video," Colt whispers to Lexi, and I've had my fill.

Storming off to the showers, I flail my arms as I enter the room, ripping down the remnants of his immature prank. Just as I round the corner, I hear Lexi's laugh for the first time, and it sucks the air from my lungs. I haven't spent twenty-four hours with the girl, and she already has me unraveling. The thing is, I can't decide how to feel about that.

CHAPTER 6

*W*ednesday morning went much like Tuesday, except I avoided stretching until I was in the locker room. Easton is far too dangerous up close and personal like that. Colton is quickly becoming my favorite Westbrook brother, but that could have more to do with the fact that he annoys the hell out of the rest of them. I like the way he makes them squirm.

The afternoon went by in a whirlwind of growls, grunts, and all-around displeasure. The softness Easton exuded on the mats in the gym yesterday was gone before we got to his office, and he only got worse from there.

By Thursday afternoon, I was ready to kill him. I'm not making any friends in the office, and that's all because of Easton, too. Everyone's scared of him, and by extension, they avoid me like the plague—everyone except Mason, who has gone out of his way to befriend me.

"Hey there, gorgeous." Mason's eyes glint with trouble I can see coming a mile away. He never misses the chance to make Easton unhappy.

I'm leaning over a table in the outer office, organizing the last of the files Easton tossed my way late last night. I've found I get more work done out here since I still don't have a desk and work better where I can spread out.

"Hey, Mason."

"What are you doing out here?" he asks playfully. Everything about Mason is striking, right down to his perfectly coiffed hair. Secretly, I'm a little jealous.

"It's either this or share Easton's desk, and that's not happening," I grumble. He doesn't need to know that I'm struggling to keep my equilibrium around our boss.

"Pfft. That asshat hasn't gotten you your own office yet?"

"My own office? Why would he do that?"

Mason's grin turns devilish, and I don't know if I should fear for myself or for Easton. Before he can cause any more trouble for me, though, I cut him off with a question.

"Why are you so comfortable around East? You don't tread water with him like everyone else does."

That grin is back, and I think Mason might be one of my favorite people ever.

"Because I grew up with that overgrown caveman. He's been my best friend since we could walk. There's not much that man wouldn't do for me and vice versa, but someone has to give him shit if we're ever going to get the old East back. I've made it my personal mission to be that guy." He eyes me for a moment too long before continuing. "But you, my dear, might give me a run for my money in that department." He winks just as Easton's voice bellows through the open door.

"Lexi?" The deep, hoarse timbre of the sound nearly knocks me on my ass as I turn to face the office.

"Keep your pants on, East. I'm busy with our new girl here," Mason yells back.

"You're going to get me into trouble," I hiss, and even though it goes against every bone in my body, I follow the sound of Easton's command.

"You know, if you stopped yelling, your throat wouldn't be so raw."

"Was Mason giving you a hard time?" Easton barks.

"No. He's actually one of the few that will talk to me."

"He … what do you mean? Are you saying my employees are unhelpful?"

"No. I'm saying you're such a tyrant they hide before I can get too close."

He scowls, and I wait for the tongue lashing, but Mason's bark of laughter has us both glancing at the open door. Mason retreats with his hands raised before Easton can say anything. If he doesn't fire me for swearing, Mason will surely get me fired with his special brand of crazy.

Easton doesn't miss a beat, and the second Mason's out of earshot, he starts barking orders. But I've made it my mission to always be three steps ahead of him.

"I need the—"

I toss two folders onto his desk.

"But the meeting—"

I set down the rest of my stack with enough momentum that the air stirs up the papers on his desk.

"You *need* the files in chronological order. You *need* the financials on every transaction for each building on that block for the last fifteen years. You *need* your travel information updated because you have to leave in," I check my watch, "forty-five minutes to meet with the Douglases' who are in New York and not returning before they leave for Europe. You *needed* all this shit an hour ago, but I couldn't get it to your grumpy ass because I'm still digging out of the mess your last assistant had going on. It's also nearly impossible to get anyone around here to help because you're such a pain in the ass they're all afraid they'll catch your wrath, so you're getting it now."

He sits back, possibly stunned. Definitely pissed, but not saying anything, so I take it as a win.

"Have you always sworn at your bosses?" he finally asks.

"Yes, when they're unbearable assholes."

"I need you to come to New York with me."

I gasp audibly. That isn't what I was expecting at all, and I feel my body tense involuntarily. Being in the south has been a needed distraction from life, but going to New York is as good as being back in Boston. Memories I've happily repressed for the last couple of months fight to break the surface of my self-imposed walls.

"For what?" The snark is so deeply ingrained that it pops out when I really want to say, 'Please don't make me.'

Instead of answering, Easton lifts a random folder. "Building #432 on Charles Street East. What are the specs?"

"It was last purchased in 1994 by Richard More. The bank foreclosed in 2001, and it has sat empty after multiple sales fell through. The historical society has its claws in it, making it difficult to turn over due to their restoration guidelines."

Easton almost smiles. His lips shift before he tamps it down, but I see it in his eyes. He's proud of me, and as much as I hate how that makes me feel, my body preens under his approval.

"That is why I need you with me, Lexi."

"You're very needy, Easton."

Standing, he places his hands on the desk and leans forward so we're almost nose to nose. "I pay you to anticipate those needs, Lex." His voice is dangerously low and causes a shiver I fight to hide.

Hating the reaction he elicits from my body, I force my inner bitch forward. "I believe I've already proven, *Easton*, that I do that better than anyone."

His eyes focus on my lips as I speak, and my tongue darts out to wet them of its own accord.

"You two look cozy," Preston jokes as he enters the office.

"Doesn't anyone fucking knock around here?" Easton growls while holding eye contact with me.

I fight the urge to fidget and focus on Preston instead. "How's your girlfriend?"

Preston stumbles, but catches himself quickly.

"Emory's great. Living together is the best thing I've ever done." His words sound truthful, but he seems surprised by them, too.

I glance back and forth between the two brothers, and I'm surprised when the ribbing I'm expecting from Easton doesn't come.

"Lexi, we have to leave soon. How long will it take you to pack?"

"Where are you going?" Preston volleys between the two of us.

"New York," Easton answers while both men stare at me. They have this uncanny ability to see through me, and it's unnerving.

"It'll only take me a few minutes to pack a bag. Preston, did you need something?"

Preston stares at me with kindness and pity, and it makes me want to throat punch him.

"I was just coming to tell you that Ash said we could ease up on your security detail. He doesn't believe you'll need it, but if you're going to New England, then—"

"She'll be fine," Easton interrupts. "Lexi will be with me the entire time."

The testosterone in the room is overwhelming. "Well, if the two of you are done planning out my life, I'll just go home to pack." I storm off, but not before hearing the beginning of their hushed conversation.

"What are you doing, East?"

"I'm trying to work."

"That's not what I mean, and you know it. Why did Mason tell me you've moved Lexi into your office instead of giving her one of her own?"

Preston may drive me fucking nuts, but his protective

streak is admirable, even if I don't deserve to be on the receiving end of it. Pausing just outside of the door, I wait for Easton's answer.

"Fucking Mason is a gossip. I don't come to your office and micromanage how you run things, so don't come in here and do it to me."

"East, listen, Lexi's struggling," Preston says under his breath. "For once, can you not be an asshole?"

"She's stronger than you give her credit for, Pres. You asked me to hire her, so I did, but I'm not going to hold her hand while she figures out her shit. We all have shit. Either she does the job I need, or you can find somewhere else for her to work."

And here I thought Preston was the asshole. Easton just took the top spot for the King Prick award.

I've heard enough. Hastily, I turn to go and run right into a smiling Mason.

"You're getting under his skin, gorgeous. It's about time someone did. Keep it up. You might just find the real Easton we've been missing all these years."

I have so many questions I want to ask, but a noise from the office has me shuffling past him in an attempt to escape.

"*W*hy the hell are you tattling on me to Preston?" Mason doesn't even pretend to be offended.

"I wasn't tattling, you toddler. I was informing—there's a difference. He asked how Lexi was doing. Honestly, if he hadn't told me he had a live-in girlfriend suddenly, I would have thought Preston had a thing for our Lexi girl."

"Don't call her that," I growl with enough venom to knock him back a step or two.

Instead of reacting, though, Mason gives me a knowing smile.

"I thought so."

"You thought what, Mason? What is it you think you know?"

"Why don't you want me to call Lexi our girl?"

"You fucking know why," I grind out.

"It didn't bother you with Alana or Emily or Mikaela."

"They were my assistants."

"So is Lexi."

"I …" Fuck, he's right. "Yeah, well, she's also family." Even I don't believe the shit that's coming out of my mouth.

"Why doesn't Lexi have a desk yet?" he asks, glancing around the room, but I know he's fishing. Mason has known me since grade school. He was there when Dillon fucked me over, and he knows where I go to hide.

"It's not ready yet," I answer while packing up my laptop. If I get out of here quickly, maybe I won't have to answer any more of his questions.

"We have a storeroom full of desks, East. Do you want me to have one brought up?"

He knows.

"No. I don't."

"Why would that be?" He smirks.

Sighing, I plop down into my chair. Mason is a goddamn dog with a bone sometimes.

"Because I made her one. It'll be here tomorrow."

The admission renders him momentarily speechless.

"You made her one?"

"That's what I said. Could you not make a big deal about it? She's going through a tough time, and … I don't know, Mas. I was inspired, okay? Is that what you want to hear? That she inspired me, and I finished the damn thing in one night?"

He narrows his eyes. "What else did you make?"

Jesus. Why do I keep this guy around? When I turned my back on everyone in my life, why the fuck did I let this asshole stick around?

"A chair."

"And?"

"Fine, I made an entire damn set, okay? Freaking sexy Lexi and her mother fucking six-mile legs inspired me, and I made her an entire set of furniture. Then I moved onto bedroom furniture, and I really don't want to fucking talk about why that is. Just leave it alone, Mason. She's broken … I'm broken. She's family and—"

"You take care of your own. I know that credence well,

39

my friend. Why do you think I'm still here after all these years? It's certainly not because of your rosy disposition or because you're a barrel of fucking laughs anymore. But, for the first time in a long time, I see potential in you, Mr. Westbrook. And, as your friend, I won't let you screw it up."

"There isn't and won't be anything to screw up, Mason. Trust me when I say Lexi doesn't even like me half the time."

"Maybe if you stopped being a dingle dick, she'd see all there is to love about you."

"Does Johnny know you whisper sweet nothings to me like this?" I tease. Mason has been with Jonathon for almost a year, but the guy rubs me the wrong way.

"His name is Jonathon, and he's very comfortable with our friendship, East. Plus, he's met you. No one in their right mind would willingly enter a romantic relationship with your grumpy ass."

I ignore the twinge of pain that little jab causes.

"Listen, East. You know I love you, but there's something about Lexi, and you know it."

"What are you talking about?"

"What happened in the copy room this morning?" Mason counters, and I have to pause to think about it.

"I have no idea." And truthfully, I don't.

"You said thank you to Michelle from accounting. It's all over the office today."

I'm beyond confused. "What the hell are you talking about?"

"When was the last time you spoke to anyone in this office, let alone thanked someone?" If Mason's eyebrows raise any farther, they'll need their own zip code.

"I'm a fair boss, Mason. I'm not a complete asshole." I don't expect him to believe the words since I can barely say them with conviction, but he doesn't fight me.

"You are. You're also an asshole that people hide from.

Either Lexi is taking all the fight out of you, or you're softening for her. I have my suspicions, but time will tell."

I keep my back to him while I pull the last of the files I'll need and stick them in my bag. I don't want to admit that there is something about Lexi that makes me want to let down my guard, and I'm not surprised Mason sees it. Instead of making any acknowledgments, I focus on getting to New York.

"I'm meeting with Douglas in New York tonight. I have to get out of here to grab Lexi on the way to the airport."

"Easton?"

Turning, I see my friend with the kind eyes and an easy smile.

"Yeah?"

"You're not broken. Sometimes life bends you a little to get you on the right path. I have faith in you, or I wouldn't still be here."

Clapping him on the shoulder as I pass, I swallow the lump in my throat. Fucking Mason. "Thanks, Mas. I'll let you know how things go with Douglas."

~

"Where are we?" Lexi glances around the private airfield, and I realize she's not nervous—she's fucking scared out of her mind.

Placing a hand on her forearm, I try to reassure her. "We're at Wilson Air Center. It's a private airport where we keep one of the smaller company planes. Are you okay?"

"What? Yes, of course I'm fine. I guess I wasn't paying attention. Why arc you staring at mc like that?"

"Lexi ..." My voice is soft. Too soft, and I feel her defenses rising. "You look like you've seen a ghost."

The car rolls to a stop on the tarmac, and she uses the

41

opportunity to escape. As she's opening the door, I catch her arm, and she instinctively rips it away from me.

"I said, I'm fine," she hisses. Once out of the car, I see her taking deep breaths through her nose.

Moving to her side, I want to comfort her, even if I don't fully understand what's going on. But Lexi has other ideas.

CHAPTER 8

LEXI

Gawd, Lex. Get your shit together. I feel Easton's large presence at my side, and no matter how much I try to rein in my fear, it grabs hold and doesn't let go. Feebly, I rub my palms up and down my pant leg, trying to rid them of their clamminess.

"Lexi?"

Easton's voice sounds as if he's in a tunnel, and somewhere I recognize I'm having a meltdown, but cannot move my feet from this spot. The sweat beads on my upper lip, and I grip my elbows at my side, making myself as small as I can out here on the tarmac.

"Lexi?" Easton tries again.

I blink rapidly, trying to bring him into focus, when I realize I'm gasping for breath.

"Fucking hell, Lex. I've got you. Okay? Can you handle getting on the plane, or is that what's causing your fear?"

My fear. My fear. No … I can't let Miles ruin me like this.

"I'm fine. I said I'm fine." My voice is so shrill I flinch at the sound, causing Easton to envelop me in his arms.

"I know you're fine, Lex." Placing an arm under my knees and one around my back, he lifts me like an injured child.

43

My body responds to his contact, and I can't control the tear that slips free.

East cradles me to his chest as he stands at the bottom of the stairs that lead to the plane. "Can you fly, sweetheart?"

Words escape me, so I nod and allow myself ten more seconds of comfort. Nine more seconds in Easton's arms. Eight more seconds of being cared for. Seven more seconds of safety. Six. Five. Four more seconds of calm. Three more, and I breathe him in. Two.

Halfway down the aisle of his plane, I push against his chest, and he sets me down. Without a word, he ushers me a few more steps. Reaching around me, he opens the door to a bedroom.

"I'll be right out here, but there's a restroom and bottles of water through that door."

Swallowing as razor blades slice me from the inside out, I manage a gritty, "Thanks," and slip past him.

Closing the door behind me, my chest heaves as emotions I can't control wrack my body. Finding my reflection in the mirror, I wonder who this girl is. This girl staring back with ashen skin and hollow eyes is unrecognizable. Splashing water on my face, I will myself to behave.

Knock, knock.

"Lex? Can I come in?"

This is a nightmare. I haven't even been working for the Westbrook Beast for a week, and I've already blown it. What the hell is he going to tell everyone? I don't get to answer him before I hear the knob turning behind me. With downcast eyes, I wait.

"Turn around," he orders. *What a prick.* "Please," he finally adds.

Slowly, I turn to face him but can't quite reach his eyes. When he remains silent, I cave and lift my gaze.

There is something so intentional in the Westbrook stare. They all have it with their perfect ocean blue eyes. I've seen it in Preston and Ashton. Mrs. Westbrook has perfected it, but when Easton turns that look on me, my inner turmoil goes up in flames. How can one look, one penetrating, heat-searing gaze take away all my pain?

"Is that the first time you've ever had a panic attack?" His question confuses me, and it takes a herculean effort not to snap at him. "I'm sure some psychiatrist somewhere would frown on this, but it's the best I can do given our circumstances."

He holds up a bottle of Belvedere and two shot glasses. I stand frozen to my spot, waiting for him to drill me with questions about my outburst, but they never come. Instead, he waltzes past me and sets the two shot glasses on the counter as the plane begins to taxi.

"Don't we need to be seated? Buckled? Something?"

Glancing over his shoulder, Easton smirks, and it makes him appear so young. And so fucking sexy. If I weren't still reeling from what he's calling a panic attack, my body would be in heat.

"When you own the plane, you get to make a few rules of your own." His cockiness is new, but not at all appealing. Okay, maybe a little appealing, but I tamp that shit down quick.

I roll my eyes at his bravado but take the shot he hands me, and I knock it back. Instantly, the burn warms me, so I hold the empty glass out for another. He eyes it curiously but smartly doesn't fight me.

"I'm not a lightweight, Easton. I won't get blasted and embarrass you at this meeting. I know how much it means to you and the WB."

Leaning against the counter, he smiles. "The WB? Sounds like you've been hanging out with Mason."

"Yeah, well, he's the only one who'll talk to me, and he's not scared of the Westbrook Beast like everyone else."

Easton's deep roar of laughter fills the small space, and it

45

takes me a minute to understand his reaction. My body is beginning to relax and chooses this instant to turn a flaming shade of red.

"Th-The Westbrook Beast, huh? That's a new one. Usually, they just call me an asshole. Someone's getting creative."

I bite the inside of my cheek until I taste copper to keep from spilling the beans that I gave him the name. My silence gives me away, though, and his laughter erupts anew.

"Lexi," he coos, "am I really that bad?"

No!

"Yes. You are," I lie.

You may not be Miles, but you're just as dangerous to my heart.

His smile fades, and I feel terrible.

"Do you want to talk about what happened out there?" he asks, changing gears so fast I have whiplash.

"Not particularly. Do you want to discuss the worst days of your life with your boss?"

He's silent as he observes me, then finally shakes his head. Holding up the bottle, he asks, "You good?"

"Yeah, I'm good. Thanks. I'm just going to freshen up if that's okay?"

Easton places a large arm on my shoulder, and the heat sears my skin through layers of fabric.

"Take your time, Lex. We have a couple of hours before the meeting. I'm going to get some work done in the cabin."

There's something in his eyes that makes me believe he understands my loss, but we'll never find out. My loss will weigh heavy on my soul until the day I die, and no one will ease that burden. I won't allow them to. It's mine to carry, and it's mine to bear.

The rest of the flight is mercifully uneventful, and we arrive at the Four Seasons in New York's Tribeca neighborhood with plenty of time before our meeting.

"Easton?" I hiss as he exits the car ahead of me. "I cannot

46

afford to stay here." I'm broke. I grew up poor, and all those old insecurities rear their ugly head. Unfortunately, I'm not in a position to care. It's better to embarrass myself in front of East than get to the counter and not even have a credit card to check in with.

He stops mid-stride, causing me to collide with his very muscular back. Turning, he removes the aviator sunglasses covering his beautiful eyes, and I catch Cartier engraved on the arm. Of course he has Cartier sunglasses.

"You know, you could get a knock-off pair of sunglasses for twenty bucks, and no one would ever know. You could probably feed a small village with the amount you paid for those."

Easton stares at the sunglasses as if he'd never given them a second thought. He probably hasn't.

"First, the company pays for your room, your food, and all expenses you accrue while traveling. Second, I do, in fact, feed multiple villages all over the globe, and that's in addition to my expensive sunglasses," he adds with a hint of snark. "If you must know, Lexi, these were my father's. You should also know that I will never feel shame for what my parents blessed me with. My brothers and I work too fucking hard to be anything but proud."

I don't know much about his father, other than they lost him too soon, but the fact that Easton can make me feel like a turd nozzle should be a giant red flag to keep my walls high. Even as he takes me down a notch, though, I find myself closing the distance between us. Then he opens his big, fat, stupid mouth.

"If you can stop thinking about the cost of things on my body for two seconds, can you manage to run the numbers with Mason one more time before we leave?" He doesn't wait for a response, so I'm left standing there, mouth agape, watching him take long strides to the hotel receptionist.

Thinking about things on his body? *Ugh, as if that's what I'd—*

Easton turns and points me out to the lady behind the counter, and all rational thought leaves my head. Holy hell. I like fighting with Easton. I enjoy being near him. I even like it when he gives me shit. Crap, that might be my favorite part. Oh, mother of mercy, I like Easton Westbrook.

Rooted in place, I watch as he converses with the hotel employee. *Lock it down, Lex.* Nothing good can come from catching feelings for a Westbrook.

"Ready?"

"Huh?" I glance up to find Easton in front of me again. *Jesus, Lexi. Get your shit together, girl.*

Easton squints like he's trying to figure me out. *Yeah, good luck there, buddy. I don't know who I am these days, so you're shit out of luck.*

"I asked if you were ready? Our room is ready."

"Oh, yeah." I take a step to follow, then realize what he said. "Wait. Room? As in one? Are you kidding me? Are you some kind of power-hungry pervert? I'm not sleeping with you just because you're my boss, you asshat."

East grabs my elbow with an almost painful grip. "Will you keep it down, Lexi? Jesus Christ, you've worked for me for less than a week, and you're already trying to ruin my reputation?"

Wrenching my arm free, I spin on him as we wait for the elevator. "Well, what am I supposed to think, huh, Easton? You said room, singular. Is that why you can't keep an assistant?"

His growl causes goosebumps to appear on my arms.

"Lexi, I know you don't know me well yet, but has my family given you any goddamn reason to think we're a bunch of fucking creepers? Ever?" he seethes.

"No, but there's always one in rich families like yours."

He takes a step toward me. "Be very careful about how

48

you label us and who you lump us in with, Lexi." The elevator doors open, and Easton shoves our suitcases inside. As the doors slide closed, he stalks me into the corner. "I don't know what kind of assholes you've spent your time with, but let me assure you, we are not them. I. Am. Not. Him."

Our bodies are so close I can feel his chest rise and fall with each angry breath. In my heart of hearts, I know Easton is a good man. Instinctively, I know the Westbrooks are all good people, but I'm a bitch. Anger is easier to deal with, so once again, I embrace it.

"I guess we'll find out," I hiss as the doors open.

"Un-fucking-believable." He grabs both of our suitcases and exits the car. Even pissed off, he's still a gentleman. I walk a few steps behind and admire how his body moves and his muscles bunch with the effort of dragging our bags. At the end of the hallway, Easton opens the door, and I pause just outside.

Glancing over his shoulder, he finds me stopped and rolls his eyes. Shoving the door wide open so I can see, he lets the bitterness saturate his words. "It's a fucking suite, Lexi. We each have our own room, but we also have a dining room and an office to get some work done. This is how I travel because I work long hours."

His jaw clenches. I think it might be his tell. Something in that statement wasn't the whole truth, but as he glances at his watch, I know we have to get moving, so I let it go for now.

"Fine." I stomp past him, grabbing my suitcase on the way by, and enter a suite so luxurious I almost trip over my bag as it drops to the ground.

What kind of alternate universe did I just enter? Greeting us in the foyer is a fully suited butler standing to the side of some life-size art display. My feet shuffle forward as I hear Easton enter behind me.

"Oh, hello. I'm sorry, Martin?" East leans forward to greet

the man with a firm handshake. "I told the front desk we won't be needing your services this trip."

The older man smiles like he's heard this a hundred times before.

"Very well, sir. Should you change your mind, just press zero on any hotel phone, and it will connect you directly to me. Would you like me to unpack you before I head out?"

My head whips to Easton. He does not pay someone to unpack his suitcase. *Does he?* East notices my expression and smirks before rolling his eyes.

"No, Martin, that won't be necessary, but thank you."

Martin nods and exits the way we came.

"Before you get any ideas, the answer is no, I do not pay people to pack or unpack for me. Preston probably does, but it's not my style."

"You guys are all wealthy beyond anything I can comprehend." I don't mean to say it out loud, but standing here in the Empire Suite, it just slips out.

"We are. But here's the thing, Lex. You can't take it with you. Some day we will all die, and we'll pass our money on to the next generation. My parents raised us to be good men first and foremost. When we're gone, people won't remember what we spent our money on. They'll remember how we treated them—how we helped them. They'll remember the people. Money makes things easier in some ways, sure, but it isn't everything."

"Yeah, I guess not." I glance around, trying not to let my naivety show, but I feel his eyes on me. "Ah, you said there's an office? I'm going to locate it and give Mason a call. What time do you have to leave?"

Easton doesn't answer me, so I turn to find him leaning against the wall, eyes blazing a hole through me.

"We, Lexi. We need to leave in an hour. We're meeting them a couple of blocks from here."

Shit. I had hoped he would leave me behind, but I'm quickly learning nothing with Easton is as I expect.

"O-Okay. I'll be ready." Turning on my heel, I leave Easton standing in the foyer.

CHAPTER 9

EASTON

*L*exi takes over the office, so I spread out on the dining room table. No matter what I do, I can't focus on anything but the expression on her face as I lifted her into my arms. I need to shake these feelings because this deal is riding on my ability to sell it to Mr. Douglas. I can't allow myself to be preoccupied with my assistant.

Grabbing a bottle of scotch from the bar, I pour two generous fingers before replacing the cap. Fucking Lexi would give me shit about the cost of this drink, too, I'm sure. Imagining the fight we would have causes me to smile, and my pants become uncomfortably tight.

What the fuck is wrong with me? Deciding I need someone to give it to me straight without rubbing my nose in it for years to come, I grab my phone to text Halton. Halt is the one brother even less interested in bull shit than me.

Easton: What are you up to?

Halton: What do you need?

Easton: What makes you think I need something?

Halton: You're texting me. I'm not really known as the brother you reach out to shoot the shit with.

Fuck. He has me there.

Halton: Ash and Colt are here. Ash wants to know how Lexi is?

Great. So much for not blowing my cover.

Easton: She's fine.

(Halton added Colton to the conversation)

Colton: Has she ripped off your balls yet?

Easton: Fuck off.

(Colton added Preston to the conversation)

Preston: Hey, fuckwads. What's up?

Halton: East texted to say, "hey."

Preston: ...

Colton: He's with Lexi in NYC.

(Colton added Ashton to the conversation)

Preston: East. What did I tell you? Lexi's hurting right now. She's off limits.

Now I'm pissed, and I can't explain why.

Easton: Don't I fucking know it. How the hell am I supposed to help the girl if no one tells me a goddamn thing about her?

Ashton: It isn't our story to tell, East. But I think you guys have more in common than you realize.

Preston: Ash, you're fucking scary with the intel you hold, you know that, right?

Halton: Not that I don't love my phone blowing up with this bullshit, but was there an actual reason you texted, East?

Easton: Nothing important. I'm meeting with Douglas tonight. Make sure you have the financials locked down, so when he's ready to sign, we can move forward.

Halton: Already done.

Colton: Have fun with Lexi-con.

Easton: Don't call her that, you moron.

Preston: Remember what I said, East.

Easton: I have to go. Talk to y'all later.

I go to turn my phone off just as a new message from Mason pops up.

Mason: Don't drool.

What the hell is this idiot talking about now?

Before I can reply, Lexi comes out of the guest room dressed in a pale blue sheath dress that matches her eyes. It hits a few inches above her knee, and although it's perfectly professional, it's sexy as hell.

"Ready?" She hardly spares a glance in my direction as she loads up some files into the bag she has tossed over her shoulder.

"Ah, yeah. Yeah, I'm … Were you able to get everything done with Mason?" Attempting not to check her out, I can't help but wonder how long it took her to get ready. She's looks fucking fantastic, so now I'm a little worried Mason didn't update her.

Sensing my unasked question, she straightens her spine before answering. "Yes, *master*. Mason and I went over all the essential details while I was getting dressed."

"I thought he was going to video conference you to show you the latest slides?"

"He did, Easton. In case you've missed this in your twenty-plus years of friendship with him, Mason is gay. He couldn't give two shits if I were running around half-naked."

"You were naked on a work call with Mason?" I yell.

"Like the day I was born." She grins, and I realize I have no idea how to tell if she's fucking with me or not. "Oh, for crying out loud, East. I'm not an idiot teenager. Of course I wasn't naked on a company call that is likely recorded."

She's right. We do monitor everything through a program our friend, Trevor, designed. I start to breathe easier, knowing Mason didn't see her rack before I did.

Wait. *Before* I see her tits? What the actual fuck is wrong with me? She's an employee. She's family. I cannot see her goddamn tits. Her next words bring my thoughts to a screeching halt.

"We FaceTimed so I could get ready while he explained the changes. You can thank him for this dress. I wanted to go with a black one, but Mason said this one looked better."

I'm going to kill him. Don't drool—that asshole.

"Great. Glad to know we put his insanely high hourly rate to good use. Are you able to walk in those shoes, or do I need to call the car service to drive us two blocks?" I have to drag my gaze away from her shoes, or I'm going to end up doing something I'll really regret. Like fucking her up against the window for all of Manhattan to see.

The mere fact that those ideas are running through my head before this meeting tells me all I need to know about tonight. I'm fucked.

"Yes, Beast. I can walk. I may appear broken to you, but something you should know about me? I'm a fighter. If my feet were bleeding from blisters and it was the difference between getting you this deal or taking off my shoes, I would get you the goddamn deal."

Somewhere in my gut, I know her words to be true.

"Never put anyone else's needs above your own comfort or safety, Lex." My voice is quiet but firm. Knowing how stubborn she is, the idea of putting herself last tears at my chest because I get the feeling that is how she's lived her life. It's probably why she found herself in such a fucked up situation to begin with, and it makes me murderous.

Standing at the door, I wait for her to exit. When she finally comes toe to toe with me, a vulnerability she fights so hard to hide breaks free.

"Is … is the dress not okay, Easton? I can change. It won't take long. I just wasn't sure what to wear, and Lanie wasn't answering her phone. Mason offered to help because I was probably freaking him out a little."

What was it she called me? The Westbrook Beast? Some-

55

how, that seems too nice for me. So, swallowing my feelings and my gut instincts, I say what I should have said in the first place.

"Lexi, you look stunning. I was … I don't know what I was," I say, running a hand through my hair roughly.

Following her into the hallway, I make sure our door locks behind us.

"Mason knows you pretty well." Something in her tone sets off warning bells.

"Oh, yeah? Why's that?"

"He said you'd lose your shit when you saw me in this dress. And then he said you'd apologize for being a lunatic and tell me how nice I look."

Sexy fucking Lexi sashays down the hall toward the elevator, and I follow like a trained monkey.

Opening my mouth to speak, I'm interrupted by the strangest sound. Cackling is the best way to describe it, but it takes me a second to realize it's coming from Lexi's handbag.

Rolling her eyes, she takes out her phone.

"Freaking Julia changes my ringtone to my grandmother laughing every chance she gets," she explains. "I have to answer, though, or she'll call in reinforcements. Ever since I went mis– ever since some stuff happened, she worries."

Nodding in understanding, I gesture for her to take the call while pressing the elevator button.

"Hi, GG."

"Well, well, well, if it isn't my little Locket. How's it going there, missy?"

Curious, I glance over at Lexi and see her smiling into her phone. An older woman I have only met once sits smiling on the screen. Preston has warned us about GG and her meddling ways, but I haven't seen them in action.

"You haven't called me Locket since high school, GG."

"Damn straight. That's the last time you locked yourself

away from me. It took well over a year to find you, but I did it then, and I'll do it again."

Lexi shifts from foot to foot, and I can tell this conversation is making her uncomfortable. When she angles her body away from me, I know it's true, so I take out my phone to pretend I'm not listening.

"I'm not locking myself away, GG. I'm in New York for work."

There's silence on the other end, and I covertly sneak a glance in Lexi's direction. Finally, GG speaks.

"Lexi Mae, I raised you. I know you better than anyone on the planet, and I know when you're shuttin' down. Remember what I told you back then?"

"The toughest job I'll ever have is lovin' myself," she sighs and the weight of her emotion sits heavy in my chest.

Lexi's voice wobbles, and every caveman instinct I never knew I possessed attempts to beat on my chest. I physically fight the urge to wrap her in my arms, and I don't know how to process these feelings. I've never reacted this viscerally to another person. Not even with Van—

"That's right, Locket. That cockamamie asstrigger, Miles, may have knocked you down, but he didn't break you. You're a Heart. We bend, but we don't break."

Jesus, that's almost verbatim what Mason said to me earlier.

"Now, I'm callin' 'cause I'm comin' to North Carolina in two days. Lanie and Dexter are flyin' me down there in some big ass plane 'cause they don't think I should be drivin'." The outrage in her voice is comical, but the woman has to be in her eighties. I'd side with Dex on this one. "We're going to unlock you again, and I have a feelin' the Grumpy Growler has the key. Where is he, anyway? His brother with the broken heart told me he was with ya. Put him on."

I'm so invested in this conversation, I forget I was

pretending not to listen, so when Lexi turns her uncomfortable gaze to me, I freeze.

"GG, don't go giving nicknames to people you don't know. We talked about this."

"Don't you go givin' me no orders, young lady. I'm still the boss, and my cards don't lie. Now put him on."

Knowing she's talking about me, I can't help but smile. I can already tell the stories Preston said about her don't do her justice, and I'm beyond curious to experience this kind of crazy firsthand. Taking a step forward just as the elevator doors open, I grab Lexi's phone from her hand, then escort her into the lobby.

Lifting the phone up, I find GG holding hers far too close to her face.

"Hello, Mrs. Heart. I'm Lexi's boss, Easton Westbrook. How are you, ma'am?"

"Cut the sweet talker bullshit, Grumpy Growler. I ain't interested in none of it."

"Ah, okay."

Lexi laughs beside me, obviously accustomed to this type of abuse.

"Can I do something for you, Mrs. Heart?"

"The name is GG. We're family, young man. Do you have any living grandparents?"

"No, ma'am." I don't tell her we never had grandparents because none of them approved of my parents' marriage.

GG squints to scrutinize me, and it makes me uneasy. I can see now why she makes Preston uncomfortable.

"Never had any grandparents, did ya? Well, now ya got me. I'll be comin' by soon to meet you proper. Locket is a tough cookie, but her center is pure gold. It's gonna take some work on your part, but fallin' for her will be worth the effort."

I choke as Lexi squeals and lunges for the phone. Enjoying the look of mortification on her face, I attempt to

58

hold it out of her reach, but with her height and the four-inch heels she's rocking, it's not easy.

"Give me the phone, Easton."

"Come on, Locket. GG wants to talk to me, not you," I tease.

"Do not call me that!" Lexi seethes, and I hear GG's laughter through the phone. The woman seriously has a cackle that could rival any Disney villain.

"Okay, GG. I need Lex on her A-game for this meeting, so I'd better hand the phone over. It was nice talking with you."

"You too, Grumpy. I'll see ya soon."

"Can't wait," I respond honestly.

Lexi huffs, takes the phone, and stomps off in the wrong direction. Jogging a couple of steps to catch up with her, I take her by the elbow and immediately regret it. I watch as her body recoils, and I reactively lower my face to her ear.

"It's just me, Locket. You're going the wrong way." After spinning us, I release her arm and gesture for her to continue. I hadn't meant to use GG's nickname, but it slipped out. I don't kid myself, though. I'm fully aware it's all kinds of fucked up that Lexi is getting under my skin like this.

She shakes out her free hand as if she's attempting to rid her body of her reactions, so I let her have some space as she leads us down the busy Tribecca streets.

My phone vibrates in my hand, and I see it's my mom calling. Glancing ahead to make sure Lexi's okay, I press the button to answer.

"Hey, Mom."

"Easton. How's New York?"

"Unseasonably warm for fall. How are you?" My mother is a special kind of angel. One you don't ever want to mess with.

"Oh, I'm fine. Keeping up with you boys is getting harder than it was when you were little, though. How's Lexi doing?"

At her name, my gaze flicks toward her like a lifeline.

"She's ... she's great, actually. We're just heading to a meeting with Douglas now."

Glancing around, I realize Lexi is about to pass the restaurant. Lowering my phone, I call out to her.

"Hey, Lex?"

She stops suddenly, and the person behind her nearly plows her over.

"Hold on one second, Mom, okay?"

I don't wait for her response as I catch up to Lexi.

"This is the restaurant. I'm just finishing up a call with my mom. Can you go get us checked in?"

She glances from the phone in my hand to the restaurant door. "Sure. Tell your mom I said hello."

I smile as I watch her enter the building.

"Lexi says hello," I tell my mom after the door closes behind her.

"I heard." I can sense my mother's smile over the phone.

"She's a great employee. She would have impressed Dad."

The words shock me as they leave my mouth. *Why the hell did I bring Dad into this?*

"I'm sure Daddy would have loved her for a lot of reasons, East." She's quiet for a moment, and I'm not sure where to go. I'm about to tell her I have to get to my meeting when she speaks again. "You're calm."

Two words, and my body stiffens.

"What do you mean?"

"I'm not sure, honestly. It's just the edge you usually carry in your voice isn't there today."

Fuck me. Am I usually a bastard to my own mother? I don't know how to respond, so I remain silent.

"It's been a long time, East—"

Knowing this conversation can only go down one path, I interrupt her.

"I need to get into this meeting, Mom. Lexi doesn't know

the Douglases. I don't want to force her into awkward small talk. We'll be home tomorrow. I love you."

She sighs, "I love you, too, East. Tell Marvin and Amy I said hello."

Sometimes I forget Mom used to accompany Dad to most of these meetings. Of course she would remember Marvin and Amy Douglas.

"I will. Talk to you soon."

"Bye, Easton."

Hanging up the phone, I stare at the busy street, collecting myself. In only fifteen minutes, three different women have been able to chip away at my carefully constructed walls, and I can't go into this meeting unnerved. *Westbrook Beast.* Lexi's nickname comes to mind, causing me to chuckle, and just like that, I'm back. I won't dwell on the fact that Lexi's voice in my head got me here. I just take it, square my shoulders, and prepare to win this bid.

CHAPTER 10

*E*ntering the restaurant, I can see the first signs of winterization as I pass through the thick, velvet curtain covering the door, keeping the cold from ambushing unsuspecting diners. Locating the hostess stand, I weave my way through the waiting crowd.

"Yes? Do you have a reservation?" the wanna-be model asks before I can even smile. I don't miss these attitudes. But, in a short amount of time, I have realized that people really are friendlier in the south. I'm pretty sure it's because of the year-round sunshine, but nothing brings it home faster than a server with snark.

Kill 'em with kindness, Lexi. My cousin, Lanie's voice, is a real buzz kill, and my snotty comeback dies on my lips.

"I do. It's under Westbrook, I believe."

"There isn't anything here under that name. Next," Snarkysnot replies.

"Oh, I—"

"Actually, it's under Douglas. It's three parties combined." Turning my head to the deep, somber voice, I feel my heart rate accelerate.

Making eye contact, the blond Adonis smiles.

Snarkysnot physically jumps at his voice. "Oh, ah, yes, of course. Right this way."

"I'm Dillon. You must be an associate of Easton's?"

Reaching out, I shake his hand. "It's nice to meet you. I'm Lexi. Easton is just outside, finishing up a call. He'll be along shortly."

When our hands collide, I'm relieved to feel nothing. Spending so much time in close quarters with Easton has caused reactions I'm not willing to acknowledge. I was beginning to worry that I'm really and truly broken. Dillon proves I can be in the presence of a panty-melting hot man and not turn into a pile of mush.

"I'm sure he will. Shall we head to the table to wait?"

"Of course." Turning, I follow Snarkysnot, who has stopped at the entrance to a private room.

Stepping inside, I'm greeted by a young woman and an older man who immediately makes my skin prickle.

Dillon steps past me to make introductions. "Pacen? Maxim? This is Easton Westbook's associate, Lexi ... I'm sorry, I didn't catch your last name."

"Heart, Lexi Heart. It's nice to meet you all. Easton will be here anytime."

"Of course. The Westbrooks never had any consideration for other people's time, anyway. Why should today be any different?" Maxim bites out. He has a hint of an accent I can't quite place.

I'm not sure who Maxim is, so I keep my inner bitch in check.

"He's just outside. The backbone of their business motto is family first, so it does not surprise me when he takes five minutes to speak to his mother. Family is the most important aspect of life, don't you think, Maxim?"

"Family doesn't pay the bills."

This guy cannot be who we're here to shmooze. Glancing around, I notice the table is set for three more people, and I breathe a sigh of relief that I don't have to impress this asshole.

"The Westbooks have built quite the business putting family first, so I'd have to disagree with you there, Maxim."

"It's Mr. Savin, Lexi."

"It's very nice to meet you, Maxim." If that fuckwad thinks he is going to intimidate me, he has another thing coming.

"Maxim," Dillon's tone carries none of the warnings he's trying to portray. "Lexi, please sit." He offers me his hand as he pulls out my chair, and I take it out of habit.

"Get your fucking hands off of her, Dillon." Easton's demand startles me, and I lurch forward. Dillon catches me, but East is to my side a second later.

"I said, let her go."

"East, you scared the shit out of her. I merely kept her from face planting in the center of the table."

Easton takes a menacing step forward, and I see his face for the first time. This is a side I've never seen in any Westbrook. The expression on his face is pure hatred. The vein in his throat so prominent, I can see every beat of his heart.

Dillon raises his hands and takes a step back as Easton glances around the table. If he was pissed a second ago, you'd think he saw a ghost as his gaze lands on Pacen.

"Ness?" Easton's voice cracks, and I suddenly realize I've walked into the middle of something far deeper than a business meeting.

Pacen swallows a sadness I recognize but shakes her head no. "No, East. I-I'm Pacen. You're not the first to confuse us, though."

I volley between everyone in the room. Maxim sits at the table, pleased with Easton's obvious discomfort, while Dillon appears almost as pained as East.

What the hell is going on here?

Pacen's voice is quiet, but she breaks the silence. "I'm

64

sorry, Easton. I ... we," she glances to Dillon, "we thought you knew we'd be here—"

"That's enough," Maxim cuts her off with the viciousness of a bully. "No one asked you to speak. Keep your stupid comments to yourself."

Pacen visibly shrinks in her seat. If I had sleeves on, I'd be rolling them up, ready to take this monster out.

"What are you doing here?" The venom in Easton's words could take out an army.

Dillon sighs. "Douglas is only in town for the night, so he asked to combine our meetings. I'm not sure why he wouldn't have let your assistant know."

Oh shit. Is this my fault? Easton's eyes cut to mine, and he gives the slightest shake of his head. Whether he's telling me it isn't my fault or that it is, I don't know.

"No." Easton's words are tight, and I can tell he's fighting with himself. "I will not sit at a table with you." The hatred in his eyes unnerves me. To be honest, I never would have guessed any Westbrook could carry this much anger; not with their welcome to the chaos mantras and open-door policies. They have more pseudo brothers than the pound has dogs, but there is no mistaking the murderous expression on his face right now.

"It's been almost eight—"

"No," Easton yells. "You, of all people, don't get to say that to me. I don't want you to say a fucking word to me ever again. Do you understand? You're not my brother. You're not a part of my life anymore. You lost that right, so now you can stay the fuck away from me."

His gaze drifts back to Pacen, and I see the pain flash across his face. I have no idea what's going on, but I have the uncontrollable urge to comfort him. Reaching out, I place my hand on Easton's forearm. He flinches but doesn't pull away. Instead, he tears his gaze away from her and focuses on me.

So many emotions play in his eyes as he centers himself,

never breaking eye contact with me. It's an oddly intimate moment, made more awkward by the audience of people Easton obviously has a history with.

"I'm sorry," he whispers before taking a step back.

"There's no amount of money, no account that is worth this shit. So you want to win this bid? Fucking take it, asshole. That's what you're good at anyway, right? Let me make it easier for you this time by walking away first."

The smirk that crosses Maxim's face informs me Easton just showed his hand and had no idea he was even playing the game. I glance around the room as East storms out. *Get a read on this, Lex.* Pacen appears to be fighting back tears. Dillon has a pained but pissed off expression. Maxim is the only one happy with the outcome we have here. *What the hell do I do? Chase after East or sit in on this meeting for him?*

"Run along, dear. Daddy Warbucks seems to need a nursemaid." Maxim's laugh echoes throughout the small room.

Well, he just made that decision for me, didn't he?

Pulling out my chair, I sit and stare straight at that asshole. Pacen sniffles, and I open my bag for a packet of tissues.

"Shut the fuck up, you sniveling bitch," Maxim curses under his breath, but the second I see his meaty palm enclose her upper arm with enough force to cause her to wince, I leap from my chair.

Slamming my fists down on the table, I send water glasses flying. "Get your goddamn hands off of her."

Maxim throws his glass of wine in my face as he seethes. "Do not speak to me that way, you fucking whore. She's mine. I will handle her however I please."

Ugh, I'm going to be sick; she's actually with this douchebag? There has to be a twenty-year age gap between them.

Taking out my phone, I quickly and obviously snap a picture of his grip that has tightened around her arm.

"He's obviously a fucking moron, but you? You just let him sit here and treat her this way? What the hell kind of man are you?" I spit at Dillon. Turning back to the disgusting pig sitting in front of me, I steady my voice as I wipe wine from my forehead. "You're the lowest of the low, you piece of shit. You degrade and bully your way into everything. I know your type. I've seen your type, and the thing I've learned is the bigger the bully, the harder they fall. You will fall, you fucking dingle dick, and when you do, I'll be there dancing on your grave. I have proof of abuse right here, and I know people who can make your life a living hell. And you," I say, turning to Pacen. "You're worth more than this. Whatever is making you stay, there are other ways. Get the fuck away from him before it's too late. If you need help, contact Ashton Westbrook. He knows people that can help you."

Maxim stands abruptly from his chair, and even though I try not to, I flinch, but I refuse to back down.

"Any man who puts his hands on a woman is no man in my book. You're a worthless piece of shit that karma will have a field day with."

The sudden sound of clapping causes me to jump. Turning in place, I see an older couple standing in the doorway.

"I see this meeting didn't go as I'd hoped," the older man sighs. "How long did Easton stay?"

"Less than five minutes," Dillon confesses.

"What the hell? Was this some sort of ambush?" Easton may piss me off, but the loyalty I feel toward him just grew exponentially.

"No, Ms. Heart. Not an ambush. We were hoping for a peace treaty, but we got stuck in traffic, and it appears everything went straight to hell. I'm Amy Douglas, and this is my husband,

Marvin." Switching gears, she turns toward Maxim. "You may go and not return. We will not be doing business with McComb Inc. so long as you're a part of their team. Pacen," her tone softens, "we will call your father in the morning to explain."

Maxim huffs and grumbles in a language I don't recognize as he storms out of the room.

"Thank you, Mrs. Douglas, but that won't be necessary. It won't make a difference at this point." Pacen casts a nervous glance at Dillon, and I have to wonder, *What the fuck is going on?*

"Thank you for trying," Dillon says as he shakes hands with Mr. Douglas and kisses Mrs. Douglas on the cheek.

"Someday, Dillon. We'll make it happen," Mrs. Douglas promises cryptically.

Standing here, soaked in red wine, I'm more lost than the moment I realized my ex had irrevocably taken everything from me. As Dillon and Pacen say their good-byes, I pack up my small purse and work bag with Easton's contracts. *We won't be needing those tonight.* My gut twists as I realize this mess was probably my fault in some way.

"Ms. Heart?"

I'm so lost in my thoughts that Mr. Douglas' words catch me off guard, and I almost fall for the second time tonight. I need to stop wearing heels this high.

Turning, I try to regain any amount of dignity I can scrounge up and smile.

"It was a very brave thing you did standing up to that man."

"Honestly, I'm so confused. I thought we were coming here for a business meeting, and everything went off the rails in the most spectacular fashion. I've been in Pacen's position before. I wasn't able to stand up for myself then. I saw her tonight, and I just reacted. Do you think she'll be okay?"

"We're working on it." The finality of his tone tells me he'll be handing out no further details.

"Okay. I meant what I told her. If she needs help, I know Ashton can do it."

Mrs. Douglas smiles. "The Westbrooks are a remarkable family."

Tears spring out of nowhere before I can blink them away, and one falls free. "They truly are."

"You don't happen to have Easton's contracts with you by any chance, do you?"

"Ah, yeah. I-I do."

Mr. Douglas smiles kindly. "May I have them? We would ask you to join us for dinner, but I'm guessing you'd like to get home and clean up."

Self-consciously, my hand reaches for my hair that is still dripping the remnants from asshat's glass.

"Marvin!" Mrs. Douglas admonishes.

"Not that you don't look lovely," he corrects, and I can't help but laugh.

"Yeah, pinot isn't really my color. Let me get you those contracts."

"If you would like to press charges on the wine tosser, we saw the entire thing," Mrs. Douglas states with matronly seriousness.

The thought has my body going rigid with fear. The idea of going to the police again for anything makes my stomach turn.

"Ah, no, I don't … I don't think so, but thank you." I hand over the contract and suddenly can't wait to get out of here.

"Our driver is out front, and he will escort you home." It isn't a request, and I'm too tired to argue, so I nod and thank them for their kindness.

Even though we're only going a few blocks, I try to call East three times, but he doesn't answer. For the first time in years, I worry about a man for reasons that have absolutely nothing to do with my safety.

CHAPTER 11

EASTON

*H*ow the fuck could I have left Lexi there with those vultures? What in God's name was I think-ing? I can't even call her because I threw my phone against the brick building so hard it shattered into a hundred pieces as soon as I left the restaurant.

Think, East. I've been pacing our hotel room for almost ten minutes, but I know I have to go back for her. However, my stomach revolts at the thought of seeing Dillon again, but I can't lie to myself. The real reason I'm struggling is that Pacen has grown up to be the spitting image of her sister, Vanessa.

God, at one time, I thought my life would be so different. Death and betrayal tend to leave you bitter, though. The pain is deeply engrained.

"Fuck." Grabbing my key, I head out the door.

The hostess tells me there was a scuffle at the restaurant, and all but two people left. I don't even bother checking to see who it is. I know Lexi's gone, and I've never felt like a bigger dick. All I can do now is head back to the hotel and wait for her.

I use the time on my walk to figure out how I will explain

this to her. Ashton is the only one in my family that knows what happened, but even he doesn't know it all. By the time I reach the Four Seaons, I'm still at a loss, and now I'm anxious in an uncomfortable, nervous way.

How the fuck did you leave her behind?

I'm still berating myself as I walk down the long hallway to our room. Stepping into the foyer, I'm relieved when I see her purse on the entry table, and I pick up the pace in my search.

"Lexi?" I shout as I round the corner.

I find her standing in the center of the family room with a towel in her hand. As she lowers it, I notice her light blonde hair is stained red, and the floor drops out below me. *Is she bleeding?* I cross the room in three long strides. Then, cradling her head in my hands, I search for a cut, a bruise, something.

"East? Wh-What are you doing?"

Taking a closer look, I notice the red has stained her neck in tiny lines that disappear at her cleavage.

"What the hell's all over you?"

Lexi rolls her gorgeous eyes and my heart beats erratically. "Wine," she groans.

"Wine? How did you spill wine in your hair?"

"I didn't."

Pulling back so I can see her entire face, I raise my eyebrows in question. "If you didn't spill it, how did it get here?" Without thinking, my index finger traces a red line down her neck.

"Freaking Maxim Savin threw it at me when I told him to stop manhandling the girl he was with. I think her name was Pacen?"

I didn't hear her correctly.

"What did you say?"

Lexi tries to step away from me, but my grip tightens in

her hair. When I see a hint of fear in her eyes, I release her, but don't allow her to step away.

"I'll never hurt you, Lexi."

"You're right," she fires back.

"Tell me what happened. Please," I whisper.

"I did. Fuckwad Maxim threw his drink in my face."

I was angry when I saw Dillon holding her hand. I was pissed off when Pacen reminded me of her sister. But, enraged doesn't even begin to explain my feelings as she recounts the messed up situation I abandoned her to.

It takes almost forty minutes for her to tell me every detail because I make her repeat it at least six times. By the time she's finished, I watch the exhaustion hit her like a freight train. I did this to her. I was so absorbed in my own pain that I didn't think about her. *My father raised me better than this.*

"Lex, I'm … I'm so sorry. None of this should have ever happened."

"We all have stories that come to bite us in the ass sometimes, East. Just be thankful you had a friend in your corner when yours came calling."

Her admission momentarily stuns me. Searching her face, I ask, "Is that what we are, Lexi? Friends?"

"Well, there are many ways to label us, East. You're my boss. Our families are what? Family?"

"We're family adjacent," I grind out. I'm not sure why calling Lexi family rankles me so much, but it does. "We coined the term when mom started taking in strays." A genuine smile pulls at my lips "But I think I might like friends better."

Friends will never be enough with this girl.

Holy shit. Where the hell did that thought come from?

"I can handle friends, but I really need a shower. Are you okay?"

"Am I okay? Lexi, you got assaulted. Why are you asking if I'm okay?"

"That's not assault, East. I've experienced assault. That was a child throwing a temper tantrum. And, I'm asking if you're okay because your story just came out of left field and hit you with a grand slam."

This isn't the first time she's used a sports metaphor, but fuck me if I don't love that she uses them correctly.

"I'm okay, Lex. Thank you. Go shower, and I'll order us some dinner."

"Oh, thanks. I'm really not hungry."

I eye her in the now ruined sexy fucking dress, and I want to ask if she's always been this thin, but I also know her well enough to know that might end in a slap across the face. So I make a mental note to ask Lanie.

"I'll order extra in case you change your mind?"

She smiles and walks to her room as a thought hits me.

"Oh, Lexi?" She turns and waits for me to continue. "Why did you stay? I know I'm an asshole for leaving you, and I'm so sorry about that. I was blindsided and couldn't see past my anger, but why didn't you just leave?"

She graces me with a sad smile. "We had a deal to close, so I closed it. Mr. Douglas said he'd have the contracts to you first thing in the morning."

I stare at her parting form, unblinking. She closed the deal. My deal. She closed it for me because I couldn't. Completely fucking blown away, I sink to the couch.

You have your work cut out for you with her. My father's voice rings in my ears with the last words he ever said to me, but this time, I don't think they're a warning. This time they sound like a promise. A promise I have no idea how to keep.

~

*L*exi didn't come out of her room for dinner, even after multiple attempts and food orders from three different places. *Why do I insist on feeding her?* I'm getting fucking weird in my old age.

Eventually, I give up and put everything away. As I'm walking through the suite turning off lights, I hear a sound that makes the hairs on the back of my neck stand on end. Pausing, I hold my breath, waiting to see if it happens again. A few seconds later, I've almost convinced myself I made it up when I hear it—a strangled sob that twists me up in an unnatural way, and I sprint toward Lexi's door.

Pulling on the handle, I curse when I realize it's locked, and I'm forced to knock. Never in a million years would I have thought I would ever be trying to break into my assistant's bedroom door, but here I am.

"Lexi?" Banging on the door, I yell again, "Lexi?" When I hear her gasp for breath, my heart stops. *What the fuck is going on?* "Lexi?" I try again, turning in a circle, looking for something to break down the door with.

"East?"

Her voice carries through the door, just above a whisper.

"Open the door, Lexi. Are you okay?"

I hear something thump lightly on the door, and my hand flies to touch the dark wood as if I can catch her.

"Lex, what the hell is going on? Open the damn door. Are you okay?"

"I'm fine, East. I'm-I'm sorry if I woke you."

"No. No, I wasn't asleep. Please, will you please open the door?" A need to see her crashes through my body so powerfully I clutch my chest, wondering if I'm the one who needs a doctor.

"I'm fine, really. I'll see you tomorrow." Her voice is lower than it should be, almost like she's sitting on the floor, so I do what my brothers and I always did when we were being little

74

shits. I lie on the floor and look under her door. Sure enough, I can see just enough to know she's slid down the door frame and is resting her back against it.

Moving closer, I sit so my head rests where I think hers is. *I might be losing my damn mind.* "Do you want to talk?" My voice is gentle, but I hear her gasp anyway.

Glancing down, I see her fingers at the door and chuckle, knowing she just dropped to look for me, too. "I'm just sitting here, Lex. I wish you'd open the door, though."

I hear her sigh through the crack near the floor and listen as she adjusts herself. When the door shifts ever so slightly, I know she's sat upright again.

"I-I just had a bad dream. Good night, East."

"You keep trying to get rid of me," I chuckle sadly.

"It doesn't seem to be working, though, does it?" Lexi's usual attitude is muted with sleep. "It's late, East. Your five a.m. workout is going to be here before you know it."

"But I'm the boss. The beauty of that is I can change my schedule whenever I want."

"Not for me."

"No, of course not. That would require me being nice, and you've already pointed out the Westbrook Beast doesn't do nice."

"Ugh, okay." I can hear her tapping her fingernails on the floor. "Maybe you have your moments."

I smile, knowing that non-compliment was hard for her.

"What was your dream about?"

"A never-ending nightmare."

Something in her voice destroys one corner of the wall I've built around my heart. I haven't wanted to care for someone other than my immediate family in years, and I'd give my left nut to crawl through this door and hold her.

This has messy written all over it.

CHAPTER 12

LEXI

A never-ending nightmare? Jesus, Lexi. Why the hell did I just say that out loud?

"Open the door, Lex."

"Not today, East."

"Can you go back to sleep?"

"Eventually." I don't admit that it'll take me hours to fall back asleep now, but apparently, Easton is learning my tells as quickly as I am his.

"Okay, so what do you want to talk about?"

"What?" I screech. "No, go to bed. It's late."

"You first."

"Fine, I will," I lie again, making no effort to move.

"Did today have something to do with your nightmare?" His voice is full of remorse, and I suddenly realize he's beating himself up for my mess.

"It could have happened, regardless," I admit quietly.

The door shakes with a loud thump. Judging by the location, I assume he just banged his head against the door.

"Hard head?"

"Jesus, Lexi. I'm so sorry. I'm so used to being alone. I just reacted. I went back for you, but you'd already left. I should never have left you with those monsters."

I know I shouldn't ask questions. I don't want to share my story, but my curiosity gets the better of me, and I can't stop myself.

"Who are they?"

Easton is silent for so long I don't think he'll answer. "Listen, I'm—"

"Once upon a time, Dillon was my family. Pacen is harder to explain. She ... she's the sister of someone I thought I knew."

Someone he thought he loved is what I hear.

"Where is she now?" *Ugh, Lexi.* I just can't stop the questions now that I've started.

More silence.

"She died. About eight years ago. I lost her and my best friend all in the same night."

My brain takes longer to comprehend what he just said than my body because I'm already in motion. I rip the door open so fast that East falls over and lands on his back between my feet.

"If I needed to grovel for an apology, there are less impactful ways of telling me." He grins, but I only see the sadness in his eyes.

I drop to my knees just as he sits up.

"East, I'm ... Geez, I'm so sorry."

He slides to the left just outside of the door and leans against the wall. I do the same inside of my room to the right, and we sit back-to-back with an open space between us. Turning my head to the open door, I can just make out his profile. Somehow, the distance between us makes me feel safer. He just dropped a bomb, and I'm not sure I'm strong enough to keep my darkness from him right now.

"You know how my mom adopted Preston's friends, like Dex, Trevor, and Loki?"

"Yeah," I say cautiously.

"Dillon and Vanessa were my versions. My mother took them in, too; her habit of collecting family started when we were kids." He shifts his face, and I see the hint of a sad smile. Lifting his gaze to mine, he whispers, "You know, I don't talk about this stuff. Ever."

Feeling guilty because I know I can't share my story, I give him an out. "I'm sorry, y-you don't have to tell me anything. I have a nasty habit of being nosy."

I watch as he nods, then closes his eyes. His strong jaw ticks as he chews the inside of his lip.

"The three of us had been best friends since we were in diapers. Dill and I were going to start our own empire. He would run the business side, and I would create elaborate furniture for the high-end hotels we created. We'd already proposed a business plan to two of my father's colleagues, and they were on board. My father's only stipulation was that we both finished school first."

As I stare at Easton, I can't help but imagine him as a teenager telling his father what he wanted to do with his life.

"Vanessa wasn't feeling well before I left for college," he continues, pulling me back into the present.

I swallow hard as Easton tells me his story.

"I wanted to stay home, but she encouraged me to go. She said it would be better for us in the long run if I went to school and continued with our plans for the future. She was going to school closer to home, and Dillon was, too, so he said he would keep an eye on her to make sure she was okay."

"Oh no," I gasp, worried I know where this story is leading.

"I FaceTimed after all her appointments, or at least I thought I was. She said she was feeling so much better, even though she was having a ton of testing done. I came home for Columbus Day weekend, and she seemed tired, but other-wise, I didn't notice anything. My family took a trip for

Thanksgiving that year. She swore she was fine, and I was going to see her at Christmas. Dillon said he was busy with school but checked on her once a week and thought she was doing well."

Needing to offer him some kind of support, I reach out with my hand, palm up, in the center of the doorway. He stares at it for only a second before placing his on top of mine. We're not holding hands. Not really, just transferring support from one hand to the next.

"The day after Thanksgiving, my mom got a call from a mutual friend who told her that Vanessa had passed away. I called her dad, but he didn't answer. I called Dillon every five minutes until his phone finally just turned off. We rushed home from Colorado, and when we got there, we found out that her husband was making all the funeral arrangements. Vanessa's husband, Dillon Henry."

"What? When? How long were they together?" My inner bitch just stood at full attention, ready to take down that asshole.

"I don't know."

"What do you mean, you don't know? You didn't ask him?"

Easton shakes his head. "We found out later that she'd learned she had stage four ovarian cancer in September. She passed away in November. I loved them, and they both betrayed me. I was mourning her loss and the loss of my best friend. I didn't see a point in explanations. As far as I was concerned, they were both dead." He pauses as his voice cracks. "I would have given up everything to be home with her, even if we only had a few months, but it was never me she wanted."

Resting my face against the wall, I stare at Easton through the doorway as I curl my fingers around his and squeeze.

"Are you hungry?"

His question catches me off guard.

"N-No, not r-really," I finally stammer. "Why do you keep trying to feed me?"

This at least causes him to laugh.

"Blame my mother. I don't know, Lex. I have a feeling if I tell you the truth, you'll slap me."

"At least you're honest." I giggle. *Since when do you fucking giggle, Lexi?*

"Have you always been this thin?"

I try to pull my hand away, but he clamps down, holding me still. He's told me his story, the least I can do is give him this.

"No, I haven't. I'm getting better, though. I lost myself for a few years, and then I lost ... well, I'm learning to live a new normal."

"It's okay to lean on us, you know. Me, Preston, even my mother, she's an amazing listener."

Giving his hand a final squeeze, I allow myself the comfort his touch brings. "Thanks, Beast. I appreciate that, but I need to fix myself."

I can see the words forming in his head, so I cut him off and decide to give him another win. Jumping to my feet, I offer him both hands.

"Come on, Beast. I'll let you feed me if that'll make you feel better," I tease.

"Jesus, don't tell me that's my new nickname? That's even worse than Grumpy Growler."

I present my hands again and smile. "Beast definitely suits you. Come on."

"Lexi, I'm six-four, 230 pounds. There's no way you're dragging me off this floor."

"You're on, Beast. One thing you need to know about me, I never back down from a challenge."

Taking both his hands in mine, I plant my bare feet on the tips of his toes. Lowering my body so my center of gravity works to my advantage, I pull.

"Beast, you cannot be dead weight. I'm not lifting you, just helping you stand, you asshat."

A full-bodied belly laugh erupts, and his breath causes my hair to shift across my cheek. Lifting my face to his, I freeze as our eyes meet, and I watch the laughter fade on his lips. His gaze doesn't leave my mouth, and immediately my chest heaves with shallow breaths.

"It was a valiant effort, Belle." His voice is dangerously low with a rasp that attacks my clit like a three hundred dollar toy. Mother fucker, this will not end well.

"I'm no princess, East." No sooner do the words leave my lips than he's giving my hands a quick tug, and suddenly we're nose to nose.

"There are all kinds of princesses, sweetheart. Some are gifted with a happily ever after, and some have to work for it, but make no mistake, you deserve it all."

"Princesses need a prince to save them, and I won't make that mistake again. My ever after will be what I make it."

"You're confused, Lex. A real prince won't create the happily ever after for you; he'll stand by your side while you build it together."

"Life's not a fairytale, East."

"It doesn't have to be a nightmare either."

The atmosphere is so thick around us as we breathe each other's air, but I can't break the spell, and he's making no effort to let me go.

"You might sue me, but … well, fuck it." His harsh words confuse me for half a second before his lips crash over mine. I'm standing bent over at the waist, and before I can blink, he's reached up and yanked me down onto his lap. On my knees, I straddle his legs as his mouth devours me.

81

CHAPTER 13

EASTON

*A*ll thoughts vanish at my first taste of her. Grasping her hips, I tug just enough that she falls forward. I hang onto her so she doesn't crash to the ground but gently guide her to straddle me.

Once seated, my hands tangle in her silky, blonde hair and tilt her face to the left. My teeth nip at her bottom lip and suck it into my mouth. When she gasps, I lick the outline of her upper lip before delving deep. Our tongues war for half a second before she shocks the hell out of me and submits, allowing me to control the course of our first kiss.

For all our back and forth, and her stubborn insistence on doing everything herself, I can tell by her body language that she wants to give up control right now. A breathy moan escapes her throat, and her hips gyrate.

Fuck me. My cock is fully erect and seeking an evacuation plan as she rolls her hips a third time. I can feel the heat of her pussy through my slacks, and it's my undoing. My hands run circles down her spine until I reach her ass. Squeezing the round globes, I grind my dick into her.

"East." Lexi trembles as I run my tongue down the

column of her neck. She arches like a cat, pushing her amazing tits right into my face.

"Lexi," I growl. "If you want me to stop, you need to tell me now." Alarm bells ring loud and clear in my head, but I drown them out. Right now, I want Lexi more than I can remember wanting anything in a very long time.

"No, East. Don't, please don't stop."

It's all the encouragement I need.

"Wrap your arms around my neck," I demand. Before Lexi answers, I've already grabbed her ass to stand. She clasps her arms behind my head as her legs encircle my waist, and I make a beeline for my bedroom. The ache in my balls is urging me to sprint across the suite.

Entering my room, we're silent except for the mingling of heaving breaths. When I reach the bed, I lower her gently. *What am I doing?* This is wrong for so many reasons, and yet, there's nothing I want more than to be buried balls deep into this infuriatingly sexy woman.

"Tell me what you want, Lex."

She bites her lip, and my shaft twitches painfully. *Why the fuck is it so sexy when she does that?* Aware that we are past the point of return, I grab hold of my dick through my pants and give it one hell of a squeeze. If I don't get that fucker under control, we'll never live through the night.

Lexi swallows and looks away. Resting a hand on her chest, I see the war raging inside of her head. My cock wants me to pounce before she has time to reconsider, but that's not how this will go with us. In a single moment of clarity, I picture tonight with Lexi. And tomorrow. And next month. Fucking hell, I can see clear into the next decade, but I need to win her over. What was it GG said? I'll have to work for it?

A slow grin spreads across my face as I realize I'm going to chase this woman. I'm going to chase her, wear her down, and make her mine. Contrary to what the world believes, I'm not always an asshole. I know she has some healing to do

83

first, and it's going to be so much fucking fun bringing my sexy Lexi back to life.

Mine. There's some fucked up caveman shit for you, but no other word will ever describe her adequately. Lexi will be mine.

"What do you want, Lexi?" I repeat.

"I want to feel, East. Make me feel … something." Her words hit me like a wrecking ball, and I feel them heavy in my heart. *You have your work cut out for you with her.* And this time, I won't fail.

"I can make you feel, sweetheart. Are you sure that's what you want?"

"Yes." There's the demanding little thing I've come to know.

Lowering myself to the bed, I rest my weight on my forearms as I spread my body out over hers. With my lips at her ear, I inhale sharply. Her scent reminds me of mountain air and lilacs, and I commit it to memory.

Rolling to my right, I use my free hand to ghost down her arm until it rests on her hipbone. Squeezing it, I ask, "Do you want to feel me here, Lexi?"

Her face shifts toward my voice as I speak, and I feel her exhale on my chin.

"Yes," she breathes.

Using my index finger, I lift her nightshirt a few inches and run my fingers across her stomach. Back and forth, but barely touching her. I use just enough pressure for her to know I'm there.

"What do you want to feel next, sweetheart?"

Lexi groans in response as my rough palms slide up her ribcage. Her skin feels like silk beneath my skin, and every inch of my body wants to own her, but I force myself to go slow. She may be giving up control, but if I spook her, we'll be over before we begin.

When my palm inches over her hardened peak, she

moans, and fireworks go off in my chest. Fucking hell, this girl is going to be my undoing.

Rubbing my palm in slow, torturous circles around her nipple, I grin when she arches into me.

"Do you want to feel here?" I ask as I pluck her nipple between my thumb and forefinger.

"Holy fuck," is the only reply she can give as I work one nipple, then the other. She's shockingly responsive, and all I want to do is unleash my tongue on her and see if I can make her writhe without even getting in her panties.

Lifting, so my weight is on my knees, I raise her shirt over her head and am met with the most fantastic set of tits I've ever seen in my life. I almost cream my pants just looking at them, and I seriously worry that I won't be able to last with her.

Allowing my gaze to rake over her entire body, I finally make eye contact. She steals my breath away without even trying. "Are you okay?"

Lexi nods, but it isn't good enough for me. I hold eye contact until I'm forced to break it when my lips meet her ear. "I want to hear you, Locket," I growl.

That damn nickname slips from my lips, and I worry I just ruined things. But when she speaks, the beast I've held at bay rears free.

"I want to feel you, Beast."

I bite down on her earlobe as my groin humps her leg, seeking the friction it so desperately needs, and I work my way lower. When my teeth graze her nipple, she gasps, so I bite down gently, flicking it with my tongue.

"Oh, God."

"Are you ready to feel me everywhere, Lexi?"

"Yes."

My bossy girl seems to be having trouble forming sentences, and knowing I'm doing that to her makes me much happier than it should. Giving her other nipple the same treatment, I finally kiss lower until my teeth graze the edge of her panties. She lifts her hips in response to my tongue, but I hold her in place with one hand on her lower belly. As I shift my weight, I notice three small scars on her abdomen.

"Did you have your appendix out or something?" Honestly, I don't even know where the appendix is, but surely you'd get a similar scar.

"Something like that," she evades and lifts her hips again.

"Not yet, sweetheart." I fucking love the groan my teasing elicits.

With my free hand, I cup her through her panties and lose my shit when I feel a hot, damp patch beneath my fingers.

"You're already wet for me."

"East—"

Lowering my face, I rub my nose on the inside of her thigh. Inhaling her musk like a starving man, I ease a finger into the band of her thong. With a sharp tug, I pull it away from her body, and I toss them to the floor.

Laying bare before me, Lexi is exquisite, and I waste no more time. I flatten my tongue, running it up her seam, and she groans. Glancing up from my spot between her legs, I find her watching, and it's the hottest fucking sight. When our eyes meet, she flushes with embarrassment. Grasping the sheets between her fists, Lexi stares at the ceiling.

No fucking way.

"Watch me," I demand. Lexi's eyes instantly flicker back to where we're joined. "Watch me," I repeat.

Sticking out my tongue, I enter her. I force it as far inside of her as I can, and bury my nose in her pussy. Shaking my head from side to side, I make sure she feels the stubble of my jaw in the most sensitive of places.

A string of incoherent noises escapes Lexi, and I grin. Lifting my mouth until I find her hardened little nub of nerves, I suck it into my mouth like a goddamn Hoover.

Adding my tongue to the mix, I flick back and forth at a frantic pace until her body starts to shake.

When I know she's about to come undone, I insert two fingers deep into her channel and curl them, searching for the magic spot. Then, finding the spongy wall of nerves, I work in tandem with my tongue until she explodes.

"Holy fuck, Easton, I'm-I'm …"

"Come, Lexi. Right now, come all over my face."

Wave after wave of pleasure wreaks havoc on her body as I consider my next move. She wanted to feel, so instead of waiting for her to come down from her high, I reach down and undo my pants, allowing my cock to spring free.

"Do you still want to feel, Lexi?"

"Yes, God, oh, fuck," she screams as her orgasm continues.

Hearing her words, I line up the head of my cock at her entrance and slam home. Once I'm buried to the hilt, I pause, allowing her body to adjust to the size of me. Truthfully, I need a moment, too. I've had plenty of sex in my life, but nothing has felt like this. I'm almost scared to move. Almost. The connection shocks every inch of my body awake, and I have the distinct feeling that nothing will ever be the same again. But, I am still a guy, and as much as this emotional awakening is freaking me out, the biological need to move finally wins out.

"Are you okay?" I whisper just above Lexi's lips.

"Yeah, I'm okay."

"I'm going to move. Are you ready?"

"Please, just fuck me already, Easton."

Her reaction causes my body to ripple with laughter, and I ease out of her slowly.

"So, so bossy." I don't allow her to respond. I ram back into her body with one hard thrust, and her words die on a sexy moan.

Tilting my hips, I grind my pelvic bone into her clit. "Are you feeling now, Lexi?"

"Holy shit. Yes," she screams loud enough to wake the neighbors.

Good. Suddenly, I like the idea of everyone knowing I've claimed her, and I piston into her again and again.

Leaning back, I watch my dick glide into her wet pussy. When I drag it out of her the next time, I reach down and spread her juices covering my cock onto her clit, and she squirms.

"No, East. It's ... I'm too sensitive," she protests.

"Do you want to feel, Locket, or do you want me to stop?"

A haunted expression fills her face, and I want to chase it away. Leaning down, I place my lips on top of hers.

"Stay with me, Lex. I won't hurt you. Feel me, okay? Let me touch you."

She squeezes her eyes shut and nods her head.

"Look at me." Her eyes fly open instantly. "Eyes on me the entire time. I'm going to shatter you, then hold you until you come back together."

Lexi's eyes are as big as I've ever seen them as I circle her clit. I feel her body tense around my cock, and I know it won't be long. Moving my fingers and cock in sync, she falls apart around me after three strokes. Her walls pulsating around my weeping cock milks me dry.

It isn't until I'm easing out of her that I realize my mistake.

"I didn't use a condom."

Lexi bolts upright as panic, then sadness, fills her eyes.

"Are you clean?" She doesn't sound as pissed off as I was expecting.

"Of course. I always use a condom."

She chuckles uncomfortably. "Everyone *always* uses a condom until that *one* time they don't, right?"

"No, Lexi, I swear. After, after Vanessa, I have never, not even once not used a condom." I notice her demeanor softens at the mention of Vanessa, and suddenly I want confrontational Lexi back. "Should I call someone? I'm sure I can get a doctor here to prescribe plan-B."

"No, we're good. I'm ... there's no chance of pregnancy. That's covered."

Her choice of words sounds off, but she's wrapping a sheet around her and getting out of bed before I can question it.

"Where are you going?" If she thinks she's going to fuck and run, she needs to think again.

Since when have I wanted to cuddle? Lexi is messing with my head.

"Ah, to the bathroom, *master*. Is that okay?" Snarky Lexi is back, and goddamn, don't I want to fuck her right back into submission.

"Oh, ah, okay. I'll get us some water," I tell her as I walk buck ass naked out the door. Glancing over my shoulder, I find her watching my ass, and I wink.

Good. The infatuation is mutual, Locket. Really fucking mutual.

CHAPTER 14

LEXI

*H*oly shit, what the hell was I thinking? *You weren't thinking, ya lil' hussy. Ya were feelin' all up in there.* Gah! Why does my conscience have to sound like GG in times like these?

Sitting on the toilet at the Four Seasons cleaning up my boss's jizz and contemplating my escape is not exactly how I envisioned my first couple of weeks at work. *Jesus, Lexi!* Glancing into the toilet, I see the water stained the slightest shade of pink. As I wipe, I know I'm going to be sore tomorrow. Just great. The doctor said I was good to go, but the Westbrook Beast doesn't only apply to Easton's bad attitude. He was freaking huge.

As much as I want to say this was a mistake, I know it would be a lie. How could the best sex of your life be a mistake? If nothing else, he got me over my fear of never being able to have sex again. Seriously, I thought I was looking at a dry spell that would span years. Freaking Easton Westbrook smashed that idea straight to hell.

I also know it can never happen again, though, so how the heck do I get out of this? Maybe he'll subscribe to the one-night stand rules that say you never discuss it, and I can just live out the best sex I've ever had in my life in my head with minimal embarrassment.

Ugh, what are you thinking, Lexi? The Westbrooks are all a hugging bunch of talkers. If they can't hug their way into your heart, they'll talk their way there. I just need to get the hell out of his room.

After washing my hands, I wrap the sheet tighter around my chest and square my shoulders like I'm getting ready for battle. I have no idea what to expect with Easton right now, so I build my wall ten feet tall and hope he doesn't demolish me.

"Where are you going?"

"Argh!" I jump and lose the sheet I'm holding when he scares the shit out of me. Scrambling to cover my naked ass, I hear him laugh. Once I'm reasonably sure that I'm covered, I turn to find him leaning against the wall next to the bathroom, still blessedly naked and unashamed. In my haste to exit, I completely missed him. "Jesus Christ, East. What the hell are you doing hiding like that?" Even as I ask, I'm inching my body away from him toward the exit.

With a smirk and a raised eyebrow, he takes a step forward for every one I take back. "Where are you going, Lexi?"

"Well ..." I search the room for my clothes, pleased when I see my T-shirt at the foot of the bed. Quickly sidestepping Easton, I grab the shirt and slide it over my head. Once it's in place, I let the sheet fall since the shirt covers all my lady bits. Avoiding Easton's steely gaze, I shuffle around the room in search of my panties, then remember they're likely ruined. My thighs clench at the memory. "Ah, it's late. I should probably get to bed." I step to the left to go around him, but he slides with me, blocking the path.

Inching toward me with a sexy grin, he crosses his arms over his chest, mimicking my stance.

"There's a perfectly good bed behind you, Locket."

Choosing to ignore the nickname, I bite my lip, contemplating what to say next. Surely, he understands what a colossal mistake this was.

"But, it's *your* bed."

"It is."

He takes another step forward, and my body tingles in response. I should not be having this type of reaction to him —to any man, for that matter. *No men, Lexi. Remember? Your man-finder is broken.* Sleeping with your boss, who is also one of your only living relatives, sort of brother-in-law, is the prime example of my epically bad choices.

I step to the right, but he blocks my path again, so I switch tactics. Turning to the side, I inch back to put some space between us. I need space where he is concerned—he has a habit of turning my brain to mush.

"And I have my own room next door."

"You do." He moves quickly, and we're caught in a game of cat and mouse. There's no mistaking who's being hunted here, though. I am the prey, and he isn't letting me go without a fight.

In another lifetime, I would have welcomed the chase; I would have thrived on it, actually. But now, I need to get us out of this landmine before one of us implodes.

"Listen, East. I know those southern manners are deeply engrained, but I'm a big girl. I can handle the truth."

His eyes narrow as he watches me. "The truth?"

"Yeah, I mean, we both know what this was. There's no point in dragging it out. This already has the chance of getting incredibly messy, and I'm not in a position where I can give up this job."

"I agree with the messy part of your spiel, but it's not anything that we can't handle. As for what *this* is? Why don't you enlighten me, sweetheart?"

"First, sweetheart is the issue. I'm not your sweetheart. I'm your assistant." *Inner bitch rising fast. Warning. Warning.*

Get your shit under control, Lex. He's trying to be nice. "Second, I'm not some clingy bitch who needs you to hold her. One-night stands are sex and only sex, and I get that. We were a good distraction for each other when some pretty heavy, emotional shit went down, but I don't need you to pretend this is anything other than what it is."

Easton cringes when I mention the catalyst for our little sexcapade, and I feel guilty. Men are wired differently. He'd probably been able to forget all about the hurt he shared with me tonight. Then I went and dragged it all back out into the open.

You're not sleeping with him again to make him forget, so don't even think about it. My clit throbs in protest, and now I know for sure I need to get the hell out of here.

"You know the expression it takes two to tango, sweetheart?" Easton is stalking closer with every word.

I'm tempted to roll my eyes, but don't because if I take them off the beast currently inches away, he might pounce. No more pouncing, Lexi!

"Of course I do."

"Well, then you should also know that there are two ways of seeing every situation. I'll acknowledge fucking phenomenal sex is a great distraction, but I don't see anything about this being a one-night stand."

"Huh?" It comes out in the least lady-like sound I've ever made. Somewhere between trying to hawk up a loogie and a fisher cat. A horrifyingly tragic sound. "Of … of course this was a one-off, Easton. You're my boss. We're fucking related, for Christ's sake. Eww, we're related?"

"Stop." His deep baritone cuts through the panic that's setting in, but only briefly.

"Wait, does this count as incest? What are the rules? Do you have to be blood relatives for that? What are we, like fourth cousins twice removed or something?"

"Locket." The fact that he is so calm and sure about life in general sets me off.

"Don't. Don't you Locket me anything. What the hell are you talking about? Not a one-time thing? You've lost your damn mind. This was the *biggest* mistake. What the hell were we think—"

Easton's lips swallow my words, and as much as I want to fight him, my body's already addicted to him like the worst kind of drug. The realization brings my world to a crashing halt. Miles was my drug for so long, I couldn't see the evil he was morphing into. *Holy shit. I'm doing it again.* I can't let Easton Westbrook be my world. My world has to be me, just me. It's the only way I can survive my future.

I push on Easton's chest as that bucket of ice-cold reality hits me, and he begrudgingly lets me go, but not escape.

With a hand holding my forehead to his, I watch as he licks his lips. "*This*, sweetheart, is not, was not, and will never be a mistake. *This*, Lexi Mae, is just the beginning."

I shake my head no, even as he nods yes.

"Get in bed, Locket. My bed."

The room tunnels in around me as a new wave of panic descends, and I do as he asks. Not because he's right, but because I can't fight for breath and my feelings for him at the same time.

Easton climbs into bed behind me, and a massive arm encircles my waist, drawing my back to his front. "Breathe, Lexi. Deep breaths. In through your nose and out through your mouth."

Following his commands, I work to regulate my breathing as he holds me so tightly against him I'm not sure where I end, or he begins. Tucked into his muscular frame, I start to relax.

"How often do you have these attacks?" he asks gently.

"It's … it's new," I say, shrugging my shoulders.

"You're safe with me, Lex. We'll fight this battle another day, I'm sure, but for now, try to sleep."

Swallowing my snark, and possibly a few tears, I lay awake until I hear Easton's soft snoring. Then, I lay here for a few minutes longer, attempting to etch the moment to memory, because this will most definitely be the very last time I take comfort in Easton Westbrook's arms.

CHAPTER 15

EASTON

lick.

Opening my eyes to the early morning sun, I smile. Unfortunately, rolling over to an empty bed immediately causes me to frown. Then I remember what woke me up and realize Lexi must have just gone into her room.

My brain wants to catalog all the hottest moments of our night, but I know I won't get out of this room without jerking off if I do. So, instead, I grab a pair of gym shorts and go to find my girl. *My girl.* It doesn't even freak me out. Maybe confiding in her about Vanessa was more cathartic than I'd realized.

I'm musing about if Lexi can be my girl without actually asking her yet when I stop in my tracks. Glancing around her room, I notice something's off. Stepping inside, I move to the en suite and realize she's gone. All her shit's gone, too.

Where the fuck did she go? I sprint to the front door when a letter on the table catches my eye.

Easton

If this is some sort of Dear John letter, I'm going to lose my fucking mind. Unfolding the piece of paper, I scroll over Lexi's neatly drawn script.

Easton,

I have some things to take care of. Don't worry about last night. One little mistake doesn't have to derail our working relationship. I'll see you on the plane.

Lexi

One little mistake? Is that what she thinks last night was? And what the fuck does she need to take care of at seven in the morning? Heading to the office, I search for the new phone the concierge delivered with my takeout last night. As it turns on, I smile, knowing I could track her phone. It's a company phone, after all, but I don't want to breach that confidence. Not yet, anyway. Instead, I text her.

Easton: ~~Where the fuck~~

Knowing that won't go over well, I try again.

Easton: Where are you?

Lexi: ...

I watch the three little dots dance for a full minute before going still.

Easton: Where are you?

Lexi: Errands.

Easton: What kind of errands?

Lexi: Girl errands.

This makes me pause. Either Lexi's telling the truth, or she's using her period to get me to leave her alone. I'm learning a lot about her on this trip, and I'm going with door number two.

Easton: What size do you need? Come back, and I'll go to the pharmacy.

Lexi: You're going to buy me tampons?

Easton: Why wouldn't I?

Lexi: Did you buy your last assistant tampons?

Easton: ~~I didn't sleep with my last assistant~~

Easton: The occasion never arose.

Lexi: You don't buy tampons for co-workers.

Easton: You're also family adjacent.

97

Lexi: I'll see you on the plane.

Easton: Come back to the room, Lex. We need to talk.

Lexi: It was a mistake, East. Leave it alone.

Easton: ~~It wasn't a fucking mistake~~

Easton: ~~We'll see about that~~

Easton: We'll have to agree to disagree on that one, Locket.

I sit with my phone in my hand for ten minutes, waiting for a reply that doesn't come. Just as I'm about to toss it on the desk, a new message comes through.

Lexi: Sometimes mistakes help you move on, but that doesn't make them right.

Easton: And sometimes, mistakes turn out to be blessings in disguise.

~

Two hours later, I arrive at the airfield to learn that Lexi has taken an Ambien and is fast asleep by the time I board. She's the master of evasion, and it's pissing me off. Unable to do a damn thing about it, I sit at the table and stare at Sleeping Beauty. Watching her sleep, I can't hang onto my anger, though, and end up pulling out the contracts I received right before I checked out of the hotel.

True to her word, Lexi closed the deal.

Ashton: Any idea why Pacen Macomb would be contacting me after all this time?

I stare at the text message, unblinking. Just seeing the name Macomb makes my body seize until I remember how scared Lexi had been for Pacen.

Easton: Lexi is worried about her.

I won't elaborate, because if I do, I'll have to admit to him why Lexi knows and I don't. Ash may be the most responsible Westbrook, but he's still a Westbrook. Leaving a man or woman behind doesn't fit well with our family creed.

Ashton: Do you want me to help her?

I don't even hesitate in my response.

Easton: Of course I do. She isn't her sister. Pacen was just a kid back then.

Ashton: She called late last night. What do you know?

Fuck. There's no getting around it now.

Easton: Not much. Lexi spoke to her, not me. She can give you more details than I can.

Ashton: You okay?

Easton: Never fucking better.

Ashton: Did you know you would see her?

Easton: No.

Ashton: Want to talk about it?

Easton: No.

Ashton: I'm here when you change your mind. How's Lexi?

My eyes seek her out at the mention of her name. How is she?

Easton: Hurting? Healing? I'm not fucking sure, Ash.

Ashton: But you want to know. That's a change for you, and you know it.

Easton: ...

Ashton: Fuck, sorry, dude. I didn't know Colt was reading over my shoulder.

New text message

Welcome to the chaos-Group

Colton: Easton and Lexi sitting in a tree. K-I-S-S-I-N-G.

Preston: What the fuck, East?

Easton: Grow up, Colt, and mind your own damn business.

Preston: ...

Easton: I don't need a lecture from you, Preston. Not fucking today.

Just as the plane touches down in Charlotte, Lexi's phone

rings, and she stirs from where she's sprawled out in the reclining seat. Perfect timing. She may think she can hide from me, but I'm done with it.

"It was bad, Ash. I don't think she's safe." Lexi's words draw me to her, and before I can put too much thought into my actions, my hand lands on the small of her back as we exit the plane. Her body tenses at the initial contact, but she doesn't pull away, so I take that as a win for now.

Stepping into the sunshine, I glance around for my driver and am shocked to see two cars waiting on the tarmac—mine and Julia's. *What the fuck?*

"Ash, can you hold for a second? ... Thanks." Turning to me, Lexi places a hand over the receiver. "I'll see you tomorrow, East."

"What the fuck, Lexi? Why is Julia here?"

She shrugs her shoulders without making eye contact. "Girls' night." I stand at the foot of the plane as she sprints to Julia, who gives me a telling wave.

Knowing there's nothing I can do about it, I watch as she gets into Julia's car and they drive off. Shaking my head because I seriously underestimated her avoidance skills, I take my phone out to text her.

Easton: I know what you're doing.

Easton: You can't hide forever. We need to talk.

Looking forward to our banter, I sit with the phone in my hand the entire way home. Disappointment fills my chest when she doesn't reply, and I know I am really and truly fucked.

~

*L*exi has successfully avoided me for three full days, and my irritation has everyone on edge. The murmurs around the office that started to die down last week are back in full force. She's met me every morning for my workout with Colton at her side. I'm ready to kill the fucker.

The three of us are in the elevator, and the only reason I'm not losing my shit is knowing that Lexi's desk arrived last night. I won't make a big deal about it, but I'm nervous to see her reaction. When I got it back from The Ironworks, I decided it needed a few more details, so I took it to my shop. It absolutely had nothing to do with nerves.

Approaching my office, I'm pissed off that Colt is still with us. I didn't exactly want an audience for this.

"Don't you have somewhere to be?" I bark.

He wraps an arm around Lexi's shoulders and smirks. "Yup, but first, I thought I'd make some lunch plans with Lexi-con here."

"We have a meeting, so you'll have to take a raincheck." Of course it's a flat-out lie, so I hurry to my office before Lexi can call me out on it and rush through the door. At least that was the plan, but I'm met with resistance and have to force it open.

Pop. Pop. Pop, pop, pop.

The second I push open the door, balloons start popping, and glitter rains from every direction.

One balloon snaps the next, and it's a chain reaction of popping glitter bombs. That asshole must have filled my office with thousands of them. Maybe more. They cover every inch of the office, and the indoor fireworks display goes on for a solid three minutes.

I stand rooted to my spot in shock. I hear Colton pissing himself with laughter. Of all the stupid shit he's done over the years, this is his most elaborate prank yet. And though I won't admit it, I'm impressed by the sheer man-hours he had to have committed to pulling this off.

"What in the ever living ..." Halton's voice trails off as he rounds the corner where a rather large crowd has gathered.

I stare open-mouthed as the last of the popping sounds

subside. A fine cloud of glitter dust still permeates the air, though, and I realize every single one of us looks like they just got a lap dance.

Considering the shit show literally happened in my face, I have to assume I have it the worst. Blinking out of my stupor, I use the back of my hand to wipe my eyes and realize I have glitter an inch thick on every exposed area.

"You had better get the fuck out of here," Halt's low voice carries through the eerily silent office.

Glancing up, I see even Halt has a smirk on his face, but everyone else who got to the office early looks like they might be sick waiting for my response.

When did I turn into the office curmudgeon? When my eyes land on Lexi's, I know I want more. So much fucking more than to spend my life in an office I'm obligated to and making everyone's life around me miserable.

Throwing a playful wink her way, I school my features and turn to face Colton. Like a battle in the Old West, we study each other, waiting for the opponent to make a mistake. There isn't much that flaps Colt, but knowing I'm coming for him will slowly eat away at him until he can't take it anymore.

"I'm coming for you, Colt. Consider yourself warned. We are on."

His eyes sparkle with mischief. He knows he has lain down the gauntlet, and I just ran away with it.

Lexi's desk will have to wait until Peter Pan cleans up his mess.

Sensing my sudden shift in mood, Lexi retreats. "Okay, well, I'm going to run to Mason's office and get a few things done before we leave tomorrow."

Dexter and Trevor are having a joint bachelor and bachelorette party. In Vegas. That means approximately twenty adults and an indeterminable amount of children will be flying out at the crack of dawn tomorrow morning. I need to talk to Lexi before this trip. I've allowed her to avoid me long enough. The chase begins now.

CHAPTER 16

LEXI

"*Lexi-loo*, where are you?" Julia's sing-song voice carries throughout the small apartment.

Didn't I lock the damn door?

Poking my head out of the bedroom, I can't help but smile at my friend. Dressed in sweatpants four sizes too big for her petite frame, she almost looks homeless.

"How did you get in here?" I finally ask, narrowing my eyes in her direction.

Holding up a giant set of keys, she jingles them like Santa Claus. "Preston has a key to everyone's place."

"He does?"

"Yup. I'm not sure why, but it was way too freaking crowded up there in his fancy-schmancy penthouse, so I thought I'd make sure you're ready. If you're packing like Lanie, I might have to kill you, though."

"I don't have Lanie's wardrobe these days, so no worries there."

"I did notice that," she says, glancing around the apartment. Julia is all kinds of awkward, but she loves hard. When she lost Trevor, it nearly broke her. If anyone deserves a happy ending of this magnitude, it's her and my cousin. "Wanna talk about it?"

"Nope."

"Didn't think so. How's East?" Her question catches me off guard, and I drop the hairbrush I was attempting to run through my hair.

"Grumpy, and glittery." I laugh. I didn't see him for most of the afternoon after Colton's glitter bomb, but Mason told me he was still trying to wash the sparkles off.

"Hmm," Jules sighs dramatically.

I know that sound. She's fishing for information, but I'm all about avoidance these days. Jesus, if I can work this closely with East and have successfully avoided him for nearly four full days, I can handle pint-sized Julia McDowell. Thankfully, a knock on the door saves me from delving any deeper.

I open the door wide, expecting it to be Julia's fiancé, Trevor. Instead, I get a scowling Beast leaning against the door. Never taking his eyes off of me, he calls into the apartment, "Jules? Trevor's waiting for you downstairs."

Julia comes down the hallway with a bounce in her step that's only recently returned. "Hey, East. Thanks. You guys coming?"

"Yes …"

"No," Easton growls at the same time. "Lexi and I have some business to go over, so we're taking a separate car. We'll see you on the plane."

"Don't you think it's weird they say see you at the plane instead of the airport like us poor underlings?"

Easton stares at her with confusion. I'm not sure how much time he's spent with her, but Julia is definitely an acquired taste. Unlike Lanie, who's just naturally sweet, Julia's a little thornier and a hell of a lot bossier. Then there's me. I'm all thorns.

Grabbing my bag, I try to sneak out with Julia. "Actually,

Easton, I'm pretty sure we covered everything in the office yesterday. There's nothing else on your schedule that can't keep until after Vegas."

I attempt to slide past him, but he tilts his hip, blocking my narrow escape, and lowers his voice to just above a whisper. "We have things to discuss, Locket. And unless you want Julia to hear how I want to bury myself balls deep in your tight, wet pussy again, you'd better let her go."

His crassness shocks me into submission, but only briefly. Steeling myself for her questions, I hug Julia. "I'll see you at the airport. Bossy beast has some work we need to finish first."

"Ah, ha. Don't *work* her too *hard*," Julia yells to Easton, even though he's less than ten steps away.

I see his lip twitch, but if he thinks he's found an ally in Julia, he doesn't know her well enough yet.

"I'll do my best," he says cryptically, then gives her a nod, which she takes as her cue to leave.

"See you soon, Lex. Luvs."

"Luvs," I reply like a sullen preteen.

The second we see her step into the elevator, Easton has my arm and slams the door shut with his foot.

"You've been avoiding me," he accuses, as his body presses mine into the wall.

"I've been working. Maybe you should spend a little more time working and a lot less time trying to play grab-ass—"

Easton's hand lands on my hip, and my breath hitches. *What are you doing, Lexi?*

Space, we need space. Twisting my body away from his, I slip free and step into the small family room.

"What did you need to discuss, Easton?" I ask in the most professional voice I can summon.

"Us."

"Bah. Huh? What? Us? There's no us, Easton. What the hell are you talking about?"

"Not yet, but there can be."

"No."

"No? That's it? No conversation about the mind-blowing sex we had? No conversation about the next steps. Just no?"

"What do you expect from me, East? A marriage proposal? We had sex. Once. So what? It was good, I'll give you that, but there's no future here beyond boss and employee. Nothing. Never."

Even as the words leave my mouth, they cause me pain. There's no denying the connection Easton and I have is explosive, but explosive chemistry leads to heartache. I am a direct line to it, and I don't want that for him.

When he doesn't respond, I continue to ramble, "One little mistake doesn't make a relationship, East. I'm not relationship material anymore, and fuck buddies with you has disaster written all over it. Trust me. I'm not worth the effort."

The world spins all around me as Easton pulls me to his chest so fast I see stars. With his hands on either side of my face, he grinds out his words.

"You can say we were a mistake. You can even say what we did was *good,* even though we both know that's a fucking lie. You can spend your days hiding from your feelings. What you can't do, is tell me how to feel about it. So, you can tell me you're not worth the effort, but I'll disagree. You can tell me it was *good*, and I'll disagree. You can tell me we are a fucking mistake, and I'll disagree because if you ask me, Locket, your perception is off."

"You're my boss," I say meekly.

"And I'll rewrite the entire employee handbook if that's what it takes."

"It was a mistake."

His face inches closer to mine. "If it was, it's one I want to make over and over again." Easton's voice is gruff with honesty.

"We can't?" It comes out as a question, and that's when I know my resolve around this man is non-existent.

"We can, Locket." The words ghost over my lips. If I pouted even the tiniest bit, our lips would touch.

"One more little mistake?" My voice comes out in a squeak and my eyes go wide.

"Sweetheart, I'll make all the mistakes you'll allow." His lips crash over mine, and I feel my resolve slipping with this kiss. I have to stop him. I can't keep doing this when there is no future for us. I have no future.

"Stop overthinking this and fucking kiss me, Lexi."

A demand like that from anyone else would result in a swift kick to the nuts. But from Easton's lips, at this moment, it makes me want to strip naked and have him kiss me everywhere.

The growl that vibrates throughout his chest teases my nipples that have hardened in my arousal. It causes an ache so deep inside of me, I don't know that it'll ever be soothed.

"Lexi-con? You still here?"

I pull away from Easton so fast I trip over my suitcase and land flat on my ass with a thud. *Jesus, that's going to leave a mark.* As if Easton had the same thought, I can see his dirty thoughts of kissing it better play over his face.

"What the … What's up, buttercup?"

"What are you doing here, Colt?" Easton barks.

"I think the better question is, what are *you* doing here?"

Ignoring him, Easton reaches down and hauls me to my feet.

"You scared the shit out of her, and she tripped over her suitcase. Don't you knock?" East grumbles.

Colton is always carefree, but I've learned quickly not to underestimate him. He is a Westbrook through and through, so when I see him staring at my just-kissed lips, I know I'm fucked.

"You feeling okay, Lex? You're looking a little piqued today," he goads.

"Yeah, I'm fine. We're just trying to finish up some work, so I don't have to see his grumpy ass all weekend." I toss a thumb in Easton's direction and he growls.

"Why wouldn't you see me this weekend?" Easton's words push through clenched teeth and Colton notices.

"Oh yeah? So, if you're not hanging out with boss man over here, who, pray tell, will have the pleasure of your company?" Colt is laying it on thick, and brother or not, I think Easton might kick his ass.

Harnessing bitchy Lexi, I stare straight into Easton's eyes as I speak. "Whoever's looking for a good time, Colt. That's all, just a good time."

Easton's hands ball into fists at my declaration, but I turn away from him before I say something I'll regret.

CHAPTER 17

LEXI

*F*lying is stressful, and there's no way to get around it. Flying with twenty-plus adults and an army of mini-humans, even on a private plane, is next-level insanity. I've done everything I can to avoid Easton, but I feel his sexy, determined glare on every inch of my skin.

I situated myself so Julia and Colton act as buffers, but my body heats when he's behind me. If he's in front of me, my eyes are drawn to him, and as he sits beside me, I nearly combust. Alcohol seems to be the only solution. Thankfully, Julia has no issues with it and keeps the Bloody Marys coming. She also spews non-stop random facts in his direction giving me a little reprieve.

While Easton is distracted, I slip out of my seat and find Lanie at the front of the plane. Staring at her is like seeing myself in a mirror of opposites. She could be my twin physically, but where I'm bitter and jaded, she's happy and hopelessly optimistic. Where she has a family, I'll always be alone. Realizing my hand has landed on my empty stomach, I tear my gaze away and grab some crackers Lanie had out for her new stepchildren.

"Hi, Auntie Lex. How come you're so sad?" Lanie's stepson, Tate, asks.

"Sad? No, buddy. I'm so excited to celebrate. Look at this awesome family you have."

"Uncle Preston told me family is what you make it, so you have to make a good one. We're a pretty good family, huh?"

You can't look at this kid and not love him. He's an old soul with the heart of a giant.

"It's an amazing family, little man."

"Yup, I'm getting a mom and a cousin, but watch out for Charlie. He's a handful." Julia's son may look just like his dad, but that boy got his mother's genes for sure.

"Shut up, Colt." Easton's voice cuts through the cabin just as an ear-piercing scream drowns him out.

The chaos that surrounds this group for once is not of the loving variety, and people are all over the place. Dexter has risen, holding a screaming, bleeding toddler. Colton is bolting over the tops of seats, and Easton is pacing in his attempt to catch him.

What the hell is going on?

"If you weren't drooling over Lexi, you might have caught little Harper before she fell," Colt teases.

My eyes dash to Easton, and I see the rage burning beneath his chest.

I'm getting to know Colton pretty well, and I can tell he's goading Easton, but this is not the time. I need to see if Lanie or little Harper need anything, but I cannot tear my gaze away from the man attempting to break down my walls.

Hushed conversations happen all around me as people tend to Harper, and it's too much. I make my escape and head to the restroom at the front of the plane so I don't have to pass Easton.

By the time I exit, everyone has taken their seats, and the rest of the flight is silent while everyone catalogs what went down.

My phone vibrates. Glancing down, I see a text from Easton.

Easton: We need to talk.

Lexi: No more talking. No more mistakes. We're good, East. Just let it be.

Easton: ...

I turn off my phone, put on headphones, and close my eyes. When I wake up, we're in Vegas, and Easton has already exited the plane. The sinking feeling that knowledge brings sucks. *What did you expect, Lexi? You told him no more, and you're getting exactly what you wanted.* This weekend is about Julia and Lanie.

"What's got ya so twisted up there, Locket?" My grandmother stands in front of me, eagle-eyed as ever.

"Nothing, GG. Come on. I'll help you to the car. We're probably sharing a room, anyway." Placing a hand around her bony upper arm, I escort her down the flight ramp.

"I hate to break it to ya, lady, but I've got my own room. Sylvie and I have a suite, and I plan on taking full advantage of it."

"What? I thought Lanie said we're sharing rooms?"

"Sharing suites, not rooms, Lexi-con. That's a bonus of marrying a Westbrook. Everyone gets their own room."

"That's not just a Westbrook thing, you dingbat," Julia chides.

"But, who am I sharing with then?" Mentally, I pair everyone up. Julia and Trevor. Lanie and Dex. Preston and Emory. That just leaves the Westbrook boys of bad decisions. This is probably going to be an enormous pain in the ass.

"Halton and Ash won the coin toss, so you're stuck with me and East the Beast," Colton chimes in happily.

"Yup, good things are coming, Locket. Just you wait and see. Big big night for you. Best you take a nap." GG waggles her eyebrows, and I feel sick.

"What do you mean it's a big night?"

"You'll see. Colton, take Lexi in your car. She's looking a little green and could probably use a distraction," Julia orders. "Jesus, GG. Don't you ever just cool it with your card reading?"

"Can't calm the chaos, Jules. Best we can do is direct it, ya know?"

"Come on, Lexi-con. Big day, *you know*?" Freaking Colton smirks while mimicking GG, and we climb into the back of a waiting SUV. "Let's go get you a drink before my mom takes all you girls shopping this afternoon."

"I'm not shopping."

He laughs. "Wanna bet? No one says no to Sylvie. Come on, she means well, and this is her way of welcoming you all. She never had any daughters, so it doesn't surprise me she wants to spoil the hell out of you. Just try to enjoy it."

The idea of shopping right now is enough to send me into a full panic attack, and Colton seems to sense it. "Drink. It'll help."

"Why are all the Westbrooks so good with people? Don't ever tell Preston or Easton I said that," I scold.

Colton chuckles, and there's a sadness behind it. "Listen, we know how lucky we are. We grew up with more privilege than most people experience in a lifetime. But, my mom grew up poor. She worked our entire lives, making sure we understood our place in life. She made sure we turned out well-balanced individuals. It was hard work on her part. It would have been so easy to let us turn into a bunch of rich assholes."

So different from the way my ex was brought up. I really need to stop comparing the two situations. The Westbrooks couldn't be more different from anyone I've ever met before.

When we arrive at the hotel, we're ushered straight to our rooms.

"Privileged," Colton whispers.

I can't help but laugh at him. He's such a dork, but incredibly sweet when he wants to be.

Just as we're about to get on the elevator, Sylvie calls out, "Colton? No games while we're here. I mean it … no shenanigans for two days."

He leans in and kisses her on the cheek. "I'll do my best, Mom, but no promises." He jumps back and lets the elevator doors shut.

"I bet you drove her nuts growing up."

His grin displays the chaos lurking in his mind. "Growing up? I still drive her nuts, but it keeps her young."

Colton leads us down the long corridor and holds up his phone to unlock the door. The space puts our New York City suite to shame, and all I want to do is explore, but I know East is here somewhere.

"Okay, where's my room?"

"Take your pick," Colt calls over his shoulder. "I'm heading to the pool. I'll see you later, Lexi-con."

I'm not sure why I've never corrected his stupid nickname. Perhaps it's because I know it would only make him use it more, or maybe it's because I enjoy feeling like a part of this crazy, big family.

"Colt?" Easton's voice comes from one end of the suite, so I run to the other side and hope it's a bedroom.

I just get the door closed when I hear Easton's chuckle from the other side.

"Open the door, Locket."

"Maybe another time."

"Lexi," he sighs. "We need to talk."

Resting my head against the door, I wish things could be different. I wish I had met Easton and not Miles all those years ago, but I've never been one to live in the realm of what-ifs, so I shut it down quickly.

"Did you ever stop to think that there's nothing to talk about? It was a mistake, East. Can't you just leave it at that?"

"Open the damn door, Lexi," he growls and I feel it in every pore.

"Not today." If I open the door, I'll lose all my resolve.

"Jesus Christ. I cannot believe we're having this conversation through a damn door."

"I have to get ready, East. You should go."

"Is that what you want, Lexi? Do you want me to leave you alone?"

No! "Yes. It's the best for everyone, trust me."

"I won't chase you if you don't want me, Lex. But, for what it's worth, it wasn't a mistake for me."

Why does my heart feel like it's shattering? This man is my boss. We had sex one time. One time! Yet, knowing he's giving me exactly what I wanted, claws at my insides.

It wasn't a mistake for me either, East. Instead of saying that, I thank him. Freaking thank him. By the time I exit my room an hour later, I know he's gone.

CHAPTER 18

EASTON

"Maybe she's just not that into you. Did you ever stop to think about that?"

"Gee, ya think? Jesus, Ash. Of course I fucking thought it. It's not what I feel, though."

"Well, maybe you need to stop thinking with your dick?"

Why did I agree to come up here?

"So what if I am thinking with my dick? It's the first time either of us has wanted anyone since ... since fucking Vanessa, okay? That has to mean something."

"So you admit it?"

"Admit what?"

"You like her."

Ashton has always been the one to see through me. "Yeah, I fucking like her, okay?"

"Good. Don't give up on her then. I didn't know Lexi before this shitstorm I'm living in with Loki, but judging by what I do know? She's good for you, but she needs time to mourn."

I suck in a breath at his choice of words. "That's a very specific fucking word, Ash. Mourn what?"

My youngest brother, who is so much better behind a

116

computer screen than face-to-face, cringes. "I just mean, the life she thought she'd have was taken from her. Lexi's future looks very different than it did a year ago. She needs time to accept it all."

Something tells me that's not what he meant at all, but I let it go for now.

"What the hell am I supposed to do?"

"Be her friend, East. I get the feeling she doesn't have many of those."

"Her friend?" *Do friends imagine each other naked every time they see each other?*

"Yeah. Now, about Pacen?"

My fists clench involuntarily.

"I spoke to Lexi. Do you know who the guy is? The one that was with her and … and Dillon?"

"No," I say regretfully. As much as I fucking hate Dillon, and regardless of how her sister shredded my heart, Pacen was just a kid when everything went down. Lexi is concerned for her safety, and if we can do something about it, we have to. It's who we are as a family. It's in our blood, and I would never forgive myself if something happened to her that I could have prevented.

"You're not going to want to hear this, East."

"I already thought the same thing. The Dillon I knew would never have allowed a man to hurt a woman. If that's happening with Pacen, the Dillon I knew would have already stepped in. But, I think we can agree that I never really knew him at all, right? So you do whatever you need to do with him. I want no part in it. He's still dead to me."

"Okay. Does Lexi know?" he asks like he's afraid of my answer.

"Know?"

"About Vanessa?"

Fuck. Sighing, I roll my shoulders, attempting to work out

117

some of the tension that's settled there. "Yeah, Ash. S-She knows."

"Good, there's hope for you yet."

I don't even want to know what he means by that.

His phone dings with a text, and I know I'm about to lose him to his work. I like to think that all five of us Westbrook boys have turned out to be good men, but there's a difference between good and great, and he's sitting in front of three computer screens. Where the rest of us try to be the good in the world, Ashton just is. He always has been, and it's why I'm not surprised he works to take down the bad guys with Loki.

"Ash?"

He glances up at me, but I can tell he's distracted.

"Are you happy?"

His fingers pause on the keyboard. "Yeah, man. I'm happy. Once I get Loki out of this mess he's in, life will settle down. But yeah, I'm happy." Holding up his hand, we fist bump.

"Welcome to the chaos, little brother."

"Welcome to the chaos, beast." His grin tells me he knows more about our comings and goings than he lets on. "You might want to hit the pool next."

"Yeah? Why's that?"

"Colton said Lexi looks sexy in a bikini." He says it so straight-faced I'm convinced he's fucking with me. Then he turns his phone around to show me a picture of Lexi's ass, and my face flames with anger.

"I'm going to fucking kill him."

Ash doesn't laugh a lot, but when he does, the world takes notice. Even in my anger, it causes me to laugh right along with him.

"He's only pushing because he thinks you're going to fuck things up, you know that, right?"

"I already did, Ash. But you're right. I can be her friend if that's what she needs. A fucking bikini, though? Today might end with me in jail if any fleabags try to hit on her."

~

"*Y*ou're in my sun." Lexi doesn't move from her chair, lift her head, or otherwise acknowledge me in any way, and it makes me freaking happy because, as far as she knows, I'm some dick bag looking to hit on her. "Listen, dude. I'm not interested. I don't need a drink, a dick, a rubdown, or a friend, so keep moving."

I don't fight the smile that explodes across my face. "That's an oddly specific and unusual way to address a stranger, Locket."

I enjoy watching the flush creep up the back of her neck, and if she were to roll over, I have no doubt it would continue down her chest.

"So, tell me … Has someone offered you a drink, a dick, a rubdown, and a friend all in the two hours since I last saw you?"

"She was also asked to take part in a threesome, a hot dog eating contest, and a wet T-shirt contest. I pushed for the wet T-shirt, but she shoved me in the pool," Colton says over my shoulder.

I hadn't even noticed him there. The second I entered the pool area, all I could focus on was Lexi. So much for keeping her in the friend zone.

"I'm going to get a drink. You want anything?" he asks, clapping me on the back as he passes.

"Sure, just a beer. Lexi?"

"Mango me up, Colty." I raise an eyebrow in his direction, and he laughs. "She's a great fucking wingman, East."

Colty? I hate the familiarity she has with my brother, and I know it makes me sound like a lunatic. I just can't bring myself to care.

"Like you've ever had any trouble getting a woman?" I grumble.

"Oh, but you see, Beast, I don't let Colty use his money. Everyone thinks he's just a poor twenty-something on vacation. It's opening up a whole new world to him," Lexi says with her face still buried in her towel.

"She's not wrong," Colt says. "I'll be back."

"You know, he would still get laid, even without the money. We're not bad people, Lexi." Finally, she raises her head to look at me. "And not all people with money are assholes."

"I know."

We have so many conversations with just our eyes. I want to reach for her, but she has her rules. She thinks we're a mistake, and as much as I want to push her, I won't. Not now.

Removing my shirt, I take a seat in the lounger next to her. I don't miss how her eyes roam my torso, but I have to look away before I sport a boner. There's no fucking hiding a hard-on in swim trunks.

"Ash is checking on Pacen," I tell her.

The sigh of relief she expels for Pacen causes an ache deep in my chest. Why is she so good at taking care of others but not herself?

There's so much I want her to tell me, and I'm about to break my own damn rule after ten minutes when a douche canoe with too much self-tanner approaches us.

"Hey, beautiful. Can I buy you a drink?"

The balls on this guy. I'm sitting right fucking here.

"No, she's with me."

Lexi swings her legs to the side of her lounger to glare at me.

"I'm not with him," she tells the stranger, "but I don't need a drink either, thanks."

"If you're not with him, you want to come hang out with

my buddies and me? We just got a bucket of beers for twelve dollars. You can buy in if you want."

"Didn't you just offer her a drink? Now you're saying she can buy in? What the fuck, dude? Go back to the playground."

The jerk puffs up his chest. "You have a problem, asshole?"

I stand from my lounger so fast the back snaps forward. At my full height, the guy immediately realizes his mistake. He's maybe five foot ten, and no match for my six-four, 230 pound frame.

"Jesus, you big oaf. I don't need you coming to my rescue. I save myself, East. I fucking save myself from now on," Lexi snaps.

She's about to storm off when Colt comes back with our drinks. He assesses the situation in half a second.

"You'd be smart to walk away, man, before my brother or our girl tears you to shreds. And I'll be honest … my money's on our girl."

With Colton and I standing shoulder to shoulder, the sleazeball backs away, mumbling under his breath.

"Easton, what the actual fuck?"

Colt interrupts by handing her a fish bowl sized drink.

"Time out, Lexi-con. Take a drink. I just made a bet at the bar, so you and East are going to have to put aside your differences for a few minutes."

"What the hell did you get us into now, Colt?" Usually, I want no part in any of his chaos, but if it means Lexi will stop scowling at me, I'm game.

"We're playing chicken in the pool. I made friends with a cute, little lady at the bar. It will be us four against the two dingle dicks that were trying to pick her up. You can't say no because I bet two grand we would win."

"Two thousand dollars, Colt?" Lexi's screech echoes across the pool, causing more than a few heads to turn.

"What the hell happened to my poor, twenty-something, normal guy?"

"I'm still normal, Lexi-con, but sometimes you have to put your money where your mouth is. And, I want my mouth on that girl, so you have to do this. It's in the wingman code."

She mumbles something under her breath, then finally stands. With her hands on her hips, and every inch of skin on display, she stares me down.

"Fine. But I'm warning you now, East, I don't lose. So, you better be ready for this."

Lexi? On my shoulders, in nothing but a teeny, tiny bikini? Perhaps there is a God after all.

Stepping into her space, I lower my face until we are just inches apart. "I'm all in with you, Locket."

There are so many meanings in that sentence. But for now, I grab Lexi's hand, drag her to the edge of the pool, and jump into the deep end.

CHAPTER 19

LEXI

*W*hy in God's name did I let Colton talk me into this? Avoiding Easton is hard enough, but sitting atop his shoulders in a pool with his hands roaming my body, holding me upright, is like setting fire to every nerve ending in my body.

We won the first two rounds easily, and while I think Colton's conquest is a floozy, they're at least holding their own in this battle.

"You ready, Lex? Last round," East calls up to me. Every time he tilts his head back to talk to me, his skull presses against my clit. It's blissful torture.

"Let's end them," I reply, with a giant smile on my face. I've always been competitive, but I haven't won at anything in a really long time. In some weird way, I need this.

Tucking my legs behind his back, Easton runs his hands up my thighs, holding me steady while he moves closer to our opponents. The girl across from me appears to have had a few drinks, but she's as determined as I am.

When we start grappling, I'm impressed with Easton's ability to keep us steady.

"Your girl's tits are hot. Too bad her top doesn't hold them in."

Glancing down, I realize the guy is just talking smack to make East lose his concentration, and it works. His grip on my left thigh loosens, and I start to spin.

"East! He's fucking with you. My tits are just fine. Concentrate."

"They look to be the perfect handful. What do you say, man? Want to trade for a bit?"

I feel Easton growl as he cranes his neck to get a look at me. When he does, my body slides, and he has to twist me completely, so we don't fall. Now his face is buried between my legs with nowhere to go.

Glancing down, I'm horrified to see his grin. Our competition comes forward, causing me to lean into Easton to shove her back. My crotch is hidden from view by Easton's face, but every time I lean forward, I feel his hot breath through my suit.

"Spin me back around, East. Hurry up," I demand. Sparing half a second to glance down, I see him lick his lips just as I lean forward again. Holy shit. If his nose hits my clit one more time, I might come right here in front of a thousand people.

"Take them down!" Colton's laugh brings me back to the present just as my competition grabs at my left arm.

Easton's hands on my ass are doing nothing to help the situation, either.

"You have to unhook your legs, Locket." At least, that's what I think Easton says. It's hard to tell because his face is buried in my pussy. The vibrations of his voice make my legs tremble. "Fuck me," he growls, and I give up.

"Stop, stop talking, Easton." I'm on sensory overload. The girl across from me gives a celebratory cheer too early, and I lunge at her.

Easton grumbles something, and I see stars. How the fuck

can I be this close to coming? Our competitors topple over with a final push, and I throw myself back, taking Easton into the water with me. Somehow, he never loses contact, and when we break the surface for air, we're face-to-face.

"That was…"

"Uh-huh." I can't catch my breath.

"You were close."

I swallow in response as he leans down to whisper in my ear.

"I'm not going to push you, Lexi, but I will never agree that we were a mistake. And I'll never forget the way you smell. Fucking delicious."

Even the cold water can't cool me off now. In another life, I would have been dragging this man to my room and done every wicked thing I can think of. But I'm not that woman anymore. Easton Westbrook deserves a woman who can give him a future. One that's whole, and that's not me, so I push away from him and swim to the edge of the pool.

"Yes, Lexi-con. You're amazing," Colt cheers as he offers a hand and helps to haul me out of the pool.

Even though I don't want to, I glance back at East, who hasn't moved from his spot in the pool. He shakes his head sadly, and I know I need to get away.

"Glad I could help, Colt. Listen, I'm going to get ready. I'll see you in the suite."

"Sounds good. What's up with East?"

I don't dare turn, so I shrug my shoulders. "Not sure. See ya."

Colton chuckles, but I grab a towel and hurry away.

Walls, Lexi. You have them for a reason. It's time to reinforce them before you get hurt again.

◦~◦

*a*n hour later, there's a knock on my bedroom door.
"Lexi? Can we talk?"

What is it with this guy? I've never known a man who wanted to talk as much as Easton Westbrook.

"I'm getting dressed," I lie. "What do you need?"

"You," he says it so softly, I finally convince myself it was wishful thinking.

"East? What did you need?"

There's a soft thump on the door, and then the light that was filtering in under it goes black. Dropping to the ground, I almost laugh when I realize he's sitting outside of my door. Again. Sliding over, I sit, too.

"Is this our thing, East? Sitting on opposite sides of doors?"

"It's the only time you'll talk to me."

He's not wrong. Maybe I feel safer with a barrier.

"I'm messed up, East. You don't want to waste your time here."

"We're all fucked up, Lexi, but I don't want to make things harder for you. I'm sorry for crossing the line in the pool with you today."

I want to tell him I liked it, that I wanted him, but I know that's not fair.

"What the fuck are you doing on the floor?" Colton's voice startles me.

"Talking to Lexi. She's getting ready. What's up?" Easton asks.

Colt mumbles something I don't catch, followed by an Easton growl I know well. My body reacts as if he touched me.

"So," Colton draws out, "remember Jessa, from the pool? She has a single friend. Do you have plans tonight?"

"Ugh," I scoff and shove back from the door as if it

126

shocked me, but I can't hear Easton's reply, so I hurry back and press my ear to it.

Why does it matter, Lexi? You have no right to him. I don't have a right to be mad, but I can't control the way my heart clenches at the thought of him going out with floozy number two.

"She's fucking hot, East. I need you to be my wingman tonight. Jessa won't go out unless I bring a date for her friend. When's the last time you got laid, anyway?"

"Fuck off, Colt."

"So … is that a yes?"

No, it's not a yes. Is it?

"Come on, East. Remember that time in Fiji? I was there when you—"

"I'll think about it, okay?" East interrupts irritably.

Ick. Seriously? He just had his head buried in my crotch, and he'll think about going out with someone else? I'm fully aware that my crazy is showing, and I don't give a shit. Well, fine. That just proves why we were a mistake.

"Locket?"

"Don't call me that," I hiss. I have no right to be pissed off, but I am, and my inner bitch is flying high. "Go to your brother's, East. I'll see you up there. We're done here."

"Open the door, Lex."

"Not today, Easton."

I stomp off to my en suite and make sure to slam the bathroom door so he knows I'm done.

Twenty minutes later, I exit my room, mostly composed, and head straight for the front door. Preston is staying three floors up, and that's where I'm meeting everyone for this stupid shopping trip.

Please, please, please don't let me run into Easton and his floozy. Knowing it's a possibility, I put on my armor. Acting like a bitch is so much easier than admitting I might be pushing away the best man I've ever known.

CHAPTER 20

EASTON

*W*hat a fucking nightmare. The girls returned from their shopping trip, and all hell broke loose. I knew the second the she-pack entered Preston's suite, one of us was in for it. Thankfully, it was Preston that managed to piss everyone off and not me.

As a war broke out between Preston and his girlfriend, Emory, I sat back and watched Lexi. She was so confident in her role as best friend and protector. There's no doubt in my mind she would have kicked Preston's ass if Emory needed her to. Shockingly, Emory took him to task herself.

Seeing Preston take the beating he probably deserved broke something inside of me, though. As it unfolded around us, I realized my big brother was in love. Real, messy, complicated love, and for the first time in years, I felt like I was missing out. I've spent so long living with hate and regrets. I don't want to do that anymore. I want what Preston has—what my dad modeled so perfectly for us. I want a life, and I think I need it with Lexi and all her stubborn, bitchy ways.

Colton is downstairs trying to persuade the girl from the pool to go out with him. I don't know the last time he worked this hard, but there was no way in hell I was going on a double date with him. Not when the woman I want is ten feet away.

Knowing she'll make me sit outside of her door, I walk to her room anyway and knock. Then knock again. When she doesn't answer, I open her door to find the room empty. *Where the hell is she?* I sigh because there's only one way to find out, so I grab my phone.

I hate that I'm about to partake in the shitshow that is group texts, but with all my brothers, friends, and their girls here, there's no getting around it.

Easton: Please tell me someone is still up for going out?

Dexter: I'm out.

Lanie: Me too. Sorry!

Halton: Working.

Julia: Having sex.

Trevor: Jesus, Jules! (Facepalm emoji)

Lanie: Yeah, girl! Get it!

Ashton: Can someone take their phones away in times like these?

Ashton: I've got some things to take care of. If I finish soon, I'll meet you somewhere.

Colton: I'm in! (Beer emoji)

Julia: Grab Lexi. She needs to get out.

Trevor: New rule. No phones during sex.

Easton: (Green puking emoji)

Lexi: No one needs to grab me. I'm out already.

Easton: WTF? By yourself?

Lanie: That doesn't sound safe. Please meet up with Easton and Colt. Luvs.

Lexi: Fine, I'm playing basketball on the roof.

Easton: Coming.

Colton: Sweet! I'll be there soon.

What the fuck is Lexi doing going out by herself? I swear this girl has been rubbing me the wrong way since Preston first stuck me with her. She's an outstanding employee, but she's a thorn in my side. She argues about every damn thing, and she has no sense of what's appropriate for an employee to say to her boss. *"Get laid and lighten up,"* after I declined her prospectus was not an appropriate reaction.

I'd love to get laid, but the girl I want keeps fucking running from me.

Now she doesn't think to call one of the twenty people on this trip to go out with her? My shoes are on in record time, and I'm at the elevator bank in seconds. The car seems to move in slow motion, and I hate that she makes me antsy. I don't have reactions like this. Ever. I'm an asshole for a reason, and I really should keep that going, but nothing with Lexi is easy, and I want her anyway.

When I finally reach the roof deck, I step out and spot her instantly—so do a hundred other red-blooded men. I'm moving before I realize it, and I don't stop until I'm standing toe-to-toe with her.

"What the hell are you doing, Lexi?" I try to shield her, and the cocksuckers behind me actually boo.

"I told you, I'm playing basketball, Easton."

"Dressed like that?"

I can't even look at her because I know one glance, and I'll be rocking a boner for the rest of the night. She's wearing a scrap of material she's calling a dress. It's white and sparkly and barely covers her ass. Every time she takes a jump shot, I swear I see her panties. Check that. There's no way she's wearing panties, and my head is about to explode.

"Hey, hey, hey! This is awesome," comes Colton's voice from behind me.

Thank God. Reinforcements.

Shoving me aside, Lexi locates Colt. "Hey, Colty, wanna play?"

Why the hell does he get a friendly greeting?

"Hells yeah I do."

Fucking Colt. As he passes, I grab his arm. "Hey, all these assholes are watching her ass. Don't you think we should get her to change before we play?"

"Get me to change? Are you kidding, East? What am I? Ten?"

"Lexi, your ass is hanging out," I yell to cheers from the peanut gallery. "See!"

"Pft. It is not. Don't get your panties in a twist. I'll tell you what, let's play for it. If I win, I wear whatever the hell I want. If you win, I'll go put on sweatpants and your sweatshirt to ensure I'm 'properly covered' for the rest of the night. What do you say, East? Think you can beat me?"

I know I can beat her. I wasn't varsity captain for three years in a row for nothing.

This was my first mistake.

"Done. Let's go."

"What about me?" Colt whines.

"You get the shots," Lexi yells. "First to ten wins. Every basket the winner and loser take a shot."

"God, I love you, Lexi! This is my kind of Vegas."

I can't help but roll my eyes at my younger brother. "Get some water, too," I shout, unbuttoning my top few buttons.

"Water? Come on, East. We're in Vegas!"

"You'll thank me later. Just get a waiter to bring everything," I tell him.

"You ready to play, or you still barking orders at your underlings?"

Stepping into her space, I lower my mouth to her ear. "If I'm paying them well enough, I'll yell whatever the hell I want."

"Asshole."

"Princess."

"Ha, ha. So far from the truth, you have no idea. You want to jump for it?"

"You want to jump for the ball? Lexi, I realize you're six feet, but I still have a few inches on you."

"Yeah, so did my teammates in college. I had to learn to jump, white boy. Did you?"

"It's *White Men Can't Jump*, Lexi, not white boy."

"We'll see about that. What do you say?"

"Sure. Colt!" I yell. "Throw the ball up for us."

Lexi gets into position opposite me, and holy fuck, her dress rides up her silky thighs even higher. I need to end this goddamn game so I can dress her appropriately.

"Clean game, kids." Colt smirks just before he sends the ball into the air.

I take my eyes off of him for a second and see the muscles in Lexi's thighs push off. It's a two-second distraction that has me biffing the tip-off. Lexi, who is barefoot, lands gracefully and takes off toward the basket. I have to sprint to catch her, and when I do, I plant myself in position, but she fakes right, then rolls left to make the left-handed layup.

As she's grabbing her own rebound, the crowd that's forming cheers. *Holy shit, she's good.*

She throws the ball underhanded straight at my gut, and it lands with a thud. "Shots, big guy."

Sure enough, Colt comes prancing across the court with shots. The three of us throw them back, and I check the ball to Lexi. I dribble a few times, getting a feel for the court, and when she comes up to defend, I move to my left. I'm about to spin when her hand comes from out of nowhere and strips the ball. She runs after it, and before I can react, she's headed to the hoop again. *Motherfucker.* I track her down enough to get a hand in her face as she pulls back for a fadeaway jump shot. I get in position for a rebound but can tell by the arc that it's all net.

"Shots!"

I get my man card back on the next couple of plays.

"Shots!"

132

"Shots!"

Lexi comes back with a vengeance. Somehow, she gets better the more we drink.

"Shots!"

"Shots!"

"More shots!" Colton yells as we come to the final play of the game. I have to win because there is no way in hell I'm walking around Vegas with Lexi's ass on my mind.

We all sling the shots back, and I shudder. "What the hell was that?"

Colt smiles wickedly. "Mind eraser. Come on, finish this game. I'm ready to dance!"

Fuck. Now I'm going to have to babysit and watch Lexi's ass.

It's my ball, and I take an easy jump shot, but I'm seeing two baskets. I hear the telltale thunk of the backboard. Lexi, fast as ever, grabs the rebound. She's cleared it at the three-point line, and I'm still trying to get the mind eraser out of my mouth. Since she's lingering near the arc, I don't pay much attention.

That was my second mistake.

"Never, ever underestimate me, East."

I look up just in time to see her go airborne for a three. It has a perfect arc, and I know she just hit the winning shot with nothing but net without ever taking her eyes off of me.

"Looks like I'll be wearing whatever I like," she says evilly.

"What do you mean?"

"Let's go, boys. I need to change before we hit the town."

~

I'm going to kill her. I'd give my left nut if she would put the first outfit back on, but I can never admit that. So now I have to walk around with a fucking steel rod in my pants because the girl I'm with is wearing a sheer shirt with a sparkly bra and hot pants. Her heels are sky high, too, putting her nose to nose with me.

I hate to dance, but as soon as we enter the club, I know I'm going to dance to any song she wants because the second I step back, there will be four other assholes ready to take my spot. I don't give a shit if she wants to dance with me or not. It's not up for discussion tonight.

Pink comes on over the speaker, and by the glint in Lexi's eyes, I know it's going to be a long night.

"Raise your glass, East," Lexi yells as I grind up behind her. I don't know if it's the shots or her, but I never want to leave the dance floor if it means I can keep her in my arms. She jumps and wiggles and writhes to the music, and I have an uneasy sense of home.

"Next!"

I laugh. "Lexi, we just got here."

"I know. I've never been to Vegas before, though. I want to hit every bar on the strip tonight! Come on, East. Please?"

She asks so sweetly I have to take a breath. That's the kind of look that could have me agreeing to anything for the rest of my life.

Apparently, even my willpower wilts to her magic. "All right, Sexy Lexi, lead the way. Where's Colt?"

We turn in a circle and find him propped up against a wall. "Oh, shit."

Lexi runs to him and holds his hand. She also gives him a mint and tells him to suck on it until he's outside, so he doesn't throw up. I've never heard of that trick before, but thankfully, it works. "Lanie was a puker," she explains. "We better take him home."

"Nah, let's stick him in a car. He'll be fine. You still have bars to hit," I say with a genuine smile and like how her reaction warms my chest.

"That's the spirit, East. Yes." She jumps in place and shocks the hell out of me when she leans in and kisses me.

I don't hold back. Wrapping Lexi's hair in my hands, I attack her lips, pressing my tongue at her seam until she opens to me. *I'm in a lot of fucking trouble.*

A car horn has us separating quickly, and I see it's our car service. We stick Colt inside with instructions for the driver. When they pull away, Lexi's eyes gleam with excitement.

"What's next, East? I want to do it all!"

~

"My feets hurts, Beast."

I stop walking, and the people behind us plow right into my back. I've had just enough alcohol that it doesn't even piss me off. I just laugh.

"Your feets hurts?"

"Yup." Lexi pops the p, and I want to kiss those lips, so I do. With my hands in her hair, I pull her face to mine.

"Get a room," someone yells from across the street.

"That's a good idea, Beast. We need a room."

I laugh again against her lips. "We have a room, two of them."

"Oh yeah." She pulls back to look at me. "My feets hurt."

Without hesitation, I turn my back to her and crouch down. "Hop on, sweetheart."

Lexi wraps her arms around my neck, and I reach back to grab her legs. When I stand, I bring her with me.

"I don't think I've had a little piggy ride since I was five."

"A piggyback ride?"

"Nope, a little piggy ride. Ask Lanie. That's what they're called."

"I'll take your word for it. If we call her now, Dex will probably have my balls."

"She's going to be such a pretty bride."

The sadness in her voice makes me pause. "You will be, too, someday."

135

I feel her shake her head against my back. Glancing around, I see a bench across the street, so I take us there and set her down.

"You will, you know? You'll be the best bride."

When Lexi's eyes raise to meet mine, time stops. This stubborn, beautiful woman shows the pain she's carrying with the single tear that escapes, and I drop to my knees before her.

"Talk to me, Locket." Even in my drunken haze, I have the urge to fix her. "Please, tell me why you're so sad."

"There's no future for me, Beast. I won't marry someone when I can't give them everything."

Oh, you beautiful, misguided, messy woman.

"Marriage isn't about giving everything, sweetheart. It's about giving what you can and letting your partner pick up the slack. Teamwork."

"You'll make a good team someday, East."

I don't know what comes over me, but suddenly, this seems like the best idea I've ever had. "Be my teammate, Locket. Tonight. Be mine. Give me what you can, and I'll handle the rest."

"What?" She laughs. "You're not making any sense. Plus, in case you forgot, I get to be team captain. I already killed you on the court. Remember?" She runs her hands up and down her body like Vanna White—a reminder of why she's dressed in hot pants and a see-through top.

Placing my hands on her thighs, I bring my face to hers. "Oh, I remember, sweetheart. Your ass in those shorts will be fodder for my showers for the foreseeable future. You can be the captain, Lexi. I just want to be on your team."

"My team? You mean for tonight?" She pauses and narrows her eyes at me as a giggle escapes her pouty lips. "Are you trying to get in my pants again?"

Somewhere in the back of my head, a voice is yelling that this is a terrible fucking idea, but I drown it out. The longer I think about it, the more I know I want to marry her right here tonight. If that means I get in her pants again, I'm all for that, too.

"Yup. For tonight, tomorrow, whatever I can get. What do you say, Lexi? Wanna be a team?"

"I'm drunk."

"Me too. But, this is a good idea. I know it is. Marry me. Be my team." *Just be mine.*

"I can't give you a future, East."

"Then give me tonight. We'll worry about the future tomorrow."

"Get married. Here?"

"Yes. Right now."

"And tomorrow we'll go back to being friends?"

"Yup."

Her laughter makes my heart feel lighter than it has in years.

"I don't think that's how it works."

"It's a good idea, Lex. I know it is."

"You want to get married tonight. And be friends tomorrow?"

"You keep saying you can't give me a future, so give me tonight. If tonight is all we have, let's do it all."

When our lips meet, I know she's mine.

CHAPTER 21

LEXI

I'm dying. I must be. There's no other explanation on the planet for why my head has a thousand-man marching band dancing in it. When I turn my head, the room spins, and I'm pretty sure I'm going to be sick. *Oh, fuck.*

Standing, I make my way to the bathroom, but seeing my reflection, I wince. I'm splashing water on my face when I hear something. Is that … is someone snoring? Poking my head out into the bedroom, I freeze.

Who's …

I sneak back into the bathroom as the events of last night come into focus. Playing basketball on the roof, dancing in the club, then sending Colton home in the car. *Fuck, I hope he made it home.* Rubbing my temples, I try to piece together the rest of the night. My lady bits are so freaking sore, so there's no mistaking the fact that Easton and I had sex last night. Again. Double fuck.

That's when I notice the giant, plastic ring on my finger, and I almost scream.

"And tomorrow we'll go back to being friends?"

"Yup."

"I don't think that's how it works."

"It's a good idea, Lex. I know it is. Be my team tonight."

"Just tonight?"

"Whatever you can give me."

Staring at the plastic ring, an enormous sigh of relief exits my lungs. Thank God, it was all just pretend. I think. I'm mostly sure, anyway. *Right?* If we'd really gotten married, there's no way I'd have a plastic ring.

What the hell, Lexi? Obviously, I cannot be trusted with that man. I have to get out of here. Maybe it's time to move home with GG until I can get my shit together. I can't keep ending up in bed with him. He deserves so much more, even if he is a grumpy asshole sometimes.

Removing the ring, I place it on the counter. Thankfully, I packed last night thinking I'd be sleeping in as late as possible today. After throwing on a T-shirt and denim shorts, I sneak out of the room. East is fast asleep on his side, his muscular back rising and falling with each breath. *Jesus, he's sexy.*

No, Lexi. Keep moving. Go.

Without another glance, I leave the suite and head straight for Lanie's room. Hopefully, she won't mind if I shower there. I'll have to make up some excuse about mine not working. When I press the button for the elevator, my gaze lingers on my ring finger. *No what-ifs, Lexi. It won't do you any good.*

Shaking out my hand, I let go of the momentary longing and go in search of my cousin. I know I'll have to see Easton on the plane, but I'm becoming a master of avoidance. If I can just get through Julia's wedding in a few days, then I'll go home and regroup. If anyone can whip me into shape, it's my crazy-ass grandmother.

Easton: We need to talk.

Lexi: I'll see you at work on Monday.

Easton: Jesus Christ, Lexi. This isn't a joke. Vegas is following us home whether you like it or not.

~

*T*he car carrying Lanie, Dex, their gaggle of kids, and I arrive at the tarmac first. Glancing around, I'm happy to see the other SUVs aren't here yet. As soon as the car stops, I jump out and practically run to the plane.

"In a rush to get home?" Dex laughs.

"Something like that."

"She's hungover. She was out with Easton until five a.m."

Did Lanie have to rat me out like that? Geez. Dex raises his eyebrows suspiciously, but I ignore him and find a seat.

"He's a good guy, you know?"

I open one eye to find Dex sitting next to me.

"Who?" I ask, hoping the squeak in my voice doesn't give me away.

"Who? Right, Lex. I wasn't born yesterday. The tension between you two is explosive. I just want you to know, I've known East my entire life. He won't hurt you."

"I know. It's not East I'm worried about."

Dex stares at me like I'm a puzzle to solve.

"I've got issues, Dex. He doesn't deserve my mess."

"Don't you think that's a decision for me to make?" Easton's deep voice vibrates through every fiber of my body, and I jump in my seat.

"Listen, I'm two for two with my *get the girl plans*. It worked for Trevor and me, so if you need my expertise, you know where to find me." Dex grins as he vacates his seat.

"He really fucking thinks he's Prince Charming, doesn't he?"

"He's the closest I've ever seen." My smile freezes in place as Easton drops into the seat next to me.

Reaching over, he grabs my hand and turns it so my palm

is facing up. Then, with his other hand, he drops the plastic ring.

"Ha, ha." It sounds forced even to me. "Well, at least it wasn't real, right?"

Easton stares at me with a blank expression for so long I begin to squirm in my seat.

"What do you mean it wasn't real, Lex?"

"Well, I mean—"

"What the hell is going on between the two of you?" Preston asks as he sits down across from us.

"Nothing," I hiss, but quickly close my palm around the ring. "Why are you so nosy?"

"I'm not nosy, darlin', but I'm not blind either."

"We're fine, Pres. Shouldn't you worry about your own girl? We just have some details to hammer out."

"His own girl?" Preston and I whisper yell at the same time.

"I'm not anyone's girl," I choke out.

Easton stands so suddenly I flinch. I hate that's my natural response, but living with Miles forced my fight-or-flight reaction, and I'm having a hard time letting it go. Just another reason running home to GG is a good idea. She might be the only one who can save me.

I'm waiting for Easton to say something when Ash interrupts. "Preston? Do you have a minute? I need to talk to you about something."

Preston bobs back and forth between Easton and me before finally rising from his seat. Glaring at East, he issues a warning, and I hate that I'm the cause of tension between the two. "Just remember what I said, East. Don't fuck around in the family pool."

East steps forward, so they're chest to chest. "Don't issue warnings when you have no fucking clue what's going on."

"Guys," Ash interrupts again. "Not here. Whatever the

141

fuck has crawled up your asses does not need to come to a head twenty thousand feet in the air."

Preston storms past, bumping Easton's shoulder on the way. Preston and I have never seen eye to eye, but regardless of my bitchiness, I know he's watching out for me. This goddamn family really has a way of making you theirs, even when you're running and screaming as fast as you can.

"I'm too hungover to fight with you, Locket, but we have a little problem." East grabs something from his back pocket before flopping back down next to me. Pressing a button, he unfolds a table to lay across my lap. Once it clicks into place, he slaps down some papers and a ring. A real ring. A really fucking big ring that's decidedly not fake.

~

We're married? Really, honest, and truly married? I keep running it through my head over and over again, but it doesn't make it any easier.

The plane touches down in North Carolina way too soon for my liking, and I still don't know what the hell to do.

"Well, come on, Missus. What the hell ya waiting for?"

Freaking GG.

"What?"

"Ya heard me, Missus. Let's get a move on. People are waitin' and all."

"Why are you calling me that?" I hiss.

GG waves her fingers at me, and I realize, somehow she just knows.

"What the hell is she talking about?" Easton whispers into the back of my head.

"Come now, Grumpy Growler. What is it you West-brooks say? Welcome to the chaos? Well, come on now, welcome to my chaos, Mister." GG reaches around me and wraps him in a hug. "She'll come around. Hang in there, Growler."

"GG!" I screech. She might have thought she was whispering, but she may as well have yelled for all of Charlotte to hear.

"Ah, thanks?" Easton grabs me by the elbow and escorts me down the stairs of the plane.

As I attempt to wiggle free, he tightens his grip.

"Lexi, there are not many times I'll force you to do something, but this is one of those times. We have shit to talk about, and it is going to happen tonight, at my house. So say your good-byes because you are coming home with me."

Every independent bone in my body wants to fight him, but I know the longer we wait to have this conversation, the trickier it will get.

"Fine. Let me go so I can tell the girls."

He reluctantly releases my arm just as Ashton walks up.

"I don't know what it is with this family and secret weddings, but you two were the last ones I expected this from."

Easton and I freeze in place. *How the fuck does he know?* Watching my face, he answers with a smirk.

"I have all of you tagged. So I get notified of everything, on any of you, anywhere in the world. It's a safety measure I never expected we'd need, but it has turned out to be rather fruitful recently." He frowns, and I see worry lines I've never noticed before. For someone so young, he seems to have the weight of the world on his shoulders. "Listen, I happen to approve of this union, but the thing is, there's shit going down, and you need to keep it under wraps for a while. Our family cannot take on any press right now."

Easton takes Ash's tone the same way I do, and I see him turn from Grumpy Growler to big brother protector in the blink of an eye.

143

"What's going on, Ash? Does this have anything to do with Pacen?"

"Pacen. Loki. It's all a clusterfuck of epic proportions. So, please, just trust me when I say keep this under wraps."

"But, we'll just get an annulment, right? Then it won't matter."

"You can't, Lexi. I'm sorry. It would end up in the papers for sure. Right now, we're lucky I got in with the judge first thing this morning to bury your license. It will give us a few months before anyone finds out, but if you go for an annulment or a divorce, it will be everywhere."

"That's not good enough, Ash. I can't stay married. So I need you to give me more than that," I hiss.

"Lives, Lexi. That's what I'm giving you by asking you to keep this quiet. People won't fucking die, and that's all I can tell you."

Ashton and Loki are the ones who rescued me, along with their partner, Seth, so I know he deals with life and death every day, but to hear it so bluntly knocks the wind out of me.

"I-I don't understand."

"And that's the way it has to stay, Lexi. Trust me, the less you know, the better."

"Ash, what the fuck is going on? Let us in, let us help. Just because Loki does this shit on his own doesn't mean you have to."

There's pain in Ashton's expression, and it's obvious he's fighting a war within himself.

"I can't, East. Just please, do as I ask."

Easton and I stare at each other, neither knowing what to say. Finally, Ash takes our silence as acceptance, kisses me on the cheek, and walks away.

"I ... wh-what do we do now?"

Easton shakes his head. "You're still coming home with

144

me. We need to figure some stuff out. Ashton needs us, even if he can't admit it."

I nod, but my entire body trembles with fear. I've witnessed first hand the kind of shit Ashton does. He's saved me from that evil once already. I'm not sure I can willingly walk into this again. Call me selfish, but I'm a hairsbreadth away from losing my mind. This might be the catalyst that finally breaks me, and I know there will be no recovering from it.

CHAPTER 22

EASTON

The ride to my house is silent. Lexi is curled up into the door, hanging onto herself so tightly I'm afraid she'll snap in two. But I don't push her. Not yet. I don't know what she went through in her past, but that has to change. *How can staying married save lives? Whose lives are we talking about? And why?* The questions run on a loop as I watch a range of emotions play over Lexi's face.

Sitting at the bottom of my driveway, we wait for the security gates to open wide. My place isn't anything like my mother's, or even Preston's for that matter. My home is a small, two-bedroom cottage that sits on the beach about three miles down the shore from where I grew up. I never have visitors, and keeping my place small ensured that family gatherings are always somewhere else. It makes leaving events so much easier.

Slowly, I drive down the narrow road that finally opens to reveal my Cape Cod style home. It's out of place here in the south; that's probably why I liked it so much.

"This is your house?" Lexi glances around skeptically.

"I'm sure there's a lot about me that would surprise you, Locket, if you only gave me a chance."

"This isn't what I was expecting," she admits.

"When I first bought it, I had to make some renovations. The former owners were half my size, so everything needed to be raised. Ceilings, counters, doorways, you name it. So basically, I tore the place down to the studs. There's very little in here I didn't have a hand in creating. Come on, let's go in, and I'll show you around while we talk."

"Honestly, East, I'm fucking exhausted. Can we just get this over with so you can bring me home? I'm hungover, scared, and feel like I could sleep for a week."

My spine tingles at her confession, and I need a minute to formulate the right words. I take a moment to get out of the car, then round the front to her side. Of course, she's already opening the door, but I reach in to stop her.

Bending at the waist, I force her to meet my eyes. "You have nothing to be scared of, Lexi. Nothing will hurt you here, I promise you."

"Yeah, that's great, East, except I can't exactly live in your garage now, can I? Loki is still out there taking down bad guys, right? Bad guys that at one time were almost my family. The same ones who took my future, so I'm pretty sure I have every reason to be scared."

Taking her hands in mine, I try to calm her down. "Lexi, Ashton removed your security detail. He wouldn't have done that if he thought you were in danger. I will find out for sure, but that leads me to believe it's not you that he's trying to protect here, okay? Come inside, please? I'll make you something to eat, and we can talk."

"You have a really bizarre obsession with feeding me, you know that?"

"All the better to eat you with, my dear." I mean it as a joke like she's Little Red Riding Hood or something, but the second the words are out of my mouth, my dick twitches painfully.

"You did not just say that." She laughs.

147

"Listen, you're not the only one hungover. Come on, in we go."

Walking to the front door, I notice I'm still holding her hand, and I fucking like it. Lexi seems to realize it at the same time because she snaps her hand away and tucks them into the pockets of her sweatshirt. It's always one step forward, two steps back with her.

Once inside, I get her settled at the kitchen island while pulling out ingredients from the fridge. The best I can do right now is burgers. So, hopefully, she will not tell me she's a vegetarian all of a sudden.

"Burgers, okay?"

"Oh my God, yes. The greasier, the better. Thanks. Can I help with anything?" It's the most enthusiastic response I've had from her yet.

"Nah, I've got it. You could go into the garage for me, though. I have an extra fridge out there filled with Gatorade and other electrolyte-heavy drinks. I think we could both use one or ten." I laugh. "It's right through that mudroom over there." I point her toward the opposite end of the kitchen.

"Sure. Any flavor in particular?"

"Anything but purple. I save those for Tate."

Lexi stumbles as she slides off the stool. "Lanie's stepson? You see him a lot?"

"Well, we grew up with Dex at our house every day. He's as much of a brother as the rest of us. 'Welcome to the chaos' isn't just something we say, Lex. When we welcome you, you're one of us forever. Tate has more uncles than he could ever know what to do with, and we'll always be there for him."

"That's … that's really great, East. Okay, no purples. Though, you realize, I asked what flavor, not what color?"

I stare at her blankly. "Listen, in Gatorade terms, flavors are the colors. My house, my rules."

She throws up her hands and stomps off toward the

garage. *She fits here, and I like it probably more than I should.* I toss in some seasonings to the ground beef and prepare the patties by hand. After a few minutes, I realize Lexi hasn't returned, and an abnormal amount of fear claws at my chest.

Rinsing off my hands, I jog toward the garage and find her standing in the center, running her hands over the desk. Her desk. Because of Colton's fucking glitter prank, I had to bring it home to clean out the sparkles. Even after sanding it down and staining it again, I'm still finding remnants of glitter everywhere.

"You made this?" Her voice is barely audible.

I have painstakingly carved her name into the top of the desk in a delicate scroll, so there's no hiding the fact I made it for her.

Suddenly shy, I grip the back of my neck. "I did."

Her finger traces the lines of her name repeatedly. "For me?"

"You're the only Lexi I know."

"But why? I mean, I'm pretty self-aware, East. I know I'm a bitch most of the time."

"You may be self-aware, but I can see self-preservation in every lash of your tongue. We work when we're bickering. It's even fun sometimes, but don't think for one minute you've hidden your pain from me, sweetheart."

"Don't, East. You're my boss. You're my ... my boss. That's why we work."

I'm inching my way closer, and I hadn't even realized I was moving. She's like a magnet pulling me to her. I couldn't stay away if I tried.

"I'm also your husband."

She winces at my statement as if I'd struck her. I won't lie, that was a fucking punch right to the gut.

"Come on, East. That was a mistake, and you know it ... a drunken mistake. If it weren't for Ash, we'd already be talking to a lawyer to fix this mess."

"Some mistakes aren't mistakes at all," I growl my displeasure.

"One little mistake with you turned into one more and one more. How many before you finally admit I'm bad luck?"

"What if you're a mistake I'm okay with making?"

She spins suddenly, and we're face-to-face. Lexi places a hand on my chest as if to steady herself before speaking, then realizing what she's done, tries to remove it. I'm too fast for her, though, and clamp my hand down over hers, holding her to me.

"Why are you pushing this, Easton? You don't even know me." Her voice cracks with the pain she won't share.

"Why are you fighting it, Lexi? I *know* you feel something when you're with me, but you refuse to allow yourself to let go. I *know* that you're hiding, and that you're hurting. I *know* that you use an abnormal amount of French vanilla creamer in your coffee, and you suck on butterscotch candy when you're nervous. I *know* that you love and protect with your whole heart, but don't allow yourself the same grace, so don't tell me I don't *know* you, Lexi. I may have a lot to learn, but that's how this works. We learn from each other with every mistake, each conversation, every kiss."

This time she does rip her hand away and turns her back to me.

"What do you want from me, Easton?" She yells, but sounds defeated. "I'm too tired to fight with you tonight."

"I want you to talk to me. Tell me your story. Tell me why you're afraid. Tell me what happened?"

"Not today."

"Then when?" I demand.

"Maybe next time." Her voice wavers, and I know she's fighting hard to hold it together.

"Jesus Christ, Lexi. Let me in!" I bellow. "I'm here. I want to help, but you have to let me in. You can't live your life in emotional lockdown like this. It's not healthy. You have to take care of yourself, and sometimes that means letting the people who love you in. Let me in, Lexi."

"Don't do that, Easton."

"Don't do what?" I scream.

"Don't use your Prince Charming complex to fool yourself into thinking you have feelings for me. I don't need you to fix me. I don't need you to take care of me. I don't need you, Easton."

Every word out of her mouth is a lie that cuts me deeply. It also pisses me off because I can see the emotion welling in her eyes.

"But do you want me, Lexi?" My words come out in a strained staccato. Will she lie to me again? Will she hide behind her words? Or will she give me this one little thing that I desperately need?

"You don't always get what you want in life, Easton. I know that better than anyone."

"Do. You. Want. Me?" I crowd her until she's backed up against the desk that bears her name. Each breath causes her hair to fan across her forehead. Before she can respond, I'm compelled to reach up and tuck a wayward strand behind her ear. When she gasps and leans in ever so slightly to my touch, I have my answer.

"Tell me, sweetheart. Do you want me?"

"I can't have what I want. It wouldn't be fair to you," she cries.

"I don't give a flying fuck about fair, Locket. Do you want me?"

"Tonight?"

Forever, I want to scream but bite my tongue and nod instead. Leaning in, I rub my nose along her jawline, waiting for an answer. When one doesn't come, I bite down gently on her earlobe. "Answer me, Locket." My hand snakes around her waist, and I pull her into my larger frame.

CHAPTER 23

"*A*nswer me, Locket." Easton's grip tightens around my waist as he pulls me flush against him. His erection presses against my stomach, and I bite my tongue to keep from moaning.

Do I want him? So much it hurts. Can I have him? Not without breaking him.

"Give in, Lex. Please, just let me be there for you." His tongue darts out to lick a line from the base of my neck up to my ear, and an unsanctioned moan escapes my lips just before I feel my knees buckle.

"It's going to be another mistake," I argue, but it's weak even to my ears.

His hands force themselves into my hair as he holds my face steady. "I was always taught that mistakes are how you learn. So what if I want to keep making these mistakes until I learn every inch of you?" His lips land on mine. "Every curve." He moves his hands down my sides until he's cupping my ass. "Every bruised and battered insecurity. I'm all for learning from our mistakes, Locket."

His teeth catch my bottom lip as I attempt to respond. Opening my mouth, he increases the pressure on the back of my head as he angles my face so he can devour me. This is wrong for so many reasons, but everything disappears when he controls my body like this. It's just him, and me. I've never felt safer or more free than when I'm in his arms, so I let him take control. In fact, I beg him to.

Placing a hand on my stomach, he guides me back onto the desk. When I'm perched on the edge, he leans into me so far I'm forced to lie down.

"Fuck, Lexi. You're so goddamn sexy. Sexy Lexi," he whispers reverently as his eyes roam my entire body.

I feel self-conscious as he stares at me like I'm a seven-course meal. I intentionally wore baggy sweatpants and a sweatshirt three sizes too big in a lame attempt at throwing him off my scent.

Easton spreads my legs and steps between them. His fingertips graze the skin just above the elastic waistband as he places a hand on each of my hips.

"Tell me, Lexi. Did you think these would make you less desirable? Or that I wouldn't fantasize about what I know is under all this fabric?"

His assumption makes me laugh. "Well, it crossed my mind," I admit.

Laying a hand down next to my face, he holds his weight up as he presses his body into me. "You could be wearing a bathrobe from 1970 with pornstaches all over it, and I would still daydream about your naked body, Lex."

I swallow as his other hand glides below my sweatshirt—the heat from his palm causing goosebumps to form in its wake. His hand pauses just below my left breast, and I ache for contact.

"Do you want me to touch you?"

What the fuck is it with him and these questions? But I have no self-control around him, and I know he'll be my undoing.

"Yes, Easton. Jesus Christ, I want you to touch me, okay?" I scream.

I feel his grin next to my cheek, and I want to punch him. His hot breath hits my ear just before his whispered words, and I shiver.

"That's all you had to say, sweetheart. That's all you ever have to say. I can't deny you." His admission does funny things to my chest, but before I can linger on them too long, he raises my shirt over my head.

My bare back presses into the cool wood, and my body comes alive with sensation. He wastes no time removing my sweatpants, and his groan vibrates throughout my body when he realizes I'm not wearing any panties.

"Are you trying to kill me?" he asks as he drops to his knees. "Open your legs, Lexi. Let me see you."

It's such an odd thing to say, but at the first swipe of his tongue, I comply. He uses his mouth like a maestro conducts the orchestra. He carefully choreographs his every movement to bring me pleasure.

Oral sex is generally a nonstarter for me. I get too caught up in my own head. *Has he been trying too hard? Am I making too much noise? Why is my body making those noises? Is it normal to be this wet?*

His tongue pauses on my clit, and I suck in a deep breath. He flicks it once, twice, three times before he replaces it with his fingers.

"Tell me what's happening in your head?" he orders while his fingers play a banjo chord over my most sensitive nerves.

I can't think. I heard his words, but I can't make mine come.

"Fuck me, Lexi. I love how wet you get for me. I love the sounds your pussy makes sucking me in because you're dripping for me. *I* fucking do this to you. I could do this all goddamn day," he growls right before he dives back in, this time using his teeth.

It's like he has a direct line to my heart and mind, and I can't take his honesty anymore.

"I-I need you to kiss me," I demand. Anything to get him to stop talking. If I'm not careful, he'll talk his way right over my walls and implant himself permanently in my heart.

"Oh, sweetheart, I do love it when you're demanding. Your wish is my command."

His lips land on mine, and I can taste my arousal. Suddenly it feels too real. Too personal. Too much. I claw at his belt buckle, and he pulls back to watch me.

"I wanted you to come on my lips, Locket. I'm not done with you."

I can't give in to him, and I can't walk away. Once again, my body and mind are at war. One of these times, the fight will actually kill me.

Frantically, I claw at his pants, but my hands are shaking too much to get them down.

"Hey? Lexi, wait. Wh—"

When my trembling hands finally wrap around his shaft, his words die on his lips. His hips jerk reflexively, and I lick his first drops of pre-cum. Easton is salty and rich. *He tastes like the man I've come to lo—*

My train of thought sends me spiraling, and I gag when his cock hits the back of my throat. Tears fill my eyes, and I'm thankful Easton will think it's from the size of his dick.

I should know better, though. Easton knows me. He sees me like no one ever has, so I'm not surprised when he hauls me to my feet and holds me close.

"Sweetheart? What the hell? What is happening in that head of yours? Did I push too hard? I-I ..."

"No, no," I sob. I don't want him to see me, though, so I bury my face in the crook of his neck.

"Lexi." His voice is loud but not harsh as he pulls me back and holds my face in front of his. Under his inspection, I feel my walls crumbling, so I do the only thing I can think of. I ask him to make me feel.

"Please, Easton. Just, please?"

155

"Please, what? What do you need?" he pleads, and I fear my brokenness is already tearing him apart.

"Make me feel like I'm not broken," I gasp. "Just for a minute, make me feel like a mistake you won't regret one day."

It's not a fair request. I know it's not, but my insecurities have taken over my brain, and for one more night, I just want to pretend. Pretend I can be his. Pretend I can live a happy life. Pretend I'm not alone in a room full of people.

"Are you okay?" The sincerity and fear in his eyes make it hard to breathe.

"Yes. Yes, just, please," I whimper because I'm unable to say anything else.

"Oh-okay," he says hesitantly.

Feeling as if I ruined the moment, I attempt to back away.

"We-We don't have to—"

Easton stops me before I get a whole step in. "I will always want you, Lexi. Always."

He backs me up to the desk and carefully lays me down. Stepping in between my legs, I see he's still unsure if I'm okay.

"I want this, East. I-I'm just broken."

It's like I've flipped a switch in him, and his eyes darken to a shade I don't recognize as he reaches into his pants for a condom.

"Hang onto the edge of the desk." Easton's voice is a deep, rumbling growl that makes my thighs clench. "Now, Locket."

My eyes never leave his as my hands find the smooth edge of the desk. When my palms rub against the carving with my name, I swallow the emotion clawing at my throat.

He enters me in one angry thrust, and it steals my breath.

"You." He thrusts again, and the table slides on the sawdust-covered floor. "Are." Thump-slide. "Not." Thump-slide. "A." Thump-slide. "Mistake." Each deep thrust punctures what's left of my soul.

156

The table has moved across the floor, so we're now against the wall. Easton pulls out and waits until my gaze finds his. "You're not broken. You're not a mistake. You're my wife." He slams back in. The veracity of his words mixed with his near violent thrusts are too much for me to take.

I come undone, and feel it in every inch of my body. My hair stands on end while my toes curl. My legs and pussy spasm around his long, thick length that pistons in and out of me with animalistic control.

"Feel this, Lexi. Feel me, only me. I'll never lie to you," he vows, but I only partly hear him because blood is rushing loudly in my ears.

Easton's body goes rigid while he pours himself into me with a long, low growl that seems to spur me to the edge again.

"Oh, Lexi. I feel you. I feel your pussy tightening. You're close again, aren't you?"

I don't know if my mind is even functioning anymore. All I can do is pant as he snakes his hand between us.

"Holy shit." I moan when I feel Easton's dick twitching inside of me, and he begins to move again.

"Only you. Only you do this to me," he whispers beside my ear while his fingers work their magic on my clit.

"I-I can't. I can't, Beast."

"You told me once to never underestimate you, sweetheart," he growls through clenched teeth. Every muscle in his body tenses as he fights for control. "I think you're capable of so much more than you realize."

With a devilish gleam, his fingers pick up speed as he grinds his cock so deep inside of me I'm sure he's branding me from the inside out.

"Give me one more, Locket." When he pinches my clit between his fingers, the world goes black around me.

Somewhere in my post-coital blackout, I hear him whisper, "I want you to stay, Lexi. Here, with me. You feel like home."

~

hy is it so bright in here?
Rolling over, I come face-to-face with a scruffy-faced Easton, and I bite my tongue to keep from screaming. *Ugh, Lexi. You're so selfish.* Staring at his handsomely chiseled face, I notice how young he appears in sleep. His scowl lines have vanished, and he seems peaceful. Happy.

We're already getting attached.

This man grew up with the TV perfect family—he's going to want the same thing. What's going to happen when he finds out you can never give him that future? Maybe I should just tell him? Then we can get this divorce over with before anyone gets hurt.

In another life, I know I could have made him happy. But Miles broke me. I'll never be the same, and it's time I started pulling my head out of my ass and figured out what my future will look like. One thing I know for sure: I can't let Easton think he has feelings for me. *I can't let myself think I have feelings for him either*. He'll feel betrayed when he finds out what a future with me would be, and I'd rather push him away than let him know what I allowed myself to become.

Swallowing the sadness that sits heavy in my chest, I creep out of bed and head toward the kitchen. I'm pretty sure my clothes are still in the garage so I can grab them and be on my way without ever waking the perfect beast.

Searching for my shirt, I find it under the desk. *My desk.* My chest cracks wide open. I have to blink rapidly to keep the tears at bay. No one has ever spent time on me like this. I don't know if anyone has ever given me enough thought to even consider it. The gesture means more than he'll ever know, and as much as I wish I could keep it, I know it would be too painful. A constant reminder of him is the last thing I can deal with.

Instead, I take out my phone and snap pictures of it from every angle. Once I'm satisfied I have every inch of it in my phone, I pull up Uber and call for a ride.

Easton's going to be pissed when he wakes up. He asked me to stay, but hopefully, someday, he'll realize it was for the best. Now I just need to get through this weekend. Then, I'll head home and pray that GG can fix my broken heart.

CHAPTER 24

EASTON

Knock, knock.

Glancing up from my desk, I allow a moment of hope that it will be Lexi. When I see Mason at the door with a shit-eating grin, I groan. *Fan-fucking-tastic.*

"What do you need, Mas? I'm not really in the mood for your shit today."

"And why would that be, my friend?" His tone gives him away. He knows something.

Tossing my pen on the desk, I scowl as he plops down into the armchair opposite me. *That's Lexi's chair,* my inner caveman screams, and I pull at my collar to calm myself down.

Mason's a talker, so I know I just have to sit here, and he'll eventually get to the point.

"Where's our Lexi girl today?"

And there it is. He's here to poke the lion.

"She's working remotely, so she can help Julia with last-minute wedding plans." It's the truth, but I also know she's using it as an excuse to hide from me.

It's been two fucking days since she snuck out of my house without a word. Then I find out she's coming into the office after midnight to drop off files and exchange them for new ones. I'm so fucking tempted to sit my ass right here until she shows up, but I don't know what else to say to her at this point. How long do you chase someone before you finally get the goddamn hint?

Knock, knock.

"East, you have a minute?" Ashton's no-nonsense voice rings out before he even enters the room. Eyeing Mason, he stops short. "Oh, hey, Mason. Uh, I'll just come back later."

"No need, Ash. I was just here giving Easton shit about his runaway."

"What?" Ash and I both ask.

"His runaway, Lexi? She's obviously avoiding him. I was hoping to find out what he did."

"I didn't do anything, Mason. She's helping her friend, that's it."

"I don't believe you, but I'll come back later to dig. Good to see you, Ash." Mason pats him on the shoulder as he walks past.

As soon as he's through the door, Ashton closes it. "Not going well with the wife?"

I hang my head. Ashton may be the best man I know, but he's still a Westbrook. Teasing is in our blood.

"She's hiding."

"She's hurting, East. Just stick with her."

"How long do you keep chasing someone before you finally let them go? She's made it perfectly clear she doesn't want to want me. She doesn't need me." My words hang bitter in the air.

"She needs time to process life, East. Did you know I sat with GG on the flight home?"

This makes me laugh. You never know what the fuck is going to come out of her mouth.

"How'd that go?"

161

"About as well as you would expect. But she knows stuff. Stuff she shouldn't. It's scary as hell."

"Something you want to tell me, Ash?"

"Nothing concrete, but Loki should have been home for Trevor and Julia's wedding by now." His use of past tense makes my ears prickle.

"What do you mean should have? He's family; we don't miss shit like this."

Ashton sighs, and for the first time, I notice how haggard he looks.

"Ash, are you okay? Talk to me. You look like shit."

A humorless chuckle leaves his throat. "Our world is spiraling, East. Bombs are flying from every side."

"Jesus Christ, Ash. What the hell is going on?" I don't scare easily, but fear has crept up my spine and has me on edge.

"All I can tell you is, Loki isn't answering his phone, and he missed his last check-in with SIA."

When I stare blankly, he finally caves.

"SIA, the Select Intelligence Agency we work for. He has to make the next mark, or I don't know what will happen. Then ..."

"What? What else?" I bark. The fact that our brother is missing isn't all that's weighing heavily on Ashton's mind.

"Just keep Lexi close."

"Is she in danger?" New fear rises like a freight train and thrums loudly in my ears.

"No, but when the shit hits the fan, you're going to need each other." Knowing I'm about to interrupt, he keeps going. "I think we have a mole in The Westbrook Group. I can't track it, but things aren't adding up. There are too many coincidences, too many lost bids we should have won."

Air leaves my lungs in a whoosh. I've also been worried about this.

162

"Any idea who? Or what department the leaks are coming from?"

"Not yet. As soon as I locate Loki, I'm going to find out." Ashton leans forward and lowers his voice. "When I get a track on Loki, I'm going to update our infrastructure. Trevor is working on a new program for us. Once it's up and running, I should be able to narrow it down. Or at least give us a starting point."

"Does Preston know?"

"Not yet. He's … well, he's got other things going on right now that are more important. I'm telling you so if it comes to it, we'll be ready to handle anything."

"What aren't you telling me?" I stare at my baby brother and see the turmoil he's living swimming in his eyes. I also see the minute he shuts down.

"I've told you all I can, East. Just be ready for anything, okay?"

I eye him curiously. Ashton is nervous, and it leaves me uneasy. "I'll be ready, Ash. Can you tell me what's going on with Lex? Why we really need to stay married?"

He searches my face for a long time before speaking. "I'm helping Pacen. Lexi was right; she's in trouble."

My gut clenches. Pacen is still a baby; she's … actually, she's Ashton's age. Right around twenty-five.

"And it's no secret," he continues, "Macombs hates you. Hates us, hates the world really, but I think he's gotten in too deep this time. He's looking for easy money. If there is a paper trail leading Lexi to you, she could become a target. For now, I buried your marriage license because the judge had some illegal, extramarital activities I could unearth. As long as Macomb thinks she's only your assistant, she's in the clear."

"Fuck."

"It's all a safety precaution, East. With everything else going on, I'm triple checking every base, every corner, every possible outcome. I know Lexi isn't happy with the idea, but staying married is the fastest and safest way for me to protect everyone right now."

"How can I help, Ash? I wasn't kidding when I said you look like shit. When is the last time you slept? You can't play hero if you run yourself into the ground."

"I'm good, East. Just keep an eye on Lexi so I can focus my attention elsewhere, okay?"

Swallowing the bile that's suddenly making an appearance, I stand and round the desk. Wrapping Ash into a Westbrook special, I'm surprised by how strong he's become.

"Okay. But when she kicks me in the balls, I'm blaming you." I go for lighthearted, even though the atmosphere around Ashton is anything but.

"She's a firecracker that lost her spark. Give her a light, East, and she'll find her way home."

"What if her home isn't where I want her?" I sound like a fucking pussy, but this girl is a marathon I haven't trained for.

"She's not a woman who will bend to your will, East. She needs to be your equal in every way possible. I think home to her will be where she feels safe, where she feels loved, and where she can learn to trust again. Home isn't always a building, brother. Sometimes, home is whoever holds your heart."

"When did you become so smart?" I chuckle.

"I've always been the smartest, asshole. I'm just finally ready to let you all know it."

Raising my fist, we meet halfway. "Welcome to the chaos, little brother."

Ashton smiles, but it's forced. Whatever shitstorm's brewing, Ashton is hell-bent on getting us through it, alone.

CHAPTER 25

LEXI

"Could Julia have chosen a more revealing dress for me?"

"You look beautiful, Lex. We all basically have the same dress," Lanie lies.

"You're full of shit, Lanie. If I tilt back even an inch, you're going to see ass crack. The back is so wide open it's not possible to wear a bra, and the silky material has my head-lights on high beam."

"But you look sexy."

"Says the girl in the spaghetti strap gown that completely covers you."

"Oh, geez. You're such a drama queen. Come on, I'm sure Julia's ready to get the party started. We can't hide out in the bathroom all night."

Crap. That was actually my plan. I've successfully avoided Easton, but I could feel his gaze on me during the ceremony like hot wax.

"Fine, let's go."

Lanie opens the door, and we barrel right into a chest I know well.

"Oh, shoot. Sorry, East. I didn't see you there," Lanie apologizes, but volleys her gaze between East and me.

"No worries, Lanes. Do you mind if I steal your lovely cousin away for a moment, though?"

"Ah, of course not. I'll see you in there, Lex." Leaning in, she gives me a kiss on the cheek so she can whisper, "Be nice."

"Ugh, I'm always nice." Both Lanie and Easton stare at me with open amusement.

"Fine, I'm mostly nice."

"We'll see you in there, Lanie." Easton's voice sends a chill down my spine. As he speaks, his eyes never leave mine.

Lanie bobs back and forth between us a few times, then must assume we're good and takes off for the ballroom. *Traitor.*

"You can't avoid me forever, Locket."

"Lexi," I correct him.

He takes a step closer, and as much as I want to take a step back, I hold my ground. I can't let anyone intimidate me again.

"I've missed you." The low timbre of his voice makes my body come alive. Another traitor.

"You don't."

"I do. I may be an asshole, Lex, but I've never been a liar." He takes another step forward. "I don't like that you keep running from my bed before I wake up."

"Huh, isn't that how one-night stands are supposed to go? Jesus, I'd want a random out of my bed before I went to sleep."

Easton crowds me before I finish the sentence.

"You are not a random, Locket. You. Are. My. Wife." The emotion behind his words scares the shit out of me.

"O-Only by mistake. We … we're not really married, East. We can't stay married."

He looks as if I wounded him, and I know I need to

escape before I say something I shouldn't. Pushing past him, I try to enter the ballroom, but Easton is close behind. I feel relief when I see Colton making a beeline for us.

"Lexi-con, want to dance?"

"Not fucking today, Colt. Back off." Easton's growl echoes in my head.

"Dude, whatever the fuck is going on, you need to get a handle on it."

"Not now, Colton."

I glance at him over my shoulder when we pass, and he gives an apologetic shrug as Easton drags me onto the dance floor. Wrapping me in his arms, he begins to move in time with the music while visions of Vegas flood my head.

Leaning in so his mouth is at my ear, he whispers, "I spoke to Ash. We are, in fact, married, princess. And for everyone's safety, we not only need to stay married, but we need to stick close together."

"What?" I screech, just as screaming erupts around us.

Easton releases one arm while we search for the commotion. He lets me go completely when we see his brother, Preston, lying limp on the floor with his girlfriend barking orders to everyone around her.

~

*I*t's been seven days since Preston collapsed, and I don't think anyone has slept more than a couple of hours. We're standing in the hallway just outside of Preston's hospital room, and I realize it's been the longest week of my life.

"Did you know?" Easton's voice is deadly as he corners Ashton. "Is that why you said I would need Lexi? Is that why you told me to be ready? Did you know his heart was giving out? That he had the same heart defect as Dad?"

Ash lowers his eyes, and we have our answer.

"I only found out recently. He wanted to get through this wedding, and then he was going to tell everyone."

"Jesus Christ, Ash. He could have fucking died, and it would have been Dad all over again. How could you keep that from us? How could you do that to Mom?"

"East," I try, but it doesn't calm him down. If anything, he only gets angrier.

"I'm sorry, East. It wasn't my story to tell. I was just as pissed as you. God, it fucking broke me when I found out, but I'm doing the best I can to keep everything together. I did what I thought was right. You would have done the same goddamn thing."

"That's where you're wrong, Ash. I'm tired of this 'not my story to tell' bullshit. Sometimes, you need to tell the fucking story. Sometimes, the fucking story is what will get you through all the bullshit. Sometimes, you need to stop pissing around—"

"Uncle East?" Tate's little voice carries down the hall, and we all freeze.

Glancing up, I see Lanie holding his hand, and my heart shudders.

East swallows a few times before speaking. "Hey, buddy. Sorry, I didn't see you there."

"It's okay, Uncle East. But, don't be mad at Uncle Ashton. It isn't his fault. Uncle Preston had a broken heart, but I told you that Auntie Ems would fix him, and she did. I told you, remember?"

"Yeah, buddy, I remember. How'd you get to be so smart?" he asks as he ruffles the little boy's hair.

"GG told me. She showed me her cards."

Jesus, GG. The kid is like six years old.

"And, I've got something for you, too. I found it digging at Nanna Sylvie's. She said I could have it, but I want to give it to you."

I watch as Tate reaches into his little pocket, pulls out an old-fashioned key, and places it into Easton's hand.

"GG told me you're having trouble with your lock's future. Maybe this key will work?" The smile on this kid would make my ovaries combust, if they hadn't already.

Easton's gaze finds mine, and my heart shatters because I know I'm about to break him.

"Thanks, Tate. I love it. Are you sure you don't want to keep it?"

"Nope, I'm good. GG says sometimes the key is staring you in the face." Tate leans in, then whispers, "But she said a bad word, too." The inappropriateness of my grandmother eases the tension as he continues, "If you can't fix your lock with your eyes, maybe the key will help. I'm going to see Uncle Preston now. We have a date to play old maid, but I told my dad I would let him win so he doesn't get too sad."

Easton scoops the little guy up into a fierce hug. "I love you, little man."

"Love you, too. Welcome to the chaos, right?"

"That's right, buddy. Go give Preston a run for his money."

Tate smiles and runs away. Lanie glances between East, Ash, and me. "Everything okay?"

"Yeah, I'm heading out," Ashton says, already turning away.

"Ash," Easton calls, but he just raises a hand and waves.

"We'll talk later, East. I have to find Loki."

"Fuck."

Unsure of what to do, Lanie gives me a hug and follows after Tate.

"God, that kid can really kick you in the love sack sometimes." Easton chuckles. "I hope my kids are half as amazing as he is."

And there we have it. The reason we can never work. He

grew up with this big, amazing family. I've only ever known dysfunction, and now, because I chose Miles Black, I can never give anyone a family. A single tear turns into two, and before I know it, the floodgates on emotions I've worked to suppress rear their ugly head.

CHAPTER 26

LEXI

"Sweetheart? What's wrong? Please, Jesus, Lex. Let me in. Tell me, what's wrong?"

I open my mouth, and slobbery mucus nearly suffocates me as I try to speak. The sobs that wrack my body cause my limbs to tremble. Easton glances around, then takes me by the hand. Leading me down the hallway, he finds an empty family room and drags me inside.

"Baby, please. Please tell me what's wrong? I-I can't take seeing you hurt like this. It's killing me that I don't know how to fix it. Please let me fix it, Locket."

I place a hand over my mouth to control the anguish trying to escape as I shake my head. How do you tell someone like Easton Westbrook that you're broken?

"Why, Lex? Why won't you tell me?"

"You push, and you push, and you push," I finally choke out. "It was so much easier when you were an asshole. I can't take you being nice to me, Beast. I don't deserve it."

"Jesus Christ, Lexi. Stop saying that," he yells.

I want to scream and cry and make him understand that my body hates me. Or that I was a terrible person in another life. Something. Anything to make him understand why I

171

deserve this pain, but I don't. I won't because even with all these reasons running through my head, I know no one wants to hear it. No one wants to hear that I might have accidentally caused this, or how my body and mind betrayed my heart, so instead I shut down. I go numb because it's easier for us all, and I tell him my story as if I were a witness and not a participant in my own life.

His anger gives me strength, and with sudden clarity, I know he won't give up on us unless I force him. He needs to know what I did so he can leave me to my misery.

"I killed my baby, Easton." It comes out detached, and I sink into an emotionless pit so I can get through this.

"Wh-What?"

"My baby died because of me. Before I knew what a monster Miles was, we talked about having kids. My periods were irregular, so we went to a specialist, someone his dad knew, and he told me I would struggle to get pregnant."

My words come out in a rush, but I have no feeling left to put behind them, and they sound monotone. Once again, I feel like a voyeur in my own life.

I turn to the window. I can't look at his pained face while I relive the worst day of my life.

"We were going to harvest my eggs and freeze them. The first round was okay. The second time, my body overstimulated from the injections, and one night I woke up in so much pain." My voice breaks, and I have to cough to regain it. "I couldn't move. I started vomiting, and Miles was convinced it was just the flu. We waited, and waited, and waited until the pain was so excruciating that I nearly passed out."

Easton makes no move to comfort me. He just sits in the silence of the room, waiting for me to finish.

"At the hospital, we found out an ovary had twisted … ovarian torsion, they called it. We waited too long, Beast. That ovary had already died."

"Okay, but there are opt—" I cut him off because there are no options, and the pain reflected in his eyes nearly guts me, so I turn back to the window.

Find your inner bitch, Lex. Let her protect you.

"Then, a few months later, I got pregnant. It wasn't planned. By the time I found out, I had already learned about Miles and his family, but … but I would have loved that baby, East. I promise I would have." This time I can't control the sob that escapes.

The tears overrun my words, and I just have to let them flow. Easton chooses that moment to take me into his arms. He cradles me like a child and ushers me to the couch.

"Here." He hands me a box of tissues that I gladly take. "Lexi …"

"No, East. I have to finish." Staring into his eyes hurts too much, so I watch my fingers as they twist the tissue around my finger in a constant loop. "I had gone home to talk to Julia's parents. I wanted to know if I could keep my baby away from Miles and the Black family. I had evidence. I needed them to help me protect her."

Easton clears his throat, and I dare a peek. He has tears falling down his face, and I know I don't deserve this man. I will only hurt him in the end.

"Mimi told me the evidence I had wasn't enough. She needed more, something concrete, but she begged me not to go back. She said there were other ways, and we had time. I was only a few weeks along. We had time. B-But I was too impatient. I-I thought if I went back, just once, I could get the information we needed."

"Locket …" Easton's voice cracks as he takes my hand in his. I shouldn't allow the comfort, but I need his strength.

"I-I went back. Back to Miles. He was already pissed that I'd left without telling him. I didn't know Loki was closing in on them at the time. Loki didn't exist in my world then. I just knew Miles was the bad guy, and I had to get away.

"He caught me going through his office the next day. He accused me of being a traitor, of turning him in. He yelled and screamed, but I felt numb. I tried to stay calm for my baby, but then a man came into the room with a needle. It only took a minute for them to hold me down, and the world went black around me.

"I woke up in a car, on a tarmac, and I knew if I got on that plane, I would never be free. He got me out of the car, and I tried to run, but the drugs he'd given me made my legs hang heavy. I began screaming for help, for anyone to help me, and that's when the bleeding started. It wasn't a lot at first, but we both saw it. By the time he got me on the plane, it was too much blood. I knew something was wrong, and I begged for him to help me. I pleaded."

"Jesus, Locket. I'm, I—"

I hold up my hand, silently begging for him not to talk. I'm not done.

"Finally, he decided I needed a doctor, but I'd lost so much blood. I-I wasn't even conscious. So I guess I should be thankful he brought me to Mass Mercey and didn't let me bleed out on his plane, but more times than not, I wish he had."

"Fuck, Lex."

"When I woke up in the hospital, they told me I had lost her, but I could already feel it. I was empty. They said it was too early to tell the sex, but I know it was a girl. I know it."

"W-Were you okay? I mean—"

"There was too much hemorrhaging ... too much damage. They did a full hysterectomy to save my life. I'm empty, broken.

"You know, all I ever wanted was to be a mom. I didn't have one, and Lanie's was an abusive drunk. My entire life, I wanted to be the mom that my own didn't get to be. I wanted to raise her to be a strong, independent woman. A caring, empathetic friend. I was going to raise her to be a good person, and because of my choices, she died."

"Lexi, I-I don't know what to say, sweetheart."

"Don't, just please don't say anything. I'm broken, East, and I can't be put back together. I don't want to be put back together. Why should I get to be happy when my baby never got to smile?"

"You can't live like this, Lex. Let me help you. Let me love you," he begs.

"Love? How can you love a monster, East? You grew up in the fucking Brady Bunch. You have this big, perfect family, and that's what you deserve. That's what you'll have. That's why we can never work, don't you see? I can't give that to you. I can't give that to anyone, so please, just stop. I'm not your problem to solve. I'm not a puzzle that can be put back together."

"Lex, it wasn't your fault."

I shake my head sadly. He just doesn't get it. "I don't fit in here, Easton. Your family is happiness and light. I'm dark and damaged. You can't be with someone like that. You need someone who can tell you to stop being an asshole. Someone that can make you smile and laugh even when you're angry. You need someone better than me."

He surprises me when he tugs me closer to him, then pulls me onto his lap. I struggle against him, but only for a moment. My confession has used up all my energy. I'm so exhausted, my body physically aches.

"Lexi? I'm so sorry for all you've gone through, but you don't get to make decisions for me. You say I need someone who can make me smile, I say I need someone that will give as good as she gets—"

Hearing his words, I force myself to stand and pull away. If I allow him to hold me, I might cave to whatever he's about to propose. I can't do that to him. I can't trust my body, my mind, or—in his case—my heart. So, I do the only thing I can.

175

I walk away, knowing I'll be leaving a piece of my soul at his feet.

"Easton. You deserve the happily ever after with someone who can give it to you. That's not me."

Without another glance, I walk out of the room. I have to get home to GG before I shatter into a million pieces.

CHAPTER 27

EASTON

I need to go after her. I know I do, but I have to figure out what to say first. I pace the small room, thinking about everything she just told me. *How could she believe all that was her fault? Do I want kids? Why is she so fucking stubborn?* So many thoughts flood my mind, I think my head will explode.

After ten minutes, I know I just need to find her. I check Preston's room first.

"Oh good, you're here." His smile is so large I have to rein in my own feelings for a minute. My brother is alive, and regardless of all the other shit going on, that's what is most important.

"Hey, yeah, ah ..." Glancing around, I notice everyone's here.

"Okay, I need a plan." Preston smiles. "I'm going to get my girl."

It's as if he just stabbed me, but I try to participate in the conversation. Unfortunately, all my brain can concentrate on is Lexi. *Where is she?*

Preston keeps talking, but I barely hear him. After a while, I've zoned out completely until I hear Lexi's name.

"What was that?" I bark. Luckily, it doesn't sound too different from my usual assholiness, and no one notices.

"The girls are going to Boston. They'll be back tomorrow."

Fucking hell.

"You have your job, East? You good?"

Somewhere I realize he dragged me into his 'get the girl' plan, but I'm just going through the motions with Lexi's cries screaming in my head. As soon as I leave Preston's room, I text her.

Easton: I need to talk to you.

Lexi: Not today.

Easton: Yes, fucking today, Lexi. I'm done letting you make all the rules.

Lexi: I'm getting on a plane. There isn't anything else to talk about.

Easton: I am still your goddamn boss.

Lexi: I quit.

Of course she does.

Easton: I'm your husband.

Lexi: Formalities. Nothing has changed, Easton. We're not good for each other.

This woman is infuriating.

∾

*E*aston: I know you're coming home today. We are going to talk.

Lexi: I can't.

Easton: I didn't ask.

Lexi: I'm going home, Easton.

Easton: When?

Lexi: Boarding now.

I stare at the phone in my hand. She's leaving. Lexi is leaving without so much as a good-bye, and I have to let her go. The pain that sat in my chest for so many years hits with the force of a tornado. *Well, hello, broken heart, it's nice to have you back.* I hadn't even noticed when she was here, but now that she's gone, I realize she took away my hurt. She made me better. She pushed me, and I don't care what she says. We were not a fucking mistake.

～

*I*t's been a week since she left, and I'm moping around like a fucking dillweed. It's nine p.m. on a Friday, and I'm lying in bed staring at the ceiling when my phone chimes.

Lexi: I'm sorry.

Two words, that's all I get after an entire week.

Easton: What are you sorry for, Locket?

I shouldn't keep using her nickname, but I can't help myself.

Lexi: If I give you a list, we could be here all night.

Easton: I don't have anywhere to be.

Lexi: No hot date?

Easton: I don't think my wife would like that very much.

Lexi: ...

Easton: Want to talk?

Lexi: ...

Easton: Goodnight, Locket.

～

*E*aston: Do you miss me yet?
Lexi: I miss working.
Easton: Come back.
Lexi: GG needs me.

179

*E*aston: Are you awake?
    Lexi: No.

A chuckle escapes at her response. We've texted every day since she's been gone, but she won't talk to me on the phone. It's driving me fucking insane. I need to hear her voice. *When did I turn into such a pussy?*

Easton: I miss your voice.
Lexi: (Voice message sent) "You're an asshole."

The first full laugh I've had since she left echoes throughout my room. *My prickly princess.*

Lexi: How's that?
Easton: Not exactly what I was hoping for.
Easton: How's the lodge?
Lexi: Old.
Easton: Do you need anything?
Lexi: No.
Easton: I'm here if you need me.
Lexi: ...
Lexi: (Voice message sent) "Goodnight, Beast."

Her voice is so soft, so unlike the thorny persona she wears like a shield.

Easton: (Voice message sent) "Goodnight, Locket."

I listen to her message until I fall asleep.

~

"*H*ow's Lexi?" Ashton asks. We're crowded around a table at Preston's penthouse because Sylvie summoned us. No one says no to my mom.

"Stubborn."

He chuckles, and it makes me smile. His laugh has always done that, even when he was a baby.

"She says she is helping GG, but she's also hiding."

180

Ashton nods. "I heard the roof caved in last winter. Do you know what she's actually helping with?"

His tone raises the hair on the back of my neck.

"Ash, if you know something, just fucking say it."

"Until Loki gets home, I've put security on everyone. It's merely a safety precaution that happens when you're a billionaire, or you're related to a spy."

I can tell he's making light, but I don't find it funny. My guts twists and I feel sweat forming on my spine.

"Spit it out, Ash."

"Lexi's team said the lodge is a lot worse than she's letting on."

"Lexi! Lexi's on the phone. Everyone, say hi." Lanie presses a button and turns the screen around to show Lexi.

Jesus, does Ash have the same dark magic as GG or what?

"Wait, slow down, Lexi. What's the matter?"

I'm out of my chair and at Lanie's side before she can utter another word. I don't miss the scowl Preston throws at me.

"The roof collapsed again ... entire crew ... GG can't afford ... I thought I could handle this."

I only catch bits and pieces of her conversation, but I've heard enough. She is going to talk to me.

"Fucking stubborn woman. I told her to let me help. Tell her I'll be there tonight. If she doesn't like that too fucking bad," I growl as I walk toward Preston's front door.

I hear the murmurs as I storm off, but I don't give a shit at this point. Lexi needs help, and she's getting me.

CHAPTER 28

*I*t's been twenty-seven days since I've seen him, but my body knows the second he steps into the lodge. GG has been great about giving me space, but now that Easton's here, I'm wondering if I should have talked to her sooner. *Isn't that why you came home?*

After his gaze roams over my entire body, he turns his attention to the lodge, and I see his eyes go wide.

I cringe because he hasn't even seen the worst of it yet.

"Why the hell didn't you ask for help sooner, Lexi?" He's as pissed off as I've ever seen him. That's good. Pissed off Beast I can handle. Sweet Beast is when I lose my panties.

"GG wanted to take care of it ourselves."

"She's eighty fucking years old, Lexi. She can't be climbing onto a roof …" He spots the ladder in the great room. "Please tell me you're not using that thing?"

"I had to get up there to see if there was any water damage."

Easton steeples his fingers and places them under his nose. Moving slowly through the space, he shakes his head at the condition of the lodge. I know he's trying to stay calm.

182

Stop being sweet, Easton.

"How did it get this bad? Honestly, Lexi, parts of this building should probably be condemned."

"Ugh," I scoff. "It isn't that bad." *Is it?* "Okay, I know it's bad, but not *condemned* bad."

"Hear me when I say we will talk, Locket, but first, we need to make this place habitable. And we're probably going to need a couple of crews to get it done quick."

Even as he's speaking, I'm shaking my head. Fear grips me when I realize GG's going to lose the lodge. "No, East, you don't understand. I've had to cancel all the reservations. No reservations means no income. We can't afford to hire a crew even if I could get one out here. They're all working other mountains right now."

Gripping the back of his neck, he rolls his shoulders, then removes his jacket.

"Grumpy, there ya are. I've been waitin' for you to show up," GG says happily as she enters the lodge. "What took ya so long?"

"I wasn't invited," he says under his breath.

"Nonsense. You never need an invitation here, Grumpy. Come, let's get you set up in your room. It's late; you can talk about everything else in the morning."

I watch in horror as she leads him toward my room. I didn't think this through. The only place he can sleep is in Lanie's bed. Lanie's twin bed that's right next to mine.

~

"*A*re you awake?" Easton asks, even though he's been staring at the side of my head for the last five minutes.

The utter ridiculousness of my life forces me to laugh.

"What? Are we doing the live action version of our texts

183

now?" Turning my head, I can just make out his facial features in the moonlight.

"It's the only time you'll talk to me. Behind a door, through text, in the dark."

"Who knew the grumpy growler was such a talker."

The low timbre of his laugh causes me to smile again.

"That is something I've never been accused of before, Locket, but I do have a lot to say."

Sucking in a breath, I prepare myself for impact.

"First, we need to fix GG's lodge, and you're going to have to accept my help in every way."

"GG won't take your money, East."

"Bullshit. She doesn't have a choice. I don't mind putting in the hard work, but we need help to make it safe first. Do you have any idea how it got so bad without anyone noticing?"

Guilt eats at my chest. "Lanie and I are all she has. We both went off and lived our lives. We should have been paying closer attention."

"Hey, Lex? I'm not placing blame. I'm just trying to understand."

"I know. Honestly, I'm not sure. Lanie was here not that long ago, and it wasn't like this. GG said she had some men in here about six months ago to do some work. At first, she thought everything was fine, but then she started noticing things."

"What things?"

"Like the wall cracking. Beams in the ceiling were suddenly sagging. I don't know, it could be a coincidence, but she has always kept the lodge well maintained. But I was looking at her bills. Everything seems off somehow."

"Do you know where she got the contractors?"

"She said they were a recommendation from Mr. Fontaine. He's the town accountant."

"The what?"

"You know how you have welcome to the chaos?"

"Yeahhhh," he drawls.

"Well, we have welcome to Burke Hollow. This little town isn't like anything you've ever experienced before."

"Okay. Well, tomorrow, I want to see all of GG's receipts and find out who she hired. I'll talk to GG, but we're going to get this place fixed."

"Thank you, East. I-I know there's probably some weird family obligation for you to be here, but I ... we ... GG and I appreciate it."

"It killed you to be nice, didn't it?" He laughs out loud, and as much as I don't want to, I join him. When the laughter dies down, he turns to me again. "I'm here because I want to be. I'll help because you're family, and we take care of each other."

"It has always been just me, Lanie, and GG. I can't imagine what your house was like growing up."

"Pure chaos." I can hear the smile in his voice, and it reminds me of how we got here.

We lie side by side in the silence for a long time. The sound of his breathing lulls me into a sense of calm I haven't had in a long time. Then he speaks. He always knows how to ruin a fucking moment.

"I've decided something, Locket."

"Oh, yeah? What's that?"

"You're not broken. You won't shatter. You're a survivor, and you'll do what survivors do."

"East, please don't ..."

"I've also decided I kind of like being married."

"What?" I screech. "How can you possibly say that? You don't even know what it's like to really be married."

"No, but I'm gonna learn." The smirk on his face glows in the moonlight. "Here's the thing, Lex. I thought about it a lot on the plane. I'm invested."

"In what?"

"In you. And, that's scary as fuck because I don't normally give a shit about anyone."

"That's not true, and you know it. You love your family."

"You're right, but I'm all in with you, Locket. I haven't cared about anyone since Vanessa, and I care about you. Whether or not we end up together, I'm invested, and I will not allow you to suffer alone if I can help it."

"What do you mean if we end up together?" My voice is almost shrill. "We have to get divorced, Easton."

"We'll see."

"I'm serious."

"So am I."

I don't know what to say to him, so I roll over in a huff. I feel his eyes on my back, and it heats my core. I don't want to have this reaction to him, especially when he's being an impossible prick, but apparently, I've lost all control over every aspect of my body.

He's invested. Who the hell says that. *A good man, Lexi. Too good for you.*

When I wake up in the morning, East is already up and pouring over files at the kitchen table.

"What are you doing?"

When he raises his gaze to meet mine, blood rushes to my head. He's so stinking gorgeous it hardly seems fair. Self-consciously, I attempt to tame my hair with my fingers, and he grins like he knows I'm doing it for his benefit.

"I happen to be a big fan of your bedhead, Locket." Then he winks. Full-on winks at me, the asshat. "But, to answer your question, I called Mason and told him to step into my position for a while. Then, I snooped until I found GG's receipts. After that, I snooped again and found her banking statements. Now, I'm about to make an appointment with this Fontaine guy because I think he's a crook. Once that's done, I'm going to have a chat with GG and hire some licensed contractors."

That's a lot to handle at seven in the morning. A Taylor Swift song plays in my head, and I almost laugh until my brain catches up with the first part of his spiel.

"Wait, why is Mason taking your job? How long do you plan to be here?"

He eyes me as he weighs his words. Then, standing to his full height, he crosses his arms over his chest as if daring me to argue. "Indefinitely."

"You can't do that." My voice comes out about ten octaves too high.

"I just did. Invested, remember?"

"Fucking insane is more like it," I grumble.

"Only because you make me that way, sweetheart." His chuckle is already grating on my nerves.

~

*T*go into the meeting with Easton, and I come out with the Westbrook Beast. I hate to admit that he might be right, but Mr. Fontaine was not happy to see us. Easton's questions made him uncomfortable, and he couldn't get rid of us fast enough.

"Did you know your grandfather leased that land to the town?"

"Well, yeah. It was kind of a joke. He wanted his own national park, and he wanted the town to have a place to hike and camp that wasn't always full of tourists."

"I mean, seriously, Lexi, who puts their land up for auction like that without a safety net in place? Did you know about the development clause? If the town chooses to lease your land to developers, it's as good as gone."

This is news to me, and will be a devastating blow for GG. It crushes what's left of my heart to know this is going to hurt her.

"No, I didn't. It shouldn't surprise me, though. Gramps

was always looking out for people. Not just for himself, but for everyone in town."

"Yeah, well, that's up for debate. Who makes a contract that leaves something this important up to the sole discretion of the mayor?"

I cringe at his words and what they imply, and before he can say anything else, I pull out bitchy Lexi. "Not everyone has unlimited money to hire every godforsaken lawyer out there, East. He did what he thought was right. I understand that you're helping us, but you will not talk badly about my grandfather."

Easton stops walking and stares at me. "I'm sorry. I didn't mean it like that. I'm just frustrated that none of this makes sense. I'm going to need to meet with the mayor and see what I can do to get the development rights before this all goes to hell."

That sounds expensive, and I know GG will never approve. If Easton is trying to purchase the development rights, that means he's willing to put out a lot of money. Money we will never be able to repay.

"You can't meet the mayor," I say, shaking out the crushing thoughts running rampant in my mind. "Not like that anyway." I make a sweeping motion up and down his body. Dressed in a black peacoat and trousers, he stands out in Burke Hollow like a sore thumb.

"What's wrong with me?"

I *almost* laugh at his expression. "Mayor Baker is ... hmm, how do I explain this? He's very protective of our town and its people. So if you want to win him over, you have to look like you belong."

"Lexi, I don't give a shit what I look like. None of that matters."

I know I shouldn't do this. He's here helping my family, and I appreciate that, I do. But it doesn't mean I want him getting too comfortable around here. "Famous last words, Beast. Famous last words."

CHAPTER 29

EASTON

When will I fucking learn not to underestimate the evil that is Lexi Heart? Standing on the sidewalk between Eggy's Eatery and Hattie's Happy Haven Hardware store sit's Fresh Lemons—a consignment shop.

"Are you shitting me?"

A smile finally graces her face, and of course, it's at my expense. "There is perfectly good clothing in here, East." Her voice is sickeningly sweet, and it clicks. This is her pushing me away. *Well, have at it, sweetheart. You may be stubborn, but so am I.*

"Fine. Let's go. Show me what I need." I walk past her to open the door to Fresh Lemons. "What is with all the business names around here?"

When Lexi doesn't move, I turn back around to find her gaping at me with wide eyes. "What?"

"You're going in?" She sounds shocked.

"You said I can't wear my clothes around here, so let's go. I already told you, I don't give a shit what I wear."

Narrowing her eyes as she catches on to my plan, I wink. She can play all the games she wants; I'm invested.

Expelling a huff, she stomps forward. When she gets to

the big lemon on the glass door, she explains, "Burke Hollow is a small, ski town. All the businesses have these cutesy names, so the tourists will keep coming back."

"Huh." I'm genuinely interested. "Does it work?"

"We're crawling with tourists year round, so I guess so."

As she enters the shop, my eyes drift to her ass, and I have to adjust myself. It's been too long since I've tasted her. *I'll have to see what I can do about that.* The thought makes me feel light as air. So as I enter the store behind her, my mood has risen considerably.

Glancing around, I school my features as I take in the racks of secondhand clothing, shoes, and household items. They're all neatly displayed, but there's something unsettling about seeing it firsthand. I'm not naïve. I'm fully aware that there are the 'haves' and 'the have nots' in this world. But seeing it in person puts my life in stark contrast to most people's reality.

"Why are you smiling like that?" She has to question every little thing.

Turning my attention back to sexy Lexi, I lean into her space, then growl next to her ear, "You don't want to know, Locket."

The sharp intake of air followed by her stammering proves I'm right. Her body wants me, even when her mind tries to push me away. *How the hell do I get them to coincide and in my favor?*

"Don't go getting any ideas, Easton. We may have to share a room, but we have separate beds."

"So did married couples in the fifties, and they still found a way to get things done, or none of us would be here, sweetheart."

She's saved when a salesperson notices us. "Well, hello there, handsome. How can I ..." The woman pauses when Lexi steps out from behind me. "It's you."

Glancing past Lexi, who appears to be attempting to hide

191

me, I see a woman about her age, but there's nothing appealing about her. She's wearing too much makeup and not enough clothes. I'll admit, I like the jealousy Lexi is showing toward me though.

"Well, hello to you, too, Jillian. So nice to see you do have manners occasionally."

"Whatever, Lexi. What do you need?"

"Easton and I will be just fine, but thanks." Lexi loops her arms through mine and drags me to the back of the store, where I can see a sign for men's clothing.

As we walk away, I whisper, "Who was that?"

"Just a mean girl who grew up to be a mean woman. She tormented Lanie when we were younger. If Julia or I weren't around, she could be vicious."

"You mean not everyone in town has eaten the happy hippy hotcakes?"

She shakes her head as she starts rummaging through the racks. I really don't care what she chooses, so I stand back and watch her in action. Within minutes she's pulled about ten outfits, and I remember Preston telling me she was a buyer for a big department store.

"Do you miss your real job? Being a buyer, I mean?"

Lexi freezes with her hand in midair, handing me a pair of jeans. "Uh …" She shakes her head as she stares at the floor. "Sometimes, yeah. I worked so hard for it. Choosing the clothes that dictated Boston fashion used to be my dream job."

"And now?" I push a little, hoping she'll keep talking.

"Now I know I don't want that life in the city. I'm not that girl anymore. Go try these on."

"Er, here?" I've never worn another man's clothes in my life, and suddenly, I'm more than a little skeeved out. "Are they clean?"

Lexi rolls her beautiful eyes. "Yes, of course they're clean, you asshat. Go." She points to a curtain behind me.

192

"Fine, Locket. You win this round, but the next one's mine."

I cannot believe I'm putting on someone else's pants. I guess I should be happy she's letting me keep my own underwear. Yuck, I may have thrown up in my mouth a little. After yanking on a pair of Levi's and a gray Henley, I pull back the curtain.

Lexi turns, and her mouth drops open. I've never been self-conscious about anything, but the way she's looking at me has me checking myself in the mirror.

"What? What's wrong with it?"

"Jeeeesus. There's nothing wrong with you. Why the hell do you Heart women get all these thirst traps?" Jillian mutters.

I hadn't noticed her walk up beside Lexi, and apparently, neither did Lexi.

She tosses a dirty look over her shoulder at Jillian and ushers me back into the dressing room. I'm not sure she even realizes what she's doing as she pulls the curtain closed around us.

"Something wrong, Locket?" The corner of my lip twitches as I observe her taking me in. She starts at my bare feet and inches her way up my body. When she reaches my eyes, she clamps her mouth closed.

"How the hell can you look so hot in second-hand clothes?"

"Guess the clothes don't really make the man after all." I take a step forward, so we're almost touching. "You think I'm hot?" I say just before my lips land on hers. I kiss her like I'll never have another chance and hope she doesn't knee me in the balls.

When she yields to my intrusion, I say a silent prayer, but it's short lived as Jillian raps on the wall next to us. "Only one person per dressing room."

Lexi jumps back and hits the wall. Her fingers touch her

lips that taste like mine, and I want nothing more than to take her right here. Fuck who hears. Unfortunately, she rips open the curtain and speed walks past Jillian and out the door.

"Fuck." Glancing around for my wallet, I tell Jillian I'll take everything. The miserable woman takes forever to check me out, and I know she's doing it on purpose.

When I get outside, I find her sitting on a bench in the park and I have a flashback to Vegas. She was so happy and carefree there. *She was drunk, Easton.* I'd give anything to get that girl back, though. Staring at her, huddled in the cold on the park bench, I'm more determined than ever to bring back that girl I got a brief taste of. It will kill me if she doesn't choose me in the end, but getting Lexi back is more important than my wants and needs.

It's time to bring Lexi back to life.

I approach her cautiously. Like a caged animal, I don't know how she'll attack.

"Hey," she says without looking up, so I take a seat next to her.

"Hey. So, I won't apologize for kissing you because I've wanted to do that since the second I did it last. But, I will apologize for not asking first." I place my hand with palm facing up on the bench next to us, much like she did in our hotel room in New York.

She side-eyes it but eventually lays hers on top of mine. We're not holding hands, just sharing a connection.

"You've had a lot taken from you, Locket. A lot of really fucking shitty things that were out of your control. I won't ever take from you again, Lexi. We'll share. We'll be a team, but I'll never take from you." I hope these simple words can convey everything I feel. "I won't be the man to fix you, but I'll hold your hand while you find your way. I will promise you, though, I'll never break you, Locket."

She sniffles but doesn't reply. She also doesn't remove her

194

hand until her phone rings next to her. *Please hear my words, Locket. Please let me be the one to help you.*

"Hello?" Her voice is shaky at best. "Oh, hi, John. Thanks for calling me back." She glances at me for the first time since I sat down, and I see forever in her tear-filled eyes. "Oh. All right. Can you call me when you get back into town? Easton Westbrook is here with me, and we'd like to talk to you about GG's mountain."

She doesn't know I already called him this morning. When her head whips to mine, I think it's safe to say she knows now.

"He did? Right. Okay, thanks, John. Have a great trip. We'll set up that meeting as soon as you're back in town. Bye." Ending the call, she turns to face me head-on. "Did you sleep at all last night?"

"I slept enough. Come on, let's head home."

Home. We both hang on the word. For the first time in my adult life, I feel like I have a home, not just a house. *Lexi is home.* Smiling like a fool, I stand and offer her a hand. She stubbornly puts hers in her jacket pocket but rises with me, and we walk side by side.

❧

"*Y*a ain't doing it, Easton. No, sir."

"GG, you don't have any other options. This place will never pass inspection as it is, and whatever is going on with your loan isn't getting any better. We're family, and this is what we do. We take care of our own, and I'm taking care of you whether you like it or not."

"Don't you go getting sassy with me, Grumpy. Just let me think for a minute."

I eye Lexi sitting in the corner and know this is hard for both of them. Lexi comes by her stubborn independence honestly.

195

"Locket, what do you think?"

I hear her sigh before coming to meet us at the table. "I hate asking for help, too, GG, but Easton's right. Unfortunately, we have no other options."

"Well, shit. I don't like this one bit. Not one, ya hear me?"

"I know, GG, but I'm not here to take advantage of you. I only want to help," I tell her honestly. I'm becoming quite fond of this meddling menace.

"It has to be a loan. With papers that I sign, that's the only way. And," she pauses, glancing around, "anything we can do ourselves, we do. I want to save every penny we can."

"You want to do some of the work yourself?" I ask in disbelief.

"Yup, Lexi and I will."

"That's not happening, GG. I'm sorry, but you're not using power tools and carting around heavy equipment."

"I can, and I will. That's final. Get me the papers, and then you can do what you need to."

Over the next few weeks, GG becomes the unofficial foreman, pissing off the actual one at every turn. If she sees something we can do, and by we, I mean me, she tells the crew not to do it. Instead of spending my days getting closer to Lexi, I'm repairing studs and hanging drywall.

CHAPTER 30

"*S*iiiiiiip." I wake, gasping for air and clutching my stomach.

"Shhh, Locket. You're okay. I've got you," Easton's voice calls out in the dark just before my bed dips with his weight. It's the third night in a row I've woken him with a nightmare. I'm broken. When will he see that? "Shh, it's okay." He rocks me until my breathing returns to normal.

Checking the clock, I see it's three in the morning. "I-I'm sorry, East ..."

"Don't," he says, rising from my bed. For the last three nights, he's crammed himself into my twin bed to hold me until I fell into a dreamless sleep. "But I'm done with this bullshit."

"Wh—" My question is cut off as he shoves his bed across the room. He pushes it right up next to mine, then climbs in and pulls me into his chest.

"I'm sorry, sweetheart. I wasn't thinking when I told you about Ash. I should have known. I ..."

"Is he okay?" Easton yells as his knees buckle beneath him. I know instantly something isn't right. "How did it happen? They all survived? I'm coming home."

197

"Beast? Wh-What is it?" I already know it's going to be bad.

When he raises his gaze to mine, my heart shatters for him. Then, as tears flow freely down his face, I run to him.

"Ash," he barely chokes out in between sobs. "Th-They were taken."

Now my heart stops. Knowing what Ashton does for work, 'taken' doesn't usually end well.

"H-He, Seth, and Loki. Th-They hurt him." As he crumbles to the ground, his words become garbled.

"No." I'm fighting the flashbacks trying to appear before my eyes. I was 'taken' not that long ago, and Ashton is the one who found me. Please, God, please let him be alive.

"Th-They tortured him. H-He's in surgery now, but the doctors say he'll never be the same. My ... My Preston said a surgeon is flying in from California to work on his f-face. Oh, God, Lex. Why Ash? Why him? N-Not him."

He cries harder than I have ever seen someone cry. With anyone else, this would make me uncomfortable. I'm not the friend you turn to for comfort. But with Easton? With Easton, I don't feel like I could be anywhere else. He's starting to feel like home.

I need to be strong for him. Come on, Lexi, you can do this. Be there for him.

"East? Can you get up? I'll go book us flights. I have no idea when we'll be able to get tickets, but if we drive to B-B-Boston, they run every hour."

The idea of returning to Boston has sweat forming on my lower back, but I will do it for Ash. I'll do it for Easton.

He shakes his head, which has fallen into my lap. "H-He won't see anyone. Mom said to stay with you until she has more information."

Unsure of what else to do, I scoot back against the wall and take Easton with me. With his head resting in my lap, I stroke his hair. My ass goes numb, but a bulldozer couldn't tear me away from him.

At some point, GG found us on the floor. Without a word, she ushered us to bed, where she brought tea and my Ambien.

Over the next few days, we learn the details of Ashton's condition. His injuries will heal, but he'll always carry a scar on his face. His emotional scars will be harder to survive.

Ashton is the one who found me in the house where Miles was holding me while Loki and Seth executed my evacuation. I owe those three men my life, and this is a reminder of just how close I was to life and death. Hearing the events of Ashton's attack has triggered old memories that only want to come out in my sleep.

"No, Beast. This is not your fault. I need to be stronger than this. I *am* stronger than this. I have to be otherwise … otherwise, Miles wins."

Easton's arms wrap tighter around me, and safely in his arms, I drift back to sleep. I'll worry tomorrow about what this means.

Over the next two weeks, we check in with the Westbrooks multiple times a day. We speak to Ash, but he only grunts in response. The monsters who attacked him damaged his vocal cords, and his voice is unlikely to recover.

"I'm scared for Ashton," I finally admit one morning over coffee. "I see the same darkness in him, but his is all-consuming."

GG sighs, then stares at me with sad eyes. "This was not in my plan for him. He has a long, painful road ahead of him. You might be the only one who can relate to that, Locket. Someday, he's going to need your strength," GG whispers as she kisses my forehead.

"Lexi?" Easton bellows from downstairs.

"Jesus Christ. I don't think he'll be happy until he has a tracker on me," I mutter, making GG laugh.

"Grumpy's worried about you, Locket. There's a lot of shit out of control in his life right now. You're the one thing he can keep safe, so he's hovering."

"More like smothering. Seriously, I can't freaking pee without him knocking on the door six times."

GG only smiles in response.

"There you are," East says happily. Pulling up a chair, he practically sits on top of me.

"I'm goin' into town. I've got to see about a girl that keeps comin' up in my cards."

Easton and I both freeze. *Who the hell is she matchmaking with now?* When she sees our expressions, she cackles only the way she can. "Now don't ya go worryin', Grumpy. Your match was set years ago. You two will make it when you pull yourselves out of the muck."

"GG," I scold.

"Don't go GG'ing me, Locket. When you learn to unlock that heart of yours, a lifetime of happiness will fall at your feet."

I gasp at her proclamation. How dare she? Also, what the fuck? Sneaking a glance in Easton's direction, I see his smirk on full display.

"That's really good to know, GG. It goes well with what I came up here to tell Locket." Easton grins like a kid in a candy store.

"Mm-hmm. Okay, then. I'll see ya's later."

I stare at the path she takes out of the kitchen long after she's left.

"So," Easton breaks the silence, and my spine stiffens, "I've decided something."

"Again?" I can still hear his voice saying he liked being married since the last time he 'decided' something.

"Yup. And I know I said I'll never take anything from you, Locket. I still stand by that, but I'm thinking I'll have to be creative to get my way."

Run! Run! Run! Alarm bells sound in my head, making me dizzy.

"Ah, I'm not sure how I feel about this."

"I know you don't. But it's happening. I've decided I want to date my wife."

I'm mid-sip when he throws that curveball at me, and I snort. Coffee flies painfully out of each nostril.

"What the hell, East? We're not dating. I'm not staying your wife."

Clinking his coffee cup with mine, he takes a sip. "First date. Coffee. I can't wait to tell everyone you blew coffee out of your nose on our first date. That will be an epic first-date story."

"Are you high?"

"High on you, sweetheart."

My phone rings, and I scamper to get it. Anything to put distance between this infuriating man and me is a good thing. Checking the screen, I see John Baker come up on the caller ID.

"It's John," I tell Easton as I answer the call and put it on speaker.

"Hi, John."

"Lexi-girl. How are you, sweetie?"

"I'm good. I hope you had a good vacation." Easton rolls his eyes, and then twirls his finger, indicating he wants me to get to the point. *Jackass.* He really doesn't know how anything works around here.

"Oh, girrrl! Mexico was on fire. We had the best time, but now that I'm back, work has piled up. That needy, little troll of a man, Fontaine, is all over my ass, so I was wondering if you and your hunka man could meet me today at Eggy's."

"He's not my—"

"How's one? Does that work for you both?"

"Ah." Easton nods his head wildly. "Yeah, I guess that's fine. We'll see you at one."

"Sounds good, baby girl. See ya then."

"Bye, John."

"Bye-bye."

Easton steps into my space, a sexy but devilish grin on his face. "Looks like we just scheduled date number two, Locket. I'm going to get changed." When he leans in, I swear he's going to kiss me, and when I don't move, I realize my body is still a traitorous bitch. Kissing my cheek, he whispers, "I'm really going to like dating my wife. How many dates until you put out?"

And just like that, he ruins the moment.

"Ugh, you're a pig. Get out of here."

His deep, throaty laugh has my clit throbbing. So much for losing my sex drive after the hysterectomy. That needy bitch is alive and kicking today.

How many dates does it take for me to put out? No, Lexi. Geez. Even my subconscious is working against me.

CHAPTER 31

*M*ayor Baker is unlike anything I've ever dealt with before. But, after fifteen minutes with the guy, I understand why Lexi insisted on the make-under. I actually don't mind it. The Levi's are fucking comfortable, but she keeps referring to them as the dead man's clothes, and my skin crawls at the thought.

"So, Mr. Westbrook ..."

"Easton, please."

"Easton. It's so nice to finally meet you. You've been the talk of the Cryer for quite some time."

I side-eye Lexi because I have no fucking clue what the Cryer is.

"Oh," John gasps. "Lexi, are you telling me you haven't added him to the list? It's a town ordinance, dear. You must. Easton, give me your phone."

I eye him suspiciously but unlock my phone and hand it over.

"He's going to hate this," Lexi informs him.

"Oh, he'll get used to it. It's nice knowing what's goin' on." He hands back my phone as it starts blowing up with texts. Worried it has something to do with Ashton, I open it.

Unknown: He ordered the open-faced turkey sandwich.

Unknown: He's so dreamy.

Unknown: I'll give him an open face (peach emoji)

Unknown: I don't care how Lexi got him into those jeans, but I feel like I should thank her for the rest of my life.

What the hell?

Glancing up, I notice most of the restaurant is looking at their phones or at me.

"It's GG's doing. It's called the Town Cryer. She says it's a safety measure, but really, it's just a thread for gossip," Lexi tells me.

"No, Lexi. Town news and important business are also spread that way. It's a fabulous form of communication that has really brought Burke Hollow closer."

If Lexi rolls her eyes any harder, she'll pop a blood vessel.

"Anyway, Easton, I'm so glad I got to meet with you today. Fontaine is about as much fun to deal with as an enema."

"I'm sorry to ..." My words drift off as something, or rather *someone* catches my eye. Someone who shouldn't be anywhere near Burke Hollow. Patrick fucking Macomb.

"Beast?" Lexi's voice sounds far away as my heart thrums loudly in my ears.

Patrick makes his way through the restaurant as if he owns it and heads straight for John.

"Mayor Baker, how lovely to see you again. I'm looking forward to our four o'clock meeting today."

"Patrick, how ... *funny* to see you here."

John doesn't sound sincere or happy to see him, and John Baker just rose ten notches in my book.

"I assume you know Easton, here."

"Once upon a time, yes." His gaze drifts to Lexi, and my hands involuntarily ball into fists. He stares at Lexi but continues speaking to me. "Such a pity, really. Hopefully, you'll be able to hang on to this one, yeah? Although it really did work out best for me in the end, now didn't it? Having you as a son-in-law would have proved useless. At least my daughter smartened up at the end of her life. Marrying your best friend must have been such a blow, but Dillon has turned out to be rather ..." He pauses, and pure evil spreads over his features. "Beneficial."

I'm about to lay this guy out, when shockingly, Lexi beats me to it. Slamming her fists down on the booth's table, she climbs over me on the bench. Before I can comprehend what the fuck she's doing, she's standing mere inches from Patrick. Face-to-face, ready to fight.

"You must be Macomb," she seethes. "Let me tell you something, you sick piece of shit."

"Oh, fuck." I stand quickly, as does John, but he places a hand in front of my chest, silently telling me to let her handle it.

"If you think you can come into my town and spew your venom, you have another thing coming. Your daughter was dying and chose not to tell her boyfriend. Your daughter chose to marry his best friend without ever telling him, then died, leaving him in the dark. She was a coward, and now I can see where she learned it from. You praise that type of behavior? You encourage lying, cheating, and who knows what other kinds of assholery, while Easton is one of the best men I have ever met in my life. He has proven time and time again that family comes first. You obviously missed that lesson in grade school, but let me be the first to tell you, that shit doesn't fly here. In Burke Hollow, we do things our way, the right way, and family always comes first. So you can just march your stuck-up, fat face right out of here."

He sneers, and I think Lexi might actually punch the guy, so I wrap an arm around her waist and pull her back into me.

"Oh, Miss Heart, I presume? You are a spitfire, aren't you? It's going to be so much fun watching you crumble when I take your grandmother's mountain."

I feel, not so much as hear her intake of breath. I also hear the commotion that bit of news has caused throughout the lunch crowd.

"You're not so tough now, are you, Miss Heart?" he sneers.

"Get the fuck out," she bites out, pointing her finger in the direction of the door.

"Gladly. Mayor? I look forward to our meeting." He glances around at the tables and the patrons, disgust written all over his face.

When the bell chimes to let us know he exited, a round of applause erupts around us—Kathy, our waitress, hands Lexi a large draft beer and smiles.

"Nice to have ya back, kid."

Lexi doesn't reply, and I can feel her body shaking as she hands me the beer. Finally, she eases herself out of my embrace and slides quietly into the booth.

As soon as we're settled, John leans in conspiratorially. "That's what I wanted to tell you. He's working with Fontaine to exercise the developmental clause on Victory."

"Victory?" I ask, confused.

"Victory is the legal name of the mountain. Everyone in town just calls it Heart Mountain because my family has owned it forever," Lexi explains. Her voice lacks any emotion.

"How the fuck did he know about it?"

"I don't know," John admits. "I can't say this as mayor, but as the Bossy Baker, I'll say, Fontaine is a shady, old geezer always out for a quick buck."

"But you're the mayor. So you have the final say, correct?"

I don't miss that Lexi remains silent.

John puffs up his cheeks and expels the air trapped there slowly. "I wish I did, Easton. I like you, and if it were up to me, I would have already signed it over. That mountain belongs with the Heart women, but Fontaine enacted an old fiscal emergency law. He says the town is on the verge of bankruptcy. And because of that, our only source of income needs to be utilized."

"GG's mountain," Lexi whispers.

"He's able to open it up to bidders after Summerfest if we have made no resolution. I'm sorry, Lexi. Truly, I am. I'm on your side, and I'll happily campaign for this hunka here, but Fontaine is already promising jobs."

"He's playing to their weakness," I mutter.

"This area is full of great people who can do amazing things, Easton, but the economy is so depressed they just don't have the chance. Find a way to make them shine, and they'll side with you."

"You really think people would vote against GG?"

Lexi makes a sound that sounds like a whimper. But when I turn to her, she's staring out of the window, so I can't see her eyes.

"If it means voting for GG or feeding their families, yeah, I do," John says honestly.

"That won't happen. When is Summerfest?" I ask, my brain already going into problem management mode.

"It's the month of June and culminates on the Fourth of July."

Mentally, I calculate what needs to be done in two months.

"Restoring GG's lodge so it's safe has to be my first priority. Then we'll make a plan. Heart Mountain isn't going to him or anyone else. I'll make sure of it. If it is the last thing I do, the mountain will stay with my girls."

Smirking, John raises his eyebrow.

Yeah, I said it. These fucking insane Heart women are mine, and I'll do whatever I need to protect them and what's theirs.

Lexi is quiet on our ride back up the mountain, and that's fine with me. I use the time to formulate a plan. I hate to tear my family apart with Ashton still in recovery, but now that he's home, I don't have a choice, and he needs to be my first call.

When we arrive at the lodge, Lexi jumps out of the truck like her ass is on fire. "I need to find GG."

"Lexi, just wait. Don't say anything about this yet—"

"You just don't get it, Easton," she wails. "There was a room full of witnesses. They probably recorded the entire thing and sent it to the Cryer before we even sat down. She already knows."

She takes off for the stairs, and I grab my phone to find she's right. Three hundred and forty-six messages. *Jesus, I need to silence this thing.*

With Lexi and GG inside, I take a seat in one of the Adirondack chairs. The wraparound porch is one of my favorite places here. Then, after collecting my thoughts, I call home.

As soon as she answers, the words spill from my lips.

"Mom? I need help." I spend the next forty-five minutes explaining everything that's happened. Apart from a few gasps and possibly even a 'shit,' she was silent until the end.

"The boys will be there tonight." She doesn't coddle or waver. She's the strength we pull from to make things right. "I don't think Preston or Loki can come right away unless you absolutely need them, but Halton, Colty, and Seth will be there. If you need Pres or Loki, though, you call, and they'll be there."

Swallowing thickly, I begin to understand how truly blessed I am. Not because I'm rich as fuck, but because I have people who will drop everything to be there for me.

"We measure life by how many people will pick you up when you fall, not how many dollars are in your account. That's how you'll know you're rich enough, son."

It's been a long time since I've heard my father's voice in my head. It's nice to have him back.

"I-I think we should be okay with the three amigos … for now anyway. But—"

"What is it, East?"

"I think we'll need all hands on deck for Summerfest. Dex and Trevor, too."

"Oh, we'll be there, Easton. That was never a question. Now, take care of Lexi, and take care of yourself, my sweet boy. Whatever they're doing to you up there, I hope they keep it up. I hear it in your voice. You're happy."

Am I? I haven't yelled at anyone or barked an order in weeks. She's right. I am happy.

"I-I think I am, Mom."

"That's all we ever wanted, Easton. I'm so proud of you."

"Thanks, Mom. How's Ash? I-I know he doesn't want to talk to anyone, but I need him and his *skills*. Do you think he's up for it?"

"I think it will be good for him, physically and mentally."

"Okay, can you put him on?"

"Of course. And, Easton?"

"Yeah?"

"I love you."

"I love you, too, Mom."

"I know you do. Make sure you spread that love far and wide. Sometimes, it's just what someone needs to hear. Here's Ashton."

"What?" A painful sounding rasp echoes through the line. My sweet, gentle, baby brother has turned into me.

"Ash? I need you."

He's silent, but I hear his heavy breathing.

"Welcome to the chaos. Email what you have and what you need." His voice is just above a hoarse whisper, and then he hangs up.

CHAPTER 32

"*I* matched Seth today," GG tells me as soon as I open my eyes.

"GG?" *What the hell is she doing in my room?* Reaching behind me, I feel for Easton, but the bed is empty.

"Uh-huh. That boy's been up for hours."

"Great," I mumble, tossing his pillow over my head. "Wait." I throw the pillow to the side and sit up. "Did you say you matched Seth? Seth Foster? The Seth that arrived around nine p.m. last night?"

"Sure did. I think they'll beat you to the finish line, too."

"Well, good, because I'm not in that race." Flopping back onto the bed, I pull the covers up to my chin.

GG wastes no time. She rips the covers off me just as she did when I was little and being a brat.

"GG!"

"I'm done with the GG'ing, Locket. It's time for some tough love."

Oh shit. GG is pissed. I've only ever seen this look once before, and it didn't end well.

"What do you mean?" I play dumb.

"Remember I told you once the toughest job you'll ever have is lovin' yourself?"

How could I forget? That was the last time she was this pissed off.

"Of course I do," I say the words, but there's no power to them.

"Well, I was wrong. The toughest job you're ever gonna' have is lettin' yourself believe you deserve the love that man is throwing at you every day. I know you went through somethin'. I know you're not ready to talk to me about it yet, but smarten up, Locket. That man loves you and will always love you. Allow yourself to receive it, and you'll be shocked as shit at how quickly your wounds can heal."

"That's just it, GG. I don't want them to heal. I don't deserve for them to heal. My mind betrayed me when I chose Miles. My body betrayed me when I lost …"

GG's eyes soften at my slip up, but I push on.

"My body betrayed me," I yell. "How can you possibly expect me to trust my heart after all that? How? I'm broken, GG. Every part of me, and that's never going to change."

"You're right."

My head whips to hers.

"You're broken until you decide it's time to move on from the pain. I just hope you don't wait so long that you lose something as precious as true love. I know you're hurtin', Locket. I feel it deep in these old bones. But I can't fix you, and I'm beginnin' to think you can't fix yourself either."

Well, isn't that just the final dagger to the heart?

"As I said, Lex. I don't know what you've been through, but if ya ain't gonna talk to me, I think it's time you went to see someone. Dr. Marshall told me Sarah Green in Danville is an excellent therapist. So if you won't talk to me or Easton, who has been here by your side every day, I think you better go see what she has to say."

"You think I'm crazy, too?" My voice is as weak as it's ever been. The one person who has always been in my corner doesn't believe in me anymore.

"No, Locket. I don't think you're crazy. I think you've been through more than one heart, and mind, can take, and you need some help to work through the feelings that brings. You're angry, and you're hurting. You're drowning in your own feelings. I can throw you the life raft, but I can't breathe for you. Let yourself breathe again, Lexi, before you suffocate in grief."

I don't notice the tears until they splash in my hand. GG moves in quickly for a hug and rocks me back and forth like I'm a little girl again. It was so much easier when she could kiss my booboos and make me better.

"I'm bringing some lunch into town for Seth and his Ari. Think about what I said. Sarah's number is on the wall next to the phone."

Wait, lunch? What time is it? Grabbing at my phone, I see it's after one in the afternoon. *Holy shit.* I haven't slept that late since I was a teenager. I roll back to GG, but she's already gone.

Thinking about Seth, I hope he's fairing okay. Our town can be overwhelming without a buffer, so I text him.

Lexi: Hope you're doing okay out there in the wild.

Lexi: You'll probably need a drink or ten by the time you get back to the lodge, so I'll take you to the Packing House tonight. Feel free to invite anyone you may meet on your excursions.

Seth: Thanks. WTF did I get dragged into?

Lexi: Welcome to the chaos?

Seth: Fucking chaos is right.

Just because I don't want to be a part of GG's match-making process doesn't mean I can't secretly hope for the best for everyone else.

Climbing out of bed, I make my way to the hall and tumble over a pair of legs sprawled out, taking up the entire

212

floor. Strong hands catch me before I hit the ground. Hands that my body knows well.

"What the fuck, Beast? What are you doing out here? Eavesdropping?"

"Not intentionally, but yes," he replies unapologetically. "And I'm sorry, but not for eavesdropping."

As I clamber to get to my feet, Easton untangles our limbs with more grace than I have at the moment, and we both rise. The hallway forces us to stand too close, so I make a beeline for the kitchen.

"Then what the hell are you sorry about?" I ask, reaching for a coffee mug.

"That GG told you I love you before I did." His voice is quiet but strong in his conviction.

The mug slips from my hands and shatters on the tile.

"Shit. Don't move, Locket. Let me get a broom."

"Don't call me Locket," I screech. *He did not just say he loves me.*

"Another good story to tell, huh?"

"What?"

He grins. "We can say the first time I told you I loved you was glass shatteringly good."

"No. No, Easton. You don't love me."

He doesn't say anything as he sweeps the floor around me. Once he has it all in a neat pile, he pushes it to the side, out of our way.

The world moves in slow motion as he stalks toward me. He's so close, I can smell the mint of his toothpaste on his breath. Forcing eye contact, he makes sure I feel the honesty of his words.

"The one thing you will never call me is a liar. When I say I love you, I mean it with every fiber of my being. Trust me, you don't make it easy. You're bitchy a lot of the time. You push me away when your body screams to keep me close. But that's why we work, Locket. That push and pull is what gives us life. You can continue to make loving you difficult, but it won't change the truth of my feelings for you. I love you, Lexi Mae Westbrook."

Clenching my jaw to keep the tears away, I shake my head no. He turns away from me, and I breathe a sigh of relief until I see him reach for a little, blue bag. A fancy, little, blue bag, the kind that has very expensive jewelry in it, and I feel my knees shake.

"I think I'm going to be sick," I admit.

Easton chuckles as he opens the bag, then the box.

"Another great story for us to share, Locket. Since you won't wear my ring yet, I got you this."

When I make no attempt to move, he reaches down and opens my palm. I feel something cold land in my hand, and my eyes drift to it on autopilot. In my palm is a pendant in the shape of an old-fashioned key encrusted with the sparkliest diamonds I've ever seen.

"I want to be the one to unlock that big heart of yours. The one you save for everyone but yourself. The one who can support Emory when my brother's being an asshole. The one that picked up Lanie when she was at her worst. The one who takes care of everyone around it but locks it away when it comes to yourself. Wear this, Lexi, please, and know that I'm not going anywhere. I can take on the bitchiness. I'll be here for the tears. I promised I wouldn't take from you, Locket, and I won't. We'll always be a team."

My throat is painfully dry as I wrap my fingers around the key so tightly I feel it cutting into my palm. Easton leans in and places the softest kiss on my lips, then turns and walks out the front door.

I sink into the kitchen chair, holding my head in my hands. A war is raging inside of me. I've never felt so out of control in my life.

I don't know how many hours pass, but I don't move. By the time the world comes back into focus, I can tell the sun is beginning to set. Standing, I make my way to the wall that still holds an old telephone, complete with the spiral, twenty-foot cord. Right beside the receiver is a business card for Sarah Green. Before I can chicken out, I dial her number and leave a message.

Staring around the kitchen I grew up in, I grab GG's favorite cup—the one that says 'Progress today, bitch tomorrow,'—and the bottle of Tito's, then make my way to the front porch with Easton and GG's words swimming around my head. Every few minutes, I squeeze my fist to feel the key press into the skin just so I know it's still there.

After pouring myself a drink, I finally open my hand. The pendant suddenly feels like a thousand pounds because I know it holds the key to my pain. I open the clasp, place it around my neck, then tuck it into my shirt so no one can see it. I'm not ready to acknowledge what any of it means, but having it closer to my heart helps me breathe a little easier.

I rest my head against the seat and close my eyes just as Seth's truck comes barreling up the drive.

Well shit. Looks like someone else had a pretty fucked up day. Running inside, I grab another glass. I step back onto the porch just in time to see Seth jump out of his truck like someone threw a bunch of spiders on him.

This should be interesting.

CHAPTER 33

EASTON

*I*t's been one week since I told her I loved her. One week since her epic meltdown on the porch.

"We're not meant to be solitary creatures, Locket." My raised voice causes her to flinch. "You're lying to yourself if you think you don't need love. That you don't crave it. That you don't deserve it. Not everyone in this world is out to get you. Not everyone will hurt you."

She bolts upright so fast I can't catch her. When she wraps her arms tightly around her middle, I recognize she's protecting herself. "We're not talking about me, Beast. None of this is about me, or you, or us. There is no us. There will not be an us. You need to know that we would never work. I'm not what you need," she screams.

And it's been three days since she's spoken to me. She may not want to talk right now, but at night, she falls asleep in my arms. So I'm calling that progress.

"Is she talking to you yet?" Colton asks as he enters the lodge.

He's given me the same greeting every day since he arrived with Seth.

"Not yet," I admit.

"Listen, I'm not trying to pry, but it's pretty obvious her meltdown on the porch wasn't about Ari and Seth. Anything you want to talk about?"

"Not really. It's all just a big clusterfuck."

Colton crosses his arms over his chest, and I'm reminded of how similar we all look. "So, what are you going to do about Lexi?"

A slow smile creeps over my face. I've asked myself this a lot over the last few days, as she avoids me at all costs. "I'm going to date her."

Colton's laugh echoes throughout the empty space of the lodge. "Yeah? How's she going to feel about that?"

I hear the front door open and snap closed. After taking a few quick steps to the door, I peer out just in time to see Lexi scurrying to the kitchen. Turning back to Colt, I chuckle. "She'll think she's going to hate it, but I can be very persuasive."

He laughs again as I follow Lexi's path.

Tiptoeing to the kitchen, I find her putting away groceries and starting dinner. I stay out of sight to observe her for a few minutes. She's so fucking beautiful it makes my chest ache. How she could ever feel unworthy of love is beyond me.

She's tied her light blonde hair in a high ponytail that sways with her movements. I fucking love her hair like that. It shows off her long neck, and I have to bite back a groan. I've learned the pulse point on her neck is a weakness of hers.

"Are you seriously just going to stand there creeping?" Lexi calls out.

Shit. I hadn't realized she caught me yet.

Smiling, I enter the kitchen and join her at the counter. "Not creeping, Locket. Just admiring," I whisper into her neck, then watch as her pulse picks up.

Lexi's movements halt but only momentarily. She may

217

withhold her mind, but her body can't hide from me. Finally, she throws an almost gentle elbow into my stomach and moves to the island.

After washing my hands, I join her. "Where were you today?"

"I had an appointment," she says without looking up from her cutting board.

"What kind of appointment?"

"What are you, the schedule police now?"

"No, I just missed you. I'm making small talk."

"Well, talk about something else."

This week, she has disappeared for a couple of hours every day but never tells me where she's going. "What's the big secret? Meeting up with Toots?"

This causes her to slam down her knife, but I can tell she's trying not to laugh.

"Toots? You mean Garrett? Who told you?"

"What do you mean? That Garrett Toots was your high school sweetheart?" I tease.

"His name is Garrett Wiley. He was not my sweetheart, but he was sweet, so you better not be giving him a hard time."

"Who me?" I scoff. "Come on, sweetheart, give me a little credit. He may have had you first, but I get you last."

I fucking love that Lexi's chest heaves after my admission. I can see her working to steady her breathing, but I want to push her just a little more.

Walking behind her, I crowd her body until she's pressed up against the granite.

"Will you let me have you tonight, Locket?" I growl beside her ear, then place both hands on either side of her.

"I …" I hear her swallow. "I don't think that's a good idea."

"Oh, it's a very good idea. Trust me," I plead as I push my pelvis into her back.

"Easton? Wh-What do you want from me?" The sadness in her voice guts me, and I spin her around to face me.

"Just you. That's all I want, Lexi. You and me as a team."

"I honestly don't know if I can give that to you," she whispers.

Raising her face to meet mine, I stare into her blue irises that pool with unshed tears. Nothing has ever hurt more than seeing the pain in her beautiful eyes.

"Then we take it one day at a time. Tonight is date three. How long do you usually hold out before you put out?" I add to lighten the mood.

The punch she lands to my gut knocks the wind out of me.

"Jesus, Locket. I was kidding. Well, sort of." I smirk. "So, date three. What are we making?"

"What the hell are you talking about?"

"We've had coffee, date number one. Lunch was date number two, and making dinner together will be date number three."

"We're not dating, Easton."

"It's the only way to keep the marriage alive, sweetheart." I waggle my eyebrows at her for effect and am fucking ecstatic when she bursts out laughing.

"That won't be necessary anymore," comes a raspy voice I don't recognize. Lifting my gaze away from Lexi, my throat closes up as my youngest brother hobbles into the room.

Immediately, I push off the counter in my rush to get to him, but he stops me with his cane pointed at my chest.

"I'm not an invalid. I don't want or need your help."

God, it sounds painful when he talks, and my stomach turns when I see his injuries for the first time in person. I truly think I might be sick.

Without a word, Lexi slides a glass of water across the island. Ashton takes it with a grateful nod.

219

"I don't want your fucking pity, East, so stop staring at me like that or walk the fuck away."

This isn't the Ash I've always known, and my heart shatters for him.

"Everything's gone to shit. You can get divorced whenever you want. Pacen is missing." He sits heavily in a kitchen chair as Seth and Loki walk in. I don't miss the uncomfortable glances they throw at Ashton, but I'm still trying to comprehend everything he just said.

"What's gone to shit? How is Pacen missing? Where did she go?" Lexi throws rapid-fire questions at the room.

I turn to Ash, but he points to Loki to explain. Even as Loki begins to speak, I can't tear my gaze away from Ashton. The scar that runs from his eyebrow, across his lip, and over his chin makes my stomach revolt in the most violent way. I have to swallow multiple times so I don't vomit.

Finally, tearing my gaze away, I seek out Lexi, who is staring at me with sadness.

"I'm sorry. I'm sorry, Loki. What did you say?"

"It's okay, East. I was answering Lexi's questions. Pacen is missing, but we don't know if someone took her or if she left on her own."

I have to lean into the island so I don't fall over.

"H-How do you know she's missing?" Lexi asks, but her eyes never leave mine. It's as if she's sending me her strength, and I'd give anything to hold her right now.

The emotion of seeing Ashton is threatening to overtake me. I close my eyes and count to ten to calm my inner turmoil when I feel a soft hand I know slip into mine. Lexi has stepped into my side and gives my hand a squeeze.

Glancing around the room, I can see that the only one who has noticed is Ashton. His expression is a mixture of pride, sadness, and something I've never seen from him before—rage. It's burning just below his surface, and he doesn't know what to do with it.

"Um." I cough to cover up the break in my voice. "Could you guys give Ash and me a minute? Please?"

Lexi glances at me curiously but gives my hand one more squeeze and takes the guys out to the porch.

"Keep fighting for her," Ashton forces out.

"What?"

"Lexi. Keep fighting for her. She wants to love you, she just doesn't trust herself. Be the trust for her." He downs his water and pops something into his mouth. I can't tell from here if it's candy or medicine.

"Ash—"

"Don't."

"I will, Ash. Someone has to. You're not yourself."

"Would you be?"

"No, I wouldn't. But I also know you wouldn't let me get away with this shit. You're angry. I can see it building, and you have to let it out."

"You have no idea what you're talking about." He attempts another drink, so I grab him a refill. I notice with each sentence his voice gets weaker.

"Tell me what you're most angry about."

"Fuck off. What do you think?"

"I know you've never given a shit about your appearance, and that your limp will heal. I think something is going on that you haven't told anyone about, and it's eating you alive. I know Lexi asked you to look into Pacen months ago, and now she's missing, and you're here instead of home recovering. So, tell me, little brother, what is it that has that rage burning in your soul?"

"Fuck you."

"Good, get it out. What else?"

Ashton's water glass goes flying by my head, and I see Loki poke his head in the second it crashes. I hold my hand up to keep them all away.

"What else, Ashton?"

221

"Pacen. East. Fucking Pacen almost got us killed, and now she's gone." Ashton struggles to his feet, then forces his way out of the kitchen.

Loki and Seth, obviously having heard that conversation, enter the room, and we all stare at each other in shock.

"How did P-Pacen almost get him killed?" Lexi's voice is barely audible.

Loki pinches his neck while Seth paces the kitchen.

"Pacen was staying with him when we were attacked. He thinks she gave someone our location," Seth finally admits.

"Oh my God," Lexi squeaks. "I-Is this my fault?"

"What? No, Lexi. No, none of this is your fault or makes any sense. I think Ashton is hurting and is grasping at straws," Loki states in earnest.

"How do you know she's missing?"

Loki and Seth exchange an expression I don't recognize before Seth answers, "Dillon called."

I sit and listen to their explanations for almost an hour before I admit I've had enough and make my way out to the porch while Lexi and GG get everyone settled.

I'm leaning back in the Adirondack chair with my eyes closed when I smell her. My body is so in tune with hers that I know she's here before she even sits down. Finally, after a few minutes, she slides into the chair next to me.

When her head lands on my shoulder, I smile despite the chaos surrounding us.

"I'm going to therapy," she says softly.

I lower my arm and draw her in closer. "That's where you've been going every day?"

She nods against my chest.

"I think that's great, Locket. Truly. Do you think it's helping?"

"I haven't killed you yet, so that's something," she replies cheekily.

"Sure is."

"You really want to date me?"

"Well, this wasn't the third date I had in mind, but fuck yes. I can't think of anything better than dating my wife."

It's the first time she hasn't flinched when I call her that, and relief floods my chest.

"Ash said we could get divorced now ..."

"We could," I agree, "but I think I'd like to date you for a while first."

"I can't promise anything, Beast. I'm still broken."

"We're all a little broken, Locket. It's how you put yourself back together that matters."

That night, when we crawl into our bed, I feel hopeful for the first time in years ... which is pretty fucked up, considering all the shit happening around us. However, with Lexi in my arms, I fall asleep hopeful nonetheless.

CHAPTER 34

LEXI

"*L*exi-con? Where are you?" Colton's voice rings out.

It's been a month since I agreed to date Easton. The lodge has also been overrun with Westbrooks for an entire month, and I'm starting to regret my decision.

"I'm out back," I yell. I'm attempting to haul out the old sheetrock, but it's heavy as hell.

GG was on board for allowing Easton to get the lodge up to code. But after that, she insisted we pay for everything, which means a lot of freaking manual labor on our part.

"Locket?" Easton bellows, and I realize I really might lose my shit.

"I'm outside," I scream just as Colton steps through the door with a pretty brunette. "Er, sorry?"

Colton laughs and wraps me in a hug. "No worries, Lexi-con. I want you to meet Rylan. She's been my best friend since we were in diapers, but she's been in London for freaking years. She finally came home and agreed to come help out for the summer since she hadn't lined up work yet."

"Excuse my overly excitable BFF." The girl laughs. "I'm Rylan."

I think I'm going to like this girl.

After wiping my hands on my shorts, I shake her hand. "Nice to meet you. I'm Lexi, even though this Neanderthal insists on calling me Lexi-con."

"Whatever, Lexi-con. Have you seen Halton? He disappeared, and I haven't been able to find him. I'm sure he'll want to say hello to Rylan."

I was standing right here when he hauled ass out the back door like he saw a ghost, but something in Rylan's expression makes me keep that information to myself.

"No, uh, I haven't seen him," I lie. However, when Rylan expels a lung full of air in relief, I make a mental note to keep an eye on her.

"Lexi?"

"Jesus Christ, Easton. I'm outside," I'm yelling as he steps into my line of fire.

"No need to yell, Locket. I'm right here." He smirks.

"Ugh. You guys all piss me off, you know that? I cannot take living in a thousand square feet with you assholes for much longer. We need to get this lodge fixed, or I'm moving in with Seth."

"Not fucking happening, Locket."

Colton ping-pongs between us, but for once he remains quiet. His shit-eating grin says enough.

"That's what I came out here to tell you," Easton begins. "We're going to go get Rylan settled at the Wagon Wheel. GG is still down there checking people in, right?"

"Yeah, she's staying down there so we can work around the clock on the lodge," I tell him.

"Sweet." Colton raises his fist to his brother before yelling, "Welcome to the chaos." Then he dive bombs me for one of their annoyingly good hugs.

"It was nice to meet you," Rylan says on their way out.

"You too," I mumble.

"What's the face for?" Easton asks.

"Nothing. How well do you know that girl?"

"Jealous?"

"Hardly. But something's off, and I can't figure out what."

"Nah, she and Colty have been besties since they were toddlers. She's good people."

"Humph."

"So, do you want to hear the news or what?"

"What news?" I hate to admit how freaking sexy he looks when he's excited like this.

"Halton figured out a loophole to ensure the mountain stays with the Heart women, but we have to move fast."

For the next twenty minutes, Easton explains how we have to pour foundations for ten future buildings. They all have to crisscross the backside of the mountain, eating up all the acreage so the town can't develop it.

"It won't get rid of Macomb, but it will at the very least buy us some time," he explains. "Why don't you look happy?"

"I'm thinking, Easton. This is my thinking face," I grumble.

"It's also your don't fuck with me face. So tell me, what's making you scrunch up that cute, little nose of yours?"

Ugh. Cute little nose? What is wrong with this man?

"I hate to burst your bubble, but it's still early spring. In Vermont."

He stares at me like I'm speaking Mandarin.

"Thaaat means," I stretch out the words, "that the mountain has constant rivers running down it as the snow melts. I don't know a lot about building anything, but I'm pretty sure you can't pour a foundation in mud."

Easton squints, furrowing his brow and chewing on his bottom lip as he takes in what I just said. It's truly unfair how blessed in the gene department these men are. I need to stop staring, but my heart rate accelerates when he's this close, and I'm like a dog in heat.

He's wearing a flannel shirt with the sleeves rolled up, and fuck me. I've never understood arm porn before, but I could stare at his corded ones all day. I'm licking my lips when I realize he caught me staring.

"See something you like, Locket?"

Yes. Yes, I did.

"Umm. I. Well …"

Like a lion stalking its prey, Easton moves with grace toward me. I'm frozen to the spot, unable to take my eyes off of his broad chest. I hope he doesn't expect an answer because my mouth is as dry as the Sahara, and my heart is attempting an escape.

"What are you thinking about, Locket?"

Swallowing, I shake my head. Words are too much effort right now.

He takes a finger and runs it along the collar of my Nirvana T-shirt. When he leans in, my senses short circuit. How can he smell so damn good after working his ass off like this? Inwardly, I groan because I know I cannot lift my arms without assaulting someone.

"Do you see how your body responds to me, sweetheart? The flush that crawls down your neck and disappears into your shirt? Do you recognize when your heart beats a little harder, a little faster in anticipation of what's to come?"

His hand snakes around my neck until he's angling my head the way he prefers. Staring into my eyes, he gives it a squeeze, and a breathy moan escapes my lips.

"You like it when I take control in the bedroom."

It isn't a question. Easton knows my body better than I do.

With a gentle tug, he pulls me into him, and his mouth finds its way to my ear. The hot, damp breath that caresses me as he speaks has me rubbing my thighs together. I've been adamant that we not be demonstrative in front of our families, but out here in the open for all to see, I'm ready to get on my knees and beg.

"Easton," I finally croak.

"Not here, Lexi. The last fucking thing I want is for my brothers to see your perfect, sexy body. Where can we go? And do not make it far because I'm ten seconds away from burying myself so goddamn deep inside of you."

He's right. I do like his dirty talk. Grabbing his hand and a blanket from the garage, I drag him to the only private place I can think of.

Our boots squish and squelch in the mud on our trek through the backyard. Finally, we reach the tree line, and I peer up into the tall pines.

"You have to be fucking kidding me, Locket."

"Come on, hurry up before someone sees us." Throwing the blanket over my shoulder, I climb the ladder my grandfather affixed to the tree twenty years ago.

"A treehouse? You want to have sex in a treehouse?"

I debate telling him it wouldn't be the first time, but he notices the second I pause, and he's on the ladder behind me a second later.

"Who?"

"Who what?" I play dumb. I know he's jealous, which is ridiculous since it was in high school.

His hand lands on my ass ... hard, causing me to yelp. "Hey. Don't do that shit. What if I fell?" I screech as I haul myself up onto the platform.

Easton is right behind me. Then he's on me, crowding me into the wall. "I will never let you fall, Locket. Never," he promises as he lifts my T-shirt over my head.

Like a man starved for touch, he rips my bra off and tosses it to the floor. His hands palm my breasts before catching the nipples in between his forefinger and thumbs.

"Jesus." I'm so far gone, I don't even know if I'm vocalizing my thoughts. When his teeth graze my hardened peak, I gasp.

"I love the noises you make. I love it when you gasp in

surprise." His hands roam lower until he's cradling my ass. "I love the moan that escapes when I enter you."

Lowering my gaze, I watch as he undoes the button on my jeans and slowly lowers the zipper. He bends to help me step out of them, and I hold my breath. Just when I think he's going to stand, he lunges and sticks his entire face into my sex. He inhales deeply, and I'm mortified. I've been sweating my ass off all day. *I should have showered. Why didn't I shower?*

My thoughts are interrupted when Easton lowers my panties and laps at my entrance.

"Jesus, I love how you smell, but I'll never get enough of your taste."

My knees buckle at his admission, and he pulls away. I can't hide my whimpered protest.

On his knees before me, he grins. "Don't worry, Lex. We're just getting started."

CHAPTER 35

"On your hands and knees." My command spurs her into action, and she complies in seconds. "I know I said I would never take from you, Lexi, but I think you want me to take control right now. Am I right?"

Turning her head, she finds me over her shoulder, and I notice she's worrying her bottom lip. *Did I misread this? Fuck.*

After an eternity, she nods. "Y-Yes."

Hope and pride bloom in my chest at the trust she's instilling in me. I'll never take that for granted, and I tell her so.

"I know that's hard for you to admit. Thank you for trusting me." I run a hand between her legs, and my dick twitches painfully when I see how wet she is. "This is going to be fast, and hard. Is that what you want?"

"Yes," she pleads. I feel like I'm fucking ten feet tall.

Standing, I quickly shed my clothes and realize I don't have a condom. "Fuck. Lex, I don't have a condom."

She peers over her shoulder, and sadness fills her eyes. "It's not like I can get pregnant, East. You're still clean, right? You-You haven't been with anyone else?"

Fuck me.

"Yeah, sweetheart, I'm still clean. I've never been one to sleep around, and you're it for me." My response is raw with emotion I rarely share.

She nods, then whispers, "Okay."

The air has shifted around us, and the last thing I want to do right now is fuck her. *She needs my love.* So, instead, I sit my ass on the ground and lean up against the wall.

"Come here, Lexi."

Confused, she sits back on her heels and glances around the room.

"Come here," I repeat.

She stands so gracefully that I'm mesmerized by the way her naked body moves. When she's in front of me, I hold out my hands, which she takes without hesitation. Then, giving a gentle tug, I pull her down to straddle me. Once she's seated, I bend my knees so she can rest against them.

"Wh-What are you doing?" she chokes out.

"I don't want to fuck you anymore. I want to love you. Let me love you, Lexi."

Tears pool in her eyes, and she glances down. That's not going to work for me.

"Look at me, Locket."

She's such a fucking good listener when she's naked. The thought almost has me laughing out loud until her sad eyes find mine again.

Grabbing my cock with one hand, I scoot her forward with the other so I can rub my length along her seam. When the ridge of my head hits her clit, I see her eyes roll.

"I want your eyes on me the entire time. Do you understand?"

"Yes."

"Get up on your knees for a second."

When she raises up, I position my shaft at her entrance. I know she thinks she will control our rhythm since she's on top, but I have no intention of letting that happen. Lowering her body, she impales herself until I'm fully sheathed by her quivering walls.

"God, you're big," she hisses.

Pulling her mouth to mine, I let our lips brush against each other. "Just breathe. When you've adjusted to me, I'll move."

We sit forehead to forehead for a few intense moments. The intimacy shared in these quiet minutes causes my heart to flutter rapidly.

"Okay," she finally exhales. "I'm ready."

Planting my feet, I wrap one arm around her waist and hold her perched a few inches above me. I leverage our weight between my feet and back that's pressing into the wall. Then, when I'm sure we're steady, I lift my hips and pummel into her wetness.

Her hands fly to my shoulders to steady herself, and when her nails dig into the skin, I growl my approval.

"Beast? Oh, fuck."

Lowering my hands to her ass, I squeeze her cheeks and use them to move her against me. When my finger grazes her forbidden hole, she moans in pleasure, and I almost come right then. *My sassy little wife likes it dirty.*

Reaching around, I coat my fingers in her juices, then return my hands to her ass. While my body moves in and out of hers, I circle her rosebud with my ring finger. She tenses and tries to pull away, but I hold her steady.

Continuing my ministrations, her muscles begin to relax as her moans become louder.

"Has anyone ever had you here, Locket?" I ask as I insert my finger to the first knuckle.

Her shocked gasp makes my dick vibrate even as she clenches around my finger.

"Deep breaths," I say calmly, then twist my finger around her tight hole. Moving it in time with my dick, I feel the two meet between her thin barrier. *Jesus Christ.* Every time my finger hits my cock inside of her, I swear I see stars.

"Beast. East. I'm … Holy fuck. Easton!" she screams, and I pick up my pace.

Lexi leans into my chest, resting her forehead on my shoulder, as I continue to pound into both her holes.

I feel the first signs of her orgasm, and I bite my tongue to keep from coming before she does. Opening my mouth, I sink my upper teeth into her shoulder. Not enough to break the skin, just enough to give her another sensation, and it pushes her over the edge.

Her walls spasm around my cock, so I remove my finger and use both hands to grind her body into my pubic bone.

"Yes, Lexi. Fucking yes," I bellow as she spasms again.

The sensations are too much for me to hold back any longer, and I come with a deafening roar.

My fingers trace her spine as we both work to come down from the high. Eventually, Lexi lifts her head from my shoulder, and we're nose to nose again. The sheepish grin she wears cements my love for her. I fucking love this girl, even if she can't love me back yet. I'll wait. I'll deal with whatever comes at us, as long as I never have to walk away.

Leaning forward, I kiss her gently. My kiss is full of promise and hope. It's my pledge to her that I'll always be her team. When I finally pull away, I hang onto her neck to keep her close.

"Are you my girlfriend yet?"

Surprised, laugher escapes her, and I join in. There isn't much I love more than hearing my girl laugh. I need to make it happen more often.

"Well, sweetheart? Are you?"

"I seem to have a lot of titles lately, Beast."

"As long as you're my wife, that's all that matters. But, I would like to tell my family at some point."

She freezes at my declaration and attempts to disentangle our bodies.

"Don't run, Lexi. Not now."

"I-I don't know how to do this, East. I'm sorry."

The sigh that escapes weighs heavily in the air.

"Can you try? I'm not asking for any declarations right now, Lexi. I just need to know that you'll try."

She's silent as she glances everywhere but at me. Finally, she whispers, "Okay."

I couldn't have heard her correctly.

"Okay? Just like that?"

"Well, what do you want? A fucking billboard?"

My body shakes with laughter. My bitchy, prickly princess.

"No billboard. Your word is good enough for me."

She opens her mouth to speak as a loud, clanging bell rings out.

"What the hell is that?"

Lexi jumps to her feet. "Shit. That's GG. She used to ring that bell when Lanie and I were up here. Or ..." She glances around for her shirt.

"Or what?"

"Or when I was in trouble." She grins.

"Hmm, I think I'm going to really like your kind of trouble."

Lexi throws my jeans to me, then smiles a full, beautiful, genuine smile that lights up her entire face. "Me too, Beast. But if you don't hurry, GG will send in reinforcements."

I've been in this town long enough to know she's not kidding, so I dress in record time. Just as Lexi is about to climb down the ladder, I pull her in for one more kiss. Then once more. She's definitely a mistake I never want to correct.

CHAPTER 36

EASTON

"*I* see ya found the treehouse," GG says by way of a greeting as I enter the lodge.

Lexi and I used different entrances, hoping to throw her off the scent, but we should have known better. This is GG we're talking about.

"Ah, yeah. It was fun to see what the girls would do as kids."

"Uh-huh. And when they were being naughty teenagers, too," she cackles.

"How's everything at the Wagon Wheel?" I know it's another property she owns. Dex said it's a motel, but I'll need to make a visit there soon if it's anything like this place.

"Oh, it's just fine, ya big worry wort. What happened to Grumpy Growler, huh? Don't go fussin' over things you don't need to be fussin' about."

"GG, you know I love you, but we need to have a talk. I have had three engineers out here over the last few weeks. And that's on top of four separate inspectors."

"Well, watcha wastin' money like that for?"

"I'm not wasting money, GG. I had to be sure that what I was seeing was true."

She skirts around the island, still nimble in her old age.

"All right, Grumpy. Lay it on me."

My lip twitches every time she calls me Grumpy. I know it's her own term of endearment, and I'd be lying if I said the sentiment behind it wasn't growing on me.

"GG, those men you hired to do work around here sabotaged you."

"Are you watchin' too many unsolved mysteries or what? No one around here's goin' to all that trouble."

"But they did, GG. I have the reports from multiple authorities. The structural issues with the lodge were all done in the last year, and they were intentional."

GG's bushy eyebrows furrow as she puts water on for tea.

"Now, Fontaine gave me those names. Are ya tellin' me he was tryin' to hurt me?"

"I don't have any proof of that ... not yet anyway. However, if his men were the only ones to do work here since your hospitality inspection last year, then yes. He had a hand in causing this."

"That shitty little troll," she curses. "Okay, Grumpy. I'm not one to sit around with what-ifs, so tell me what we've got to do."

"Well ..." I pinch the back of my neck. I kind of hoped I'd have backup for the bad news.

"Just spit it out already. I'm not gettin' any younger here."

My face smiles even as my gut clenches, knowing what I'm about to tell her. Lexi definitely comes by her sass honestly.

"You know how the town has to open the mountain up for a vote at Summerfest?"

"Sure do. Stupidest thing my Benny's ever done if ya ask me."

"I don't disagree with you there, but he did put in a sneaky little safety clause for you. For it to work, though, we have to move fast."

"Ya got my attention, Grumpy. What do we have to do?"

Reaching into the bag I'd brought with me, I pull out all of Halton's maps and estimates. Once they are all laid out before her on the table, GG grins.

"Do you know what these are?"

"I'm guessin' you're building houses for all my kids."

This woman is smarter than anyone gives her credit for. She may come across as a crazy, old lady, but her mind is all business.

"That's right. We can't get them all built before the vote, but Benny was very intentional in his verbiage. All that has to be completed are the foundations."

GG furrows her brow again and glances out the window.

"Lexi already informed me of mud season," I assure her. "It makes it harder to pour foundations for sure, but not impossible. I'll have a team of engineers working on the drainage issue. In order to get them all done in time, we have to start tomorrow."

"I'm proud of you, Grumpy."

The sudden words of praise catch me off guard, and emotion I wasn't prepared for smacks me in the face.

"Th-Thanks, GG."

She places a bony hand on my cheek and gives it a pat. "She's worth the fight, Easton. I hope you know that."

"I do, GG. She's not making it easy, but somewhere between calling me an asshole and naming me Beast, I fell in love with her. Maybe I'm the one who should be in therapy, huh?" I chuckle.

"Just keep bein' her strength when her darkness comes. It will keep comin', but hold her up, and you'll get to where ya' want to be."

"I'm trying, GG. Really, I am—"

I'm interrupted by a pissed-off Halton entering the kitchen. "I'm not doing it, Colton, so fuck off."

Colton enters right behind him with a carefree grin and a bounce in his step.

"You have to. This is how we're going to win over Burke Hollow. I'll even let you choose your station first."

Halton points a menacing finger at our younger brother. "Fuck. Off."

"Now, this should be good. Grumpy, grab me some cookies." I stare between her and my brothers. "Yes, I want cookies for the show, so move it." She shoos me away with both hands.

I hurry to the pantry, pull out the cookie jar shaped like a bear, and set it down in front of her.

"Halt, I've done the research. So, this is the route we're going, and you can't turn your back on family."

"Colty, I swear to God ..."

"What's going on?" I finally interject.

"I made the plan for Summerfest, and Halton is being even testier than normal."

"He wants to auction me off," Halton bellows. "He wants to auction me off for a date."

"I told you that you could have the first pick. It doesn't have to be 'date the billionaire'."

"For fuck's sake." Halton throws his hands in the air, and I'm confused but secretly loving his discomfort.

"You can do the kissing booth if you'd rather," Colton says happily.

"You're out of your goddamn mind if you think I'm signing up to kiss a bunch of strangers. Haven't you ever heard of herpes, Colt? Jesus, have you even thought about this?"

"I have," he says calmly. "I went over everything with GG, and she agrees. It'll make Summerfest what it used to be. The Westbrooks will be responsible for bringing nostalgia back."

"No," Halton barks.

"Hold on. What's going on?"

"So glad you asked, big bro. We're going to market ourselves as the approachable billionaires—the ones who want the town to succeed on its own merit for a long time to come. To do that, we're going to make ourselves accessible for the entirety of Summerfest."

"Oh-kay," I drawl. "That doesn't sound so bad. So what has Halt's panties in a twist?"

"One way we're going to show we're everyday people is to put ourselves out there. We will be sponsoring Burke Hollow Happily Ever After."

When I don't respond, he continues, "I told him he can either do the bachelor auction or the kissing booth, but he has to do one of them. I'll do the other. I'm going to stick Ash in the dunk tank."

"What the hell is Easton going to do?" Halton's sulking tone doesn't fit with his scowling face, and I laugh.

"He's the MC, so he can't participate in the events."

"Such a shame," I playfully grouse.

"Easton is as much of an asshole as I am … why is he the MC?"

"Because, you big baby, the town already knows him. He's put in the time, and since he looks like he's wearing a homeless person's clothing, I'd say he's paid his dues."

"Yup, this is going to be the best Summerfest yet. Just ya wait and see, Fibby."

In slow motion, we all turn to face GG. I already have my name. She matched Lexi and me almost a year ago. So that means whoever she's calling Fibby is her next target.

"GG?" I finally ask.

"Times not right. But it's coming. And when it does, there'll be fireworks for sure."

"What the hell is she talking about?" Colton whispers. "Who is Fibby?"

I see the panic all over his ordinarily smiling face and shrug my shoulders. Then, desperate to see Halton's reaction, I turn to my left to find he's snuck out. Again. *Interesting.*

"Summerfest for the ages, that's what it'll be," GG continues more to herself than anyone in particular.

"I've got to get out of here. I'm going to find Rylan. See ya later."

Raising my fist, he bumps it. "Welcome to the chaos." I laugh.

"Yeah, this chaos just keeps getting weirder, though."

My laughter fills the room as he leaves the lodge.

"Oh, that boy ain't seen nothing yet," GG cackles ominously.

Now I'm convinced she really is a scary fucking witch.

hy doesn't GG have any freaking tissues in here? I'm sitting in her truck after today's therapy session, beginning to think I'm paying someone to make me cry, and it fucking sucks.

Every day Sarah Green gives me a new assignment. Yesterday it was to be nice to Easton. Today is much more complicated. Today I'm supposed to talk to GG. Sarah assured me the fear that she'll be disappointed in me is unwarranted, but it doesn't change my worry.

Grabbing the collar of my T-shirt, I pull it up to my forehead, then use it to dry my tears. Like a child who thinks they are invisible when they hide, I sit like this for far longer than is normal. Hiding feels safe. *So does being in Easton's arms.*

God, my inner bitch is going soft.

Finally, I pull my shirt down. I don't even bother glancing around to see if anyone saw me. At this point, the whole damn town knows I'm broken.

I drive slowly back up the mountain. Today's therapy session is rattling around in my head as I listen to Lewis

Capaldi's "One". The tears hit me like a tsunami, and I have to pull over.

"I'm not okay," I say to an empty truck. Easton has spent almost a year trying to put me back together, and I've spent that time pushing him away. The realization that he loves me anyway causes me to sob harder than I've ever done before.

I cry for the baby I lost, for the children I'll never have, and for the pain I've kept hidden for way too long.

Images of Lanie and Julia with their kids flash before my eyes, and jealousy cuts through me like a knife. I don't want to be the bitter auntie that can't look at her nieces and nephews without longing squeezing my heart, but that's how I've lived for over a year. I'm angry and jealous and mourning a life I'll never have.

My mind drifts to Easton and Tate outside of Preston's hospital room, and I slap my hand over my mouth to keep from throwing up. My Beast was so good with little Tate. Is it fair of me to take this piece of life away from him?

"There are other ways to make a family, Locket. Right now, I just need you." His voice is so clear in my mind, I would swear he was sitting next to me.

The Westbrooks are big on chosen family. Will he really be okay with a family that wasn't his blood, though? Will he grow to resent me one day if he never has children of his own?

I don't know how long I sit there, but when I put the truck in drive again, my shirt is soaked through with tears.

The drive goes by in a blur, and before I know it, I'm entering GG's kitchen. The second her eyes meet mine, my walls come tumbling down in loud, messy, agonizingly brutal wails.

"I-I almost died. I lost my baby, and now I'll never get the chance to carry one again. I-I'm broken, and I don't know how to make it better. I don't know how to feel. I-I can't get past my pain, GG. What do I do?"

She moves fast for an old lady and wraps me in an embrace so tight I struggle for breath in between my sobs. As she holds me, I feel her strength and her love, and it grounds me.

"Loss is a terrible, terrible thing, Locket. There are lots of stages and no right or wrong way to handle them. You've been angry for so long you kept those feelings buried. Now they're comin' out, and it's gonna hurt. It's gonna test you, too, but you're my girl, Lexi. I'm here to pick you up when you can't, and you have a man around here that's bustin' his ass just to keep you close. It's time to let us in. It's time to let us carry you for a while."

"I-I don't think I know how, GG," I sob in between hiccups. "What if I'm too broken? What if I can't ever get past my grief? Wh-What if I'm too much work and he decides he can't handle me?"

"Lex? You've put that man through so many paces, I'm convinced he's not goin' anywhere. He's in it for the long haul. You just have to accept him. As for bein' too broken? There ain't no such thing. The heart can do wondrous things when it's ready."

"How will I know? How will I know I'm ready?"

"You're here, ain't ya? That's the first step in healin'. Why don't ya tell me what beat my baby girl down? Then we can talk about lettin' Grumpy's love in."

"I-I think I already have, GG. No one's ever loved me like this, though. I don't know how to handle it. How can I say I love him back when I don't even love myself?"

"Oh Locket. Lovin' yourself will always be the hardest thing you do. It's in there though, and Grumpy's kind of love only comes around once in your lifetime. You're on the right path. I see you opening up to it before it's too late. Come on now. Let's go to the porch, and you can tell me all about what's causin' your heart to bleed."

Time stands still as I tell GG about my life over the last

few years. How Miles started off as the perfect boyfriend. What happened when it all changed, and why I was scared to ask for help. When I tell her about the child I lost and the subsequent hysterectomy, I see her cry for only the second time in my life.

"Things have a funny way of workin' out, Lexi. You may not get your family in the way you always hoped, but a family is coming your way. I promise you that."

GG has a way of making things happen, and I don't dare question her predictions. I'm not ready to go there yet. But the knowledge that all hope isn't lost for a family eases the constant ache in my chest. It's a pain that's resided there for over a year, and suddenly I feel myself breathe a little easier.

We sit in silence, hand in hand, until the sun begins to set. I nearly jump out of my skin when the front door crashes open and Ashton storms outside.

"Lexi?" he attempts to yell, not realizing we're sitting right here, but it comes out with a painful rasp instead.

I jump to my feet, somehow knowing something's wrong.

"Is East okay?" I ask before he can attempt to speak again.

Ashton's eyes soften for a split second as he takes in my appearance. I'm sure I look like shit after the emotional dumpage that just happened.

"Yes. Easton is fine. I need your help. I-I can't go into town with strangers," he croaks.

It hasn't gone unnoticed that he hides himself away now. The insecurities about his appearance are suffocating him, and none of us have been able to help him.

When I place a hand on his forearm, he flinches, and my heart hurts for him. Instead of backing away, though, I lunge at him and wrap him in a hug. He may need it even more than I do.

Ashton freezes in place, then eventually pats my back awkwardly. It's nothing like the Westbrook squeeze these men are known for. "I need your help, Lexi," he repeats.

I pull away. "Anything, Ash. What do you need?"

～

For the first time in my life, I feel like a traitor. I try to call East for the twentieth time and get his voice mail. Again. The one freaking time he's not around, and I need him. I need Easton in my life, and I have to tell him what I'm about to do.

If I didn't love Ashton like a brother, I would have told him to go fuck himself. But that's not the Westbrook way. *Holy shit, I'm a Westbrook now.* My thumb absently rubs the ring finger of my left hand, and I suddenly wish I had agreed to wear his ring sooner.

With an irritated sigh, I try Easton one more time.

"You've reached Easton Westbrook. Please leave a message. In the event of an emergency, please contact my assistant, Lexi Heart, at 802.555.2524."

Beep.

"Beast? It-It's me. I need you. I-I have to talk to you, it's important. Please call me back as soon as you get this. I …" The words I love you are on the tip of my tongue, but I can't bring myself to do it over voice mail. "I'll talk to you soon."

Ending the call, I peer out over the steering wheel of GG's truck. I haven't been here since high school, yet the old, yellow Victorian looks the same.

I'll give Easton five more minutes to call, then I'll be forced to go in and pray that he'll understand.

Well, five more minutes couldn't hurt, right? I sit watching the clock, and when he doesn't call back after ten minutes, I take a deep breath and exit the truck.

I walk up the stone path to the town memorial library and push the door open. As soon as I enter, I'm assaulted by the scent of old books and lemon Pledge. An antique desk

245

that I know Easton would admire sits in the crook of the stairs, in the foyer of the old home.

Turning left, I make my way through the sitting room. I admire the books lined up on every wall. As a kid, I never appreciated the work that went into turning this old home into a library, but entering now, I have a newfound respect.

Sitting at one of the workspaces I used as a teenager is Dillon Henry. Crossing the room, I take the three steps up to the old parlor and see him up close. His hands are clasped in front of him, and his head is bowed. He hasn't seen me yet. If I didn't already know he was despicable, I'd think he was a man in pain.

With my hands on my hips, I rock back and forth from leg to leg. I'm antsy, and I don't want to be here. Dillon must catch sight of my movements because he raises his head, and our eyes lock.

Jesus. Staring at him, he appears lost. My judgment of character is seriously flawed. This is just more proof that I can't trust myself in these decisions.

"Ms. Heart? Thank you for meeting me. I-I know this is probably the last place you want to be, so I appreciate it. Ashton was supposed to meet me, but ... well, I'm sure he told you."

"Before you give me whatever information Ash needs, I want to tell you what a piece of shit you are."

A sad smile twists the corners of his lips. "I'm glad East has found a guardian. He was always the best man I knew."

"So good that you married his girlfriend? So good that you let her die without ever giving him the chance to say good-bye? God, you're worse than the worst kind of human."

"Things are not always what they seem, Ms. Heart. Please, have a seat."

I glance from him to the tables that are set up for learning. The chairs sit side by side, and I hate that I'm about to get that close to this asshole.

"Ashton fucking owes me. Big time," I grumble as I take a seat. "Let's get this over with. What do you have that Ashton needs?"

"I promise, I'm not the bad guy here. I hope Easton can see that someday."

"Listen, asshole. I'm not here to talk about Easton," I hiss. "Tell me what you need to say so I can go."

Dillon sighs, and I feel the weight of it in my bones.

Do not go soft for this guy, Lexi. Remember what he did to Beast.

Dillon removes a stack of papers from a briefcase I hadn't yet noticed and sets it on the table. Leaning forward, I scan the documents. Then, I fan them out in front of me, trying to make sense of what I'm seeing.

"Is this ... But, why didn't you ever tell him?"

"Un-fucking-believable," a deep, angry voice yells. I know without lifting my head that it's Easton, and I hang my head lower because of how this looks to him. When I'm able to keep it together, I find his eyes and am frozen by the pure hatred staring back at me.

CHAPTER 38

EASTON

"That's quite the production. Are you sure you can pull it off in time?" Baker asks.

I observe him as he leans back in his office chair. He's in a baby blue dhoti today, and he rests his joined hands on his protruding belly. Regardless of his position and what it could mean for my girls, I like this guy.

"I'm a Westbrook, sir. We thrive under pressure. I have no doubt this will all come to fruition. My teams will have the last of the foundations poured by the end of the day. That will at least pause the development deals, and my brother brought in reinforcements from our offices in North Carolina to help facilitate our portion of Summerfest."

"Burke Hollowians will want to participate you know? I hope you're not just bringing in your own men. The point of this is to get the town to trust you."

"I'm very aware of what our job is, Baker. He brought in experts to help plan. Man power will be strictly Westbrooks or residents."

Baker smiles as he clasps his hands behind his head. "Sounds like you've got a good plan then, son. Fontaine is going to hate it, but I believe in you and love those Heart women."

Hearing Fontaine's name is like nails on a chalkboard. I know I shouldn't accuse without proof, but I have to let him know where my head is.

"Listen, Baker. I'm sure you can tell there's a history between Macomb and me. It's nothing good and nothing I wish to discuss, but the fact that he's working with Fontaine worries me. Especially since I have proof that someone tampered with the Heart Lodge."

Baker's smile fades as he leans forward. "What do you mean tampered with?"

"I've had multiple independent engineers and inspectors come out to look at the damage. If you compare GG's hospitality inspection from last year to the mess I found when I arrived, you can see someone knew just where to strike to make the foundation unstable. They also notched the ceiling's support beams in strategic places. That's why the roof caved in so suddenly."

"Woo-wee. That's a big accusation, Easton."

I pinch the back of my neck and roll my shoulders. This is a fight I'm all too ready to take on. "I know it is, but GG only had two people out to work on the lodge all year. Both of them were recommendations from Fontaine. And, you're really not going to like this part."

Baker leans in even farther. I forget that this man lives for gossip almost as much as GG.

"What is it?"

"My brother, Halton, is the head of finance at The Westbrook Group. He's been going over the town's financials, and something isn't adding up there."

"Like what?" Baker gasps.

"Over the last ten years, hundreds of thousands of dollars have gone missing from the general fund. It was never in large sums. Nothing that would tip anyone off unless you knew what you were looking for."

"And Halton knows what to look for?"

"He's the best," I admit. "We don't know where the money has gone. Not yet anyway, but he's sure it's missing. That's why the town suddenly has a fiscal catastrophe."

"But, how? How could that much money just disappear?"

"There's only one person with direct access, correct?"

Baker's eyes go comically round. "Fontaine."

"Fontaine," I agree.

"I don't know what kind of angel landed you on my doorstep, but I'm going to say a little prayer for you tonight. Tell me what we need to do."

~

*I*t's late in the day by the time I leave Baker's office. I don't miss that Fontaine is sitting on the bench across the street when I exit. *Yeah, your day's coming, buddy. No one messes with my girls.*

Feeling my pockets, I realize I don't have my phone. I glance in the window of the truck and see it sitting on the seat, so I quickly unlock the door, and my heart sinks when I see fourteen missed messages from Lexi.

Shit. Pressing Lexi's name, I wait for the call to connect, but it goes straight to voice mail. Rechecking the screen, I notice I have a message from her.

"Beast? It-It's me. I need you."

I don't even listen to the rest of the message. I can hear it in her voice—something's wrong.

I call her number again, and again, but she doesn't answer. Panic I've never felt rises in my throat, and I'm finding it difficult to breathe.

Where are you, sweetheart? Her phone! I can track her phone. Pulling up the Westbrook Security's app Trevor installed last year, I search for her phone. It takes longer than it should because the cell service in this area is hit or miss. Finally, her name appears on the screen. Turning in a circle, I realize she's on the other side of the town square, and I take off running.

When my circle is almost on top of hers, I pause to glance around. Then, checking my screen, I realize she must be in the library, and the hairs on the back of my neck stand on end. Nothing about this feels right.

As I make my way up the walkway, our circles overlap. Lexi is definitely in here, but why would she have sounded so upset? Opening the door, I seek her out.

The library is old, and very quiet. Closing my eyes, I listen for any sound. That's when I hear her voice coming from the left.

"But, why didn't you ever tell him?" Lexi's voice is soft, but I'd know it anywhere. Following the sound, my heart stops when I find her.

She's head-to-head with Dillon Henry, and I'm numb. The blood rushing in my ears drowns out the rest of their words, and before I can think, I'm charging him.

"Un-fucking-believable," I scream. Fuck the library rules. When Lexi bows her head in shame, I dry heave.

It's happening again. He's taken her from me. Lexi, of all people, knew what this would do to me.

"H-How could you do this to me?" My voice is deadly.

"Beast, it's—"

"Don't," I rage. "Don't make up shit, Lexi. I can see it with my own two eyes. Does he know he can't legally marry you first since we're already married?"

"What?" she screeches.

"East—"

"Shut the fuck up, Dillon. Doing this to me once wasn't enough? What the hell did I ever do to you? And you!" I turn back to Lexi. "After everything I've done for you. I've been

251

here for months busting my ass to make you happy, and it wasn't enough?" My voice cracks, and it enrages me further.

"I gave you my heart. I gave you everything, and it wasn't good enough? I loved you with everything I had."

I attempt to leave, but the pain I'm feeling needs to lash out. Turning, I take in her appearance and shake my head. "I knew you were a bitch, Lexi, but I didn't think you were heartless, too. I guess the only good thing about us being together was that I couldn't procreate with you."

Her shocked gasp and hurt expression do nothing to ease my heartache. "You were right about one thing, though. You were the biggest fucking mistake of my life."

"Easton," Dillon interrupts, but I've had enough. Kicking the chair in front of me, I rush out of the old house, gasping for air. When I still can't breathe, I jump in my truck and peel out so fast gravel goes flying behind me.

How could she do this? I thought we were making progress. This doesn't make any sense. She said she would try. Unable to return to the lodge, I drive to the Wagon Wheel in search of my brothers.

When I arrive, I find Ashton and Preston sitting on the front stoop. My body is shaking when I approach them, and I can't hide my emotions as I get closer. The weight of Lexi's betrayal sits heavy on my soul. Lifting my gaze to my brothers, it finally crushes me and I collapse to the stairs in front of them.

Remembering the sight of Lexi with Dillon seeps deep into my heart as ice fills my veins. I'm suddenly frozen in grief while my body shakes with hurt.

"Jesus Christ, East. What the hell happened?" Preston asks as he lifts me onto the top step.

"I-I fell in love, and she chose him, too. She chose Dillon over me," I croak as a tear slides down my face.

Preston holds me at arm's length and inspects me like a mother hen.

"Fuck. Easton? What do you think you saw?" Ash forces out.

"It's not what I think, Ash. I saw Lexi with Dillon."

"Please tell me you didn't do something stupid," Preston groans, shaking my body slightly.

"Me? Me, do something stupid? I just told you I fell in love with Lexi, and I found her with Dillon. Just like ... just like Vanessa."

"This is nothing like Vanessa, East." Preston's voice carries misdirected anger, and I rip free from his hold.

"You're right. This is so much fucking worse, because I loved Lexi with my whole heart. A love I didn't know existed, and she broke me like I never mattered."

"East, Lexi met with him for Ashton. And," Preston turns to Ash, then back to me, "what happened with Vanessa isn't what you think either."

My body deflates, and a new ache takes residence in my chest. "What do you mean?" I ask through clenched teeth. Eight years of hatred are simmering inside of me, ready to fight for the pain I've endured.

"East, I don't know why Dillon never told you, but they were protecting you. They were protecting our family."

"Fuck you," I scream. "How was marrying my dying girl-friend protecting me?" My head is trying to explode, and I feel my heart ripping in two. I don't know how much more I can take.

"When you went off to college, Vanessa learned her father was planning to use her to get to Dad. When Dad died, he turned his hatred to you, to me, to anyone with the name Westbrook."

"Why?" I ask, but my voice is barely audible. Hatred and hurt sit heavy in my throat.

"The best I can figure so far is that Dad blocked him from three projects in a row because he knew Macomb was cutting corners, making the projects unsafe. Macomb lost his shirt because of it and blamed us."

"That doesn't explain why he married her," I bite out.

Preston sighs, steps closer, and lowers his voice. "East, I know you had love for Vanessa, but really stop and think about what that means. You feel betrayed, and you have every right to that anger, but listen to Ash, then ask yourself if the love you felt can even compare to what you're feeling right now."

He gives me a pointed glare, and his words knock the wind out of me. My brain is reeling with too many thoughts at once. I know what he is getting at, and he's right, but it doesn't make it hurt any less. I did have love for Vanessa. She was one of my best friends, and I would have married her because it was the right thing to do. But her betrayal felt nothing like the soul killing heartache Lexi has caused.

"I did have love for Vanessa," I admit. "But I was in love with Lexi in a way I didn't know existed." A sob breaks free, and I lower my head.

"Then listen to what Ash is telling you, brother."

Remembering the way Lexi looked when I found her with Dillon causes my chest to heave with new pain. A pain so visceral I can't breathe, so I focus on the hurt I've grown accustomed to.

"That doesn't explain why he married her." I repeat the words even as my heart bleeds from the massacre Lexi inflicted.

CHAPTER 39

LEXI

reston: He's here.

        Lexi: On my way. Do not fucking let him leave.

Preston: You going to tell me what he did?

Lexi: Ash will fill you in. The rest is between Easton and me.

Preston: Fair enough. We're out front.

Pulling into the driveway, I beeline it for the front stairs.

"That doesn't explain why he married her," Easton's voice is gritty, and full of emotion.

Stepping forward, I answer the question because I'm the only one with the answers. "Because Vanessa knew she was dying."

Easton's body tenses at my voice, but he keeps his head down as I continue to speak. "If she passed away unmarried, her father would have gotten her inheritance and used it to come after you."

"I would have married her." He forces the words out as if they tasted bitter on his tongue.

My poor Beast. "There was a strange clause to her inheritance. If she married above her 'class,' she gave up the rights to her inheritance. Her father knew that. By marrying Dillon, she ensured he was well taken care of. She knew you wouldn't need the money the way he did. They never imagined not telling you all of this. But then Macomb went after Dillon, and he made a split-second decision. By keeping Macomb close, he could thwart his attacks on you. He's been doing it ever since."

Easton jumps to his feet, but Ash shoves him back down. "It's the truth, Easton. Every word. I checked it out myself when Dillon contacted me about Pacen."

Easton shakes his head from side to side as he cradles it in his hands. I can tell he's waiting for the next blow, and I recognize the second he realizes he hurt me for no reason. He opens his mouth to speak, but I hold up a hand to cut him off.

"I know you're hurting, Beast. I know this is a lot to take in, but you destroyed me with your words tonight."

He stands suddenly, but Preston holds him back, and I worry he might punch out his own brother.

"Let me go, Pres. Let me go," he pleads, but Preston holds on tight.

"Listen to what she's saying, East," Preston whispers, but the words carry on the mountain air.

Swallowing, I force my words to come. "You came into my life like a wrecking ball of bad decisions, and as much as I tried to hate you, it was impossible. You pushed, and you pushed, and you pushed ..." A sob I can't hold in falls from my lips. "Un-Until my walls came crumbling down." Tears are streaming down my face, and I see the pain reflected at me in Easton's eyes. This all fucking hurts.

"But the thing is, Beast, you don't get to storm into my life. Force me to open my heart. Make me love you just to have you walk away. That's not how we're going to handle things. We're adults, and we'll fight like adults. You do not

256

get to love me one day and throw me away the next. I won't let you."

"Locket." My name is a plea on his lips, but I need time. I've made so many mistakes. I don't want Easton to be one of them.

"No, Beast. You hit me where you knew it would hurt the most, and it did. I need time. You need time."

"Not away from you. Please let me make this right," he begs.

"I-I will, I promise. But not right now. I don't want this to be a mistake we regret. You have so much old baggage to sort through right now, and I—" I choke back a sob. "I need to feel less broken before we talk again."

"Please don't leave like this, Locket. I'm so sorry, please let me fix this."

"I'm going to stay with Julia and Lanie for a few days. You can fix it by first sorting through all you learned tonight. We'll talk when we're both in a better place."

"Lexi, I ... God, I'm so sorry for what I said."

My shoulders shake with unshed tears. "I know."

I turn to go, but Easton breaks free from Preston's grasp, and barrels down the steps until he's in front of me. His hands grasp the back of my head, and he forces our foreheads together.

"I'm so sorry, Locket. I'm so sorry. Please tell me I didn't fuck us up. Please."

"We're not broken, Beast. Just a little bent, but we both need time."

Behind him, Preston and Ash slink away.

"God. The things I said," his voice breaks, and I have to look away. "I didn't mean it, Locket. I-I was hurting and needed you to hurt too. I was so wrong. I'm so sorry," he says again. "I don't want you to leave like this. I don't want to leave us like this. Tell me how to fix us."

I shake my head sadly. "We just need time."

"You said you loved me back there. Do you still love me?"

"I think I always have, Beast. But I don't like you very much right now. You just found out that years' worth of pain wasn't what you thought. You have a chance to get your friend back. You need to make amends and forgive Vanessa, and I need to forgive you. And myself. We both have a lot of work to do before we can ever be a team."

"But you'll try?"

The agony in his words almost makes me cave. Almost. However, I meant what I said. He can't be a mistake I regret.

"I promised you I would."

"When can I see you again?"

"I ... East, I'm not sure. Do your homework. Fix yourself, then we can fix us."

"I've never wanted to be an 'us' so badly in my life. You're my team, Lexi. Someday, you'll tell the world that you're my wife?"

I know he needs reassurance. Can I give it to him? Staring into his eyes, I see a future somewhere in those depths, so I concede and give him what he so desperately needs.

"Someday," I promise. "But not today. I-I have to go, East."

He leans in and kisses my cheek. That's when I notice his are wet with tears. We're both hurting, but we need the space to work on ourselves. Therapy has taught me that. You can't be a team until you can love yourself.

Slowly, I pull away and walk on trembling legs back to the truck. I need to get to Julia's before I break down completely. After putting the truck in gear, I pull out of the parking lot. I've never been so happy to have my girls home as I am right now. I'm going to need them.

∾

I wake to tiny fingers lifting my eyelids. "You 'wake, Auntie? You 'wake?"

"Harper! I told you to leave Auntie Lexi alone," Lanie scolds.

"It's okay, Lanes. She's fine."

"You sure?" she asks, while worrying her bottom lip.

When I arrived last night, I had diarrhea of the mouth and spewed my life story from the last three years. The only thing I held back was my Vegas wedding. I'm not sure why, but I want to keep that just for myself right now.

"Lanes, I love your kids. Yes, it's painful sometimes, but it doesn't mean I love them any less."

"Wexi woves me. Wexi woves me," the little girl chants, making me laugh out loud.

"I do. I do woves you." And for the first time in a long time, I say it without my chest trying to suffocate me.

"Are you sure?"

Rolling onto my back, I drag Harper with me, and she erupts into a fit of giggles. It's nearly impossible not to be happy when a toddler gives you a full belly laugh.

"Yeah, Lanes. I'm sure."

"You know, I think Easton's good for you."

Staring at the ceiling, I think about her words. "I do, too, Lanes."

She comes to lie next to me—our heads together on the pillow, just like when we were kids.

"I'm sorry I was so wrapped up in my life that I didn't see yours crumbling around you."

"I got really good at hiding. You didn't see because I didn't want you to."

"Can I ask you something?"

"Of course. Ah, on second thought, it depends on what you're asking. I'm not sure what kind of kink you're into these days," I tease, and enjoy watching my cousin's skin turn crimson.

"Geez, Lex. I just wanted to ask about something you said last night."

My body tenses, but I prepare myself by counting to ten. "Shoot."

"You said the first round when you harvested your eggs? That round worked?"

I sigh because I know she's hoping for a miracle.

"Yeah, it worked, but I can't find the eggs. Mimi and I have been searching databases everywhere, and they're nowhere to be found. I-I trusted Miles then. I assumed he had our best interests at heart, but he told me I'd never find them when I was trying to leave."

"And now he's—" Lanie breaks off, not wanting to upset me further.

"Now he's dead, and I have no way of knowing if he stored them properly or if he destroyed them. The unknown is the hardest to live with, but I'm working through it in therapy."

"You know? Sarah helped me a couple of years ago, too."

Rolling to my side, I stare at my beautiful cousin. "I had a hunch. GG doesn't usually make a habit of keeping shrinks on standby."

We laugh, and Julia enters the room.

"Well, looky here." She smirks, but climbs into bed between us. Lanie and I are both over six feet tall. Julia is just a touch over five feet—we've always been her bookends. "I've missed this."

"Me too," I admit.

"Awe, me three. I *luv* you girls so much."

"Luvs," Julia and I say in unison.

"Soooo." Julia drags the word out in a way that tells me trouble is brewing. "How are we going to make him pay?"

"Who?" Lanie asks.

"East. How are we going to make him grovel?"

Gah! I love these girls, but Julia is freaking nuts.

"I'll bust his balls, for reals. Trevor and I have been taking self-defense classes together. I can take down a full-grown man in under three seconds."

"Jesus, Jules. No. No physical violence. I'm sure Easton's in his own personal hell right now. He doesn't need us adding to it."

"Are you going to call him back?" Lanie asks, holding up my phone.

Taking it from her hands, I see six missed calls and twenty-four text messages.

"No," I finally reply. "I meant what I said. We need some time apart. We both have things to work through before we can try being a couple."

"Well, let me tell you from experience. Those Westbrook boys don't give up easily. So if he wants something badly enough, you'd better believe he'll make it happen."

I groan, knowing she's right. "I just can't afford to mess this up. He has to deal with the pain of everything he learned last night, and I might always be a work in progress. We can't start a relationship with two broken pieces."

"Okay," Julia sings. "Don't say I didn't warn you. Now get up. We've got shit to do for Summerfest today. Colton has already been blowing up my phone, asking for help to set up his booths. That guy has more energy than a light socket."

Laughing, I watch as Lanie crawls out of bed with Harper, and Julia makes her way to the door.

"Be ready in thirty minutes. The LUV Club's on a mission."

"The LUV Club?" Lanie and I both ask.

"Yup. GG's in a matchmaking frenzy. Summerfest might as well be known as Loverfest if she's right."

"Good Lord. Who's she matching now?"

"She hasn't said, but it's either Halton or Colty, and

they're both shitting bricks while we wait for it to play out," Julia whispers conspiratorially. "Thirty minutes," she yells over her shoulder.

"Lex?"

I turn to my cousin.

"Just make sure you're keeping East at arm's length for the right reasons, okay? Everyone makes mistakes, but he's a good man, and we can all see how much he loves you."

Choked up, I nod, and she pulls the door closed as she leaves.

My phone buzzes in my hand and startles me. Bringing it to my face, I see another message from East.

Easton: I love you.

Easton: And I'm so fucking sorry for being an unbelievably stupid asshole.

Lexi: I know you do, and I know you are.

Easton: ...

Lexi: Have a good day, East.

Easton: You too, Locket.

Reading my nickname, my hand immediately searches out the key charm around my neck. I haven't taken it off since the day he gave it to me, but I squeeze it in my palm to know it's real.

CHAPTER 40

EASTON

"*I*s she talking to you yet?" Preston asks as we take a seat on the picnic table at the town square.

Handing him a bottle of water, I shake my head no.

"Jesus, Easton. I told you to be careful with her."

"I love her, Pres."

He punches my shoulder, then bumps it with his. "I know you do, little brother. And I think she's good for you. It's nice to have you back."

"I'm happy here, Pres."

He cautiously observes me before speaking. "I can see that. I was wondering how long you would suffer through The Westbrook Group before you realized it wasn't for you."

I swing my gaze to him so fast I nearly fall off the table. "What?" I ask, shocked. I had no idea he knew I was unhappy there.

"I remember the plans you had with Dillon once upon a time, East. Those dreams don't just go away."

"No, but life happens, and responsibilities pile up. I couldn't leave you to figure it all out on your own."

"And I appreciate that more than you'll ever know, but we have a well-oiled machine now. So maybe, now that you've found your girl, it's time you figured out what will make you happy."

"I can't just walk away from The Westbrook Group, Pres. It's our legacy." Placing my forearms on my thighs, I stare at the ground.

"Maybe not, but perhaps roles can change, and we can expand into a market better suited to your talents."

I stare at him, confused.

"I saw Lexi's desk at the office, East. You're amazingly talented, and I think working with your hands makes you happy."

It does. More than he'll ever know. But I never thought about incorporating it into The Westbrook Group.

"Let's get the Heart women settled here, then we can talk about the next steps, okay?"

"Yeah, okay. Pres?"

"Hmm?" he hums distractedly.

"You scared the shit out of me when your heart stopped. Don't hide shit like that again."

"Yeah. I think we all need to agree to no more secrets. For a family that's so close, we sure do hide a lot of shit in the name of protecting each other."

"No more secrets?" I hold up my fist, and he meets mine.

"No more secrets. Welcome back to the chaos, little bro."

I'm about to show him just how little I am when a voice stops me cold. *Fucking Fontaine.*

I inhale deeply before turning around, but Preston is already running interference.

"I know what you did," Fontaine accuses.

Crossing my arms over my chest, I watch him step back a few paces. "Oh yeah? What's that?"

"You think you're so smart pouring foundations so the town can't develop that land. But you just wait until the people of Burke Hollow find out how devious and sneaky you are. They will not take kindly to being jilted out of that opportunity—an opportunity that would bring much needed jobs to the area. Oh, and believe me, I plan to tell everyone." His words slither through the air like a snake.

I take three steps forward before Preston places a hand on my chest, silently telling me to stand down.

Narrowing my eyes, I puff out my chest, making myself as large as possible. "You do that, Fontaine. I'll even hand you the microphone in two days to do just that. But, while you're busy spewing your lies, I'll be letting everyone know how the town is missing over six-hundred thousand dollars. The money you manage, if I'm not mistaken."

My words have the desired effect and knock the wind right out of his sail.

"I …. Ah, I-I, how dare you. Are you accusing me of something, Westbrook?"

"I'm just stating facts. The truth will come out, eventually. It always does, especially since I offered to hire an independent forensic accountant to audit the town."

Fontaine pales and starts to fidget.

"Be careful who you threaten around here, Easton. You may not like the consequences."

I take another step forward. "You forget where I come from, Fontaine. You also forget the resources I have at my disposal. So I suggest you take your empty threats and shove them up your ass. It might come in handy in the federal prison system."

"Tone it down, East," Preston whispers beside me. "You have an audience."

Glancing around, I notice the crowd we've drawn.

"We have to get going. Summerfest is getting some Westbrook flair this year. Have a good day, Fontaine." I spit the words as I pass him.

"He's going to skip town now, you know that, right?" Preston mumbles so no one else can hear.

"Let him try. Ash already hacked him. We'll be able to track his every move."

"Jesus. Don't tell me shit like that, East. Plausible deniability is a thing, you know?"

I chuckle but acknowledge he's right. Unfortunately, we still don't know how or why Macomb is tied up in this. Or why Pacen has gone missing.

When we reach the gazebo, Preston breaks away to search for his wife while I pull out my phone to text Lexi.

Easton: Can I see you yet?

Lexi: Not today.

Easton: Tomorrow?

Lexi: We'll see.

Easton: I'm going to meet with Dillon tomorrow afternoon.

I don't know why I tell her this over text, but it seems like something she would want to know.

Lexi: I'm glad. I really hope you're able to get some peace with that part of your life.

Lexi: How do you feel about it?

Easton: I'm confused.

Lexi: It's a lot to work through.

Easton: I wish you were going with me.

Lexi: Some things we have to do on our own. We can't come together until we're strong enough alone.

Easton: I disagree. I think we'll always be stronger together, even when we're both a little broken.

Easton: We will, right? Come together?

Lexi: We're married, East. There has to be a resolution here, too.

I don't like the sound of that.

Easton: The resolution is me putting your ring back on your finger.

Lexi: ...

Easton: I wish I had given it to you sooner. Will you wear it when we get through this?

Lexi: I hope so.

Lexi: Have a good day, East.

Easton: I love you.

Lexi: I know.

That night I'm laying in our bed, cradling Lexi's pillow like a fucking stalker, when there's a knock on my door.

"Come in," I groan, knowing it's one or more of my brothers.

The door crashes open, and they all pile into the room. Preston, Halton, Colton, Dexter, Trevor, Loki, and Seth crowd the small space.

"Ah, what's up, guys?" I ask uncomfortably. This looks suspiciously like an intervention.

"You fucked up. We're here to help," Dex says happily.

"Listen, I know you love playing the merry fucking fairy, but I don't need your help."

Colton makes a show of glancing around. "You don't need help? So, Lexi's here? Lexi-con, Lexi-con, come out and play," he sings.

"You fucking moron."

Grinning, Colton plops his ass down on the bed next to me. "It's either us or GG. Who do you want to confide in?"

"Where is GG?"

"Baking pies with-with Ry," Halton growls while watching the door.

"You have somewhere to be?" Preston asks, noticing Halton's odd behavior.

"Actually, yeah. I have to find Ash. Get your shit together, East," he grumbles on his way out the door.

"When did I become the most fucked up brother?"

"When you turned into a pecker and hurt your girl so badly, she ran away from her own home," Loki deadpans. "I've been there, dude. We both hurt our girls on purpose, and women may forgive, but they never fucking forget. You need an epic gesture to win her back."

Fuck. Are they right?

I listen as Dexter throws out one ridiculous plan after another while my mind drifts to Lexi. Showy isn't her style, but they're right ... I'm going to need something big to get through to her.

~

I'm back at the scene of my crime. The old, yellow Victorian stands against a clear, blue sky, mocking my foul mood. I need answers, though. Answers only he can give me.

"Forgiveness is a powerful thing, Easton. Only the strongest people possess that power. There will be times in your life when you're tested. Times when it's easier to hold a grudge, but bitterness weighs heavy on a man's soul. A true test of character is the ability to acknowledge your pain without drowning in it, then throwing the life raft to those who hurt you."

My father's words are coming more frequently lately, and I realize it's because of Lexi. She forced me to open myself up again, and in doing so, the love I've pushed away for so long invades my consciousness.

"Welcome to the mother fucking chaos," I whisper just before I pull the door open.

I find Dillon at the same table in the backroom, but this time pain replaces the rage. With the veil of hatred lifted, I notice the years have not been kind to my old friend, and misplaced guilt tears at my gut.

My movements alert Dillon I'm here, and he stands uncomfortably. "East, I-I'm glad you came."

Unsure of what to say, I nod and grab a chair from a neighboring table.

"I'm so sorry, East. It was never supposed to go on this long. I ..."

"I just don't understand, Dill. If everything Ash says is true, why wouldn't you have come to me?"

"I couldn't, not at first. Ness didn't have sufficient information. She overheard just enough of a conversation to know Patrick was coming after your family. When she got sick ..." He tears his gaze away. "It was hard, East. It was so hard not to tell you, but we were just kids. We thought we were protecting you."

"It's been eight years, Dillon." My voice raises to an unacceptable level, and we get shushed.

"The plan was for me to work for him. Just for a few months to get the proof we needed, and then I was going to come to you. But, East? The longer I was in, the more shit I found out, and it just snowballed. Suddenly, it became easier for me to sabotage from the inside than to get to you. The more time passed, the harder it became to explain."

"So you just, what? Spent your life protecting mine? Knowing I hated you? We were all you had, Dillon. We were your family. You had to have known you could come to us. How could you not have come to us?"

"I was a kid, East. We both were. Ness was scared for you when she died. You were our best friend. The best person we knew. So I promised her on her deathbed that I wouldn't allow her father to hurt you."

"That doesn't make any fucking sense, Dillon. My family would have fixed this."

He finally makes eye contact, and I see the pain I've carried all these years in his expression.

"Why? Why would have given up everything you loved to do this?"

"Because you were my brother, Easton. You would have done the same thing."

Would I have? Could I have become a martyr to protect

those I love? I rest my head in my hands as eight years' worth of pain fights to be set free.

"I'm sorry we hurt you," he whispers. "But Patrick is fucked up, East. And … And I'm afraid for Pacen."

"That's why you're telling me now?"

"I had to make a choice, East. I know you can protect yourself now, but Pacen? She's an innocent. He's used her as a pawn for years. He's forced her into so many dangerous situations I couldn't protect her from. I tried, I did. But now … now I think she's in real trouble. She's the only family I have left, and—" He breaks down before me.

Forgiveness. He needs my forgiveness.

"She's not the only family, Dill. You'll always be a part of the chaos."

Welcoming him back into my world releases the last part of my heart that pain had locked away.

"I can't, Easton. As much as I loved being part of your family, the second Macomb finds out I turned on him, he'll kill me. I can't put you in that kind of danger."

Staring at him, I shake my head. "I think it's been too long."

"What do you mean? You won't help me find Pacen? East, I've known her for a long time. She's not capable of what Ashton's accusing her of. I'd bet my life on it."

"You're done laying down your life, Dill. I meant you've been gone so long you forget how we do things around here. We take care of own." My words break as emotion consumes me. My mind and heart are at war for what's right. It's hard to just turn off eight years of feelings, but I know Ashton. He leaves no stone unturned. So if he believes Dillon, I should, too.

"I-I …" he stutters while shaking his head no.

"I learned recently that feelings don't change overnight. We have work to do, but we were always stronger together."

Dillon stares at me, obviously confused by my words.

Hell, I'm shocking myself. Two days ago, I never would have imagined I'd be sitting here with him, let alone welcoming him to the chaos, but here we are.

"Trust will take time, but forgiveness is an easier road to take, and right now, I need all the easy I can get. I-I just need to know …"

"Ness never stopped loving you, East. You were her shining star. Her biggest regret was that our actions might dim your light. I'm sorry that it did for so long."

His words are like a punch to the throat, and I'm having trouble keeping the tears at bay. The relief of knowing the two people I loved like family didn't betray me after all is more than I can handle.

"Thank you, Dill. Let's get you out of here, okay? You should probably come back to the lodge with me. Ashton and Loki will know how to help you. Can you believe they ended up actually being super-spies?"

His laughter is like a salve over an old wound, and I feel a little piece of my soul mend.

"You always said they'd end up in the CIA." He chuckles.

"Even better than that. Special Ops—SIA."

"No shit?" he says, obviously impressed.

As we exit the old building, I feel lighter than I can remember being in the recent years. *This must be what Lexi meant by working on me.* She was right, but isn't she always? With this piece of my past behind me, I'm ready to grab my future. I'm ready to make Lexi mine.

CHAPTER 41

*E*aston: I'm ready.

Lexi: Ready for what?

Easton: To make you mine.

Lexi: ???

Easton: Are you ready to be my wife?

Lexi: We've already covered that. Legally, I am.

Easton: That's a piece of paper. Are you, Lexi Mae, ready to be my wife?

I can't help but smile.

"How long are you going to punish him?" Colton asks from across the room.

"Colty! That's none of your business. He said some pretty shitty things," Rylan scolds.

I knew I liked this girl. Her relationship with Halton is another story, though. I have noticed they're never in the same room, but I did catch them in the hallway yesterday. I pretended not to see their angry stance, but a blind bat couldn't miss that kind of tension.

"I'm not punishing him," I sulk. "I'm-I'm just—"

"She's scared," Julia interjects, unhelpful as ever.

"I am not."

"Ya kinda are," Preston buts in.

"Ugh. I ..." *Shit. I am scared.*

"Take a seat, Locket," GG orders from across the room. "Guys? Give us a minute, yeah?"

Everyone has a job to do since Colton's Hollow Hearts mission starts today with the Billionaire Bachelor Auction, so they take their supplies and head out the door.

I hate to admit it, but every single female in the tri-state area has turned up in Burke Hollow today. Colton is deceptively good at his job.

"I can't sit, GG. We've got work to do."

"Work will always be there, young lady. Matters of the Heart won't wait."

Grabbing the box with auction paddles, I take a seat next to her so I can number them while she scolds me. The second I sit down, she grasps my hands, and my plan goes out the window.

"I know you're scared, Lexi. You've been through more than your share of heartache."

"You mean I've made more than my share of mistakes," I joke, but it falls on deaf ears.

"Mistakes are all about how you look at 'em. Sure, some mistakes bring unimaginable pain, but some bring the purest kind of love."

Resting my head on her shoulder, I take comfort in the woman who has always been my rock. "I've made a lot of mistakes, GG."

"That's part of life, girly, but you've made some pretty great mistakes, too."

Confused, I pull away to see her eyes. "What do you mean?"

"One little mistake in Vegas brought you a man who pulled you from your grief. He brought you back to life. I'd say that's the best kind of mistake."

I stare at her, open-mouthed. Shock doesn't begin to

describe what I'm experiencing right now. "You've known? This entire time you've known?"

GG cackles in a way that's so uniquely her I laugh right along with her.

"I knew ya' was drunk, missy, but I didn't realize you were that drunk."

"What do you mean?" I ask, genuinely confused.

GG pulls her phone out of her pocket, presses a few buttons, and hands it to me.

There, on her screen, is a picture of Easton and me in front of an Elvis impersonator. We're kissing in the background with our ring fingers on display for the camera.

"You were there?" I screech.

"Grumpy is a gentleman, Locket. He couldn't marry you without askin' my permission, and you said you needed a witness. Sylvie drove me, so ya got the both of us." She swipes the image on her phone, and a picture of the four of us is staring back at me.

Sylvie and GG look exhausted. I cringe, realizing we must have dragged them from bed for this, but their smiles are happy. What really catches my eye, though, is the way Easton is staring at me. While I'm gazing straight ahead at the camera, he's focused solely on me. He's looking at me as if I'm his entire world.

"That there is what a man in love looks like, Locket. I think he's proved time and time again you can trust him. Now, I know he messed up, and trust me, he'll do it again, but I think it's time you allow yourself his love."

I don't notice my tears until GG swipes them away.

"What do ya say? Ya ready to go get your man?"

My man.

"Yeah, GG. Yeah, I think I am."

"Hot damn," Betty Anne hollers from the next room. "'Bout time. Let's go get that hunka man candy."

"Did you know Betty Anne was in there?" I grumble.

"Betty Anne's my partner in crime, girly. Course I knew she was there. She missed the weddin', she didn't want to miss this, too."

I stare from GG to her best friend with the blue-tinted hair and laugh. "Only in this freaking town."

"Let's go, let's go. That Westbrook auction is starting at one. We can't be late. I've saved all month for that man," Betty Anne squeals.

"Betty Anne! He could be your grandson," I admonish.

"I'm old, chica, not dead. Now let's go."

Peace washes over me as I take these two old biddies out to the truck. I'm going to get my man.

Lexi: I'm ready.

exi: **I'm ready.**

"Holy shit." My voice booms out over the crowd.

Fuck. I forgot I'm mic'ed up for this stupid auction. Okay, it's not stupid. Colton is a crazy genius because Baker has never seen so many people at the Summerfest kick-off, but Christ. Lexi is ready. Wait, I hope that means what I want it to mean.

Easton: Does that

No!

"Preston," I yell into the crowd, "my phone died. Give me yours."

"East, this place is ready to revolt. You have to get the show on the road. Good luck. I'm headed to the kissing booth. Tell Halton to try not to look like he has to take a giant shit on stage, okay?" Colton slaps me on the back, then nudges me toward the front of the platform.

I don't get stage fright, but I scan the crowd, searching for her. I can't find her on my first or second pass over the people inching forward.

"You okay?" Halton mumbles, and I force myself to concentrate.

"Thank you all for coming today," I address the crowd, but my heart is seeking its mate. "My family and I are so honored to be here, sponsoring Summerfest's first annual Hollow Hearts fundraisers. We're looking forward to expanding into Burke Hollow and working with you all to revitalize the town and bring forth the qualities that make it so special.

"Before we begin with the auction, your lovely mayor, John Baker, would like to address some concerns."

A collective groan rings throughout the predominantly female crowd as Baker takes the stage.

"I have to find Lexi. If I'm not back by the time you're done, just introduce Halton," I whisper before handing him a microphone and the notecards Colton prepared for me.

"You got it, kid. Good luck," he yells before turning to the impatient crowd.

I hear him speak, but I'm on a mission to find my wife and weave my way through the throngs of people. *Where the hell are you, Locket?*

There's too many freaking people here, so I make my way to the outskirts of the audience and stalk the perimeter. Between her height and mine, it shouldn't be this hard to find her. Just as I'm about to turn around, I spot her. Then I nearly knock over three people in my quest to reach her.

"Locket," I sigh when she's finally within reach.

Turning slowly, I realize it's not Lexi.

"Lanes? Have you seen Lexi?"

"No. Ah, Dex? Where did she say she was going?"

"Oh my God, he looks fucking miserable. Doesn't he know how to smile anymore?" Loki asks, coming up beside me.

"What?"

Loki points to the stage. "He looks like he's going to throw up."

Following his line of sight, I see Halton on stage, and if I didn't feel so bad for him, I might laugh. He really does look miserable.

"Jesus. I told you to make sure he didn't come out on stage like that," Colton grumbles beside me.

"What do we do?" Preston asks, appearing out of nowhere.

"Ah …"

"Just look at this sexy hunka man here. Halton, do a little spin for us, will you?" Baker's voice rings out over the speakers.

Halton's eyes widen to the point of pain, and we all stand there staring at him.

"Ten bucks he spews his lunch all over the stage," someone chimes in.

I'm so focused on the shitshow happening before me, I can't even tell you who's speaking.

"This is his worst nightmare. He has stage fright. I assumed he'd grown out of it."

Turning toward the voice, I see Rylan watching him.

"How do you know he has stage fright?"

"Colty, you have to do something. This isn't okay."

Turning back toward Halton is like a traffic accident. You can't move, and you can't look away.

"Colton," she snaps, "do you have a credit card on you?"

We all watch as he absentmindedly hands her his wallet.

Raising a paddle, she yells out, "Twenty thousand dollars."

"Ba-uh. Twenty thousand going once," Baker splutters. "Going twice."

"It was him," Colton says beside me.

Oh, shit. I recognize that tone in his voice.

"Sold, to the lady in pink for twenty thousand dollars."

The crowd stands in silence. The previous bid had only been fifteen hundred.

"It was you," Colton screams toward the stage. "You're the

reason she left. You're the reason she wouldn't come back. You fucking bastard."

Before any of us can move, Colton is charging the stage.

"Shit, grab them," Preston bellows, and just like when we were kids, we all charge in.

By the time I reach the stage, Colt has knocked Halton to the ground, and they're a tangle of limbs rolling around.

Preston and Dex grab Colton, while Seth and Loki grab Halt and pull them apart.

"Get talking, East," Dex mumbles while Colton continues to thrash and yell obscenities.

"Ah, sorry to any kids in the audience. It's a little late to yell, 'Earmuffs!' I guess." Thankfully, the crowd gives me a polite chuckle, so I continue. "Well, Burke Hollow. This is us. We're a big, loud, crazy family. We love …" I glance over my shoulder to see two of my brothers still being subdued. "We love, and we fight big, but we always have each other's backs. And we're committed to having yours, too, if you'll have us."

That's when I see her. My girl. My wife. My future is standing in the back of the crowd with a crooked smile on her face.

"Ah, so, we'll get back to the auction—"

"Yes, I'll take you for two hundred," someone yells.

"Ha, thanks. Yeah, I'm not up for auction. We're only auctioning off single men today, and I am very much taken. I don't think my wife would appreciate me dating anyone else."

The crowd groans, but it's my brothers behind me that I hear the loudest. Peering over my shoulder, I grin and give them a shrug. "Sometimes, Vegas follows you home."

The shocked expressions on each of their faces are priceless as I return to the crowd.

"You see, once upon a time, there was this girl in Vegas."

Staring at Lexi, it's like we're alone in a crowd full of people.

"She could be a real bitch sometimes, and she thought she hated me. She also kicked my ass on the basketball court and gave me my first lesson: never underestimate a Heart woman."

All eyes shift around until they find Lexi. Slowly, the crowd parts, and they begin to usher her toward me.

"Our journey hasn't been easy, but life never is, right?" Lexi pauses and shakes her head. "You see, that night in Vegas, one little kiss turned into one little mistake that turned into forever. I want to be your forever, Locket. I want you to choose me."

When she doesn't move, I jump off the stage, so we're on even footing, and I wait for her. This has to be her choice. *Please, for the love of God, let her choose me.*

"I think I fell in love with you the first time your sassy mouth called me Mr. Sunshine."

Her lips twitch with amusement.

"Put that dang song on now," I hear GG yelling in the background, but I can't take my eyes off Lexi.

"The first time we danced, I knew I was in trouble."

"You're a terrible dancer," she laughs.

A song I should recognize but don't blares over the speakers, and Lexi throws her head back and laughs. The sound reverberates in my chest, and I know she'll always be home for me.

"Choose me, Lexi," I yell over the music.

Her grin warms me from the inside out, and when she swings her dress from side to side, recognition hits. It's the song from the movie *Dirty Dancing*.

"Do it," I yell. "I'll always catch you, sweetheart."

When people start to sing all around me, I remember every member of Burke Hollow is here with us. At this moment, I understand why she needed to come home. These people are her chaos collectors. They're the ones who picked her up when she was down. The ones who cheered her on when she was at her best. This is her home, and these people are her family.

"Let me be your family, Lex. Do it," I command.

With a look of pure determination, Lexi sprints toward me just as the song crescendos. Bending my knees when she leaps into the air, my hands find her waist, and I lift her over my head.

The applause around us is deafening as I let her slide down my body.

"And the crowd goes wild," she teases.

"They always do when the home team wins. Are we winning today, Lexi?"

"I never lose."

A happiness I didn't know existed fills my chest.

Placing my forehead on hers, I whisper, "Stubborn to the end."

"You wouldn't have it any other way."

"No, I wouldn't." Sliding my hands into her hair, I pull her in for a kiss. "I love you now and forever."

"I know." She smirks.

Clasping her hand, I turn to the crowd. "She said yes to forever."

The applause is smaller this time, and glancing around, I see why. Colton and Halt are nose to nose in a heated but quiet argument.

"What do you think that's about?" I whisper so only Lexi can hear.

She stares at me like I have two heads, then rolls her eyes —my prickly princess.

"Two words," she finally says. "Rylan Maroney."

My head jostles back and forth between Lexi and my brothers. When Halton storms off, I can't help but wonder what kind of shitshow we're in for now.

EPILOGUE

Six months later

"*I*'m pretty sure the girl is supposed to plan the wedding," Dillon says, entering the lodge.

We've come a long way in six months. It was rocky at first, but I have to admit, it's nice to have my friend back. He's a brother by choice, and once I got past my hurt, I was humbled by the sacrifices he made.

"Lexi isn't your typical girl. If I don't do it this way, it'll never happen."

"All right, man. You know her best." Colton laughs.

"Yeah, but she loved me first," Mason says, entering the room.

"Listen, asshole. You can have my job, but you'll never get my girl."

"He's kicking ass in your old job, actually. Makes me wonder what the hell you even used to do."

Fucking Preston with the jabs, but he isn't wrong. Mason was born to run Westbrook Development. My dad would have been proud.

"Anyone heard from Ash today?" I ask. I'd be lying if I said

282

I wasn't worried about him not showing up. It's become his MO as of late.

"He'll be here," Loki assures.

Dillon takes a seat next to me on the bench. "He was in the office when I left, but he had his suit on."

Dillon has gone to work for Envision. Ashton hired him to help look for Pacen, but Loki told me he's been invaluable in keeping tabs on Macomb and Fontaine. Fontaine, as expected, skipped town during Summerfest, but nothing gets past Ash. When he's ready to bring him in, he'll know exactly where to find him.

Thinking about Pacen makes my heart hurt. It's been over six months with no leads. It's as if she just vanished, and I can't tell who's more upset, Ashton or Dill.

"She's coming," Julia screams from the back hall.

Jesus, that woman is her own brand of crazy.

"I said, she's coming," she yells again.

"We heard you, Jules. The whole damn town did," Halton grumbles from his corner.

"Okay ... well, hide," she hisses.

"Julia, we're all crammed into this room for a reason. Just don't let her come in here."

"Right, okay. Hush. See you soon." She slams the door, and I hear her feet pitter-pattering down the hallway.

"Think she's going to like it?" Preston asks, patting me on the shoulder.

"Never know with her." I chuckle.

"What the freaking hell?"

"That was Lexi," Preston says in a panic.

I swallow so hard it makes an audible gulp sound.

"Sure was." *Maybe this was a mistake. One little mistake. Again.*

"Easton! Beast!" she screams just before the door swings open.

Lexi stands in the doorway in a robe I know they got at

the spa. I know because I planned out every minute of this day.

"Out." She stands to the side of the door, her finger pointing wildly at all my brothers.

They each grimace in their own way, then hurry out the door.

"What are you doing?"

"Calm down, Lexi."

"Mistake number four hundred and six. Don't ever tell me to calm down. It only pisses me off more."

Her insistence that we were a mistake has become a running joke for just about everything in our life.

"Okay, listen. How much do you remember of our wedding night?"

"A whole lot more once Sylvie showed us the video," she pouts.

Oh yeah, they've been sitting on that for a long time.

Crossing the room, I take her hand and lead her to the chair.

"Do you remember what I said to you on the bench?"

She scrunches up her nose while she thinks. It's become one of my favorite things about her because she has no idea she's doing it.

"It's a bit blurry," she finally concedes.

"I told you that you were going to make a beautiful bride someday. Someday is today."

"Beast," she says gently, "we're already married. This isn't necessary."

"Maybe not, but I want to give this to you. I want this for us, for our friends and family. I want everyone to witness our love."

She purses her lips, and I think she's going to fight me.

"Locket?"

She turns to face me.

"I've been planning this day since Summerfest. I want this for us."

Reaching into my pocket, I pull out the small box I've been carrying around for two weeks. When she doesn't move, I open her palm and set it down.

"Open it."

Lexi's eyes well with tears. They've been doing that a lot more easily these days. With a resigned sigh, she opens the box and pulls out a small locket, and freezes.

Moving so I can kneel in front of her, I open the small charm, hoping I'm not making the biggest mistake of my life.

"Oh. Oh my God," she cries. "East. H-How?"

"Well, GG helped with the picture of your mom."

Lexi whimpers, and I move quickly. Sitting in a chair, I drag her down onto my lap. "The other side took a little research."

"Pink diamonds," she whispers.

"She would have been born in April. The birthstone for April is a diamond. I went with pink to represent her." Undoing the clasp, I reach around her neck and help her fasten it. "Now, you can keep them both with you always. I never got to meet them, but I love them just the same because they're a part of you. I will love you forever, Lexi. I will love our family no matter the size."

She cries against my shoulder while I hold her. We do this sometimes, and I'll always be her strength.

I'm shocked when she pulls back suddenly, though.

"Okay. Let's do this," she says, rising to her feet with determination written in her beautiful features. "I saw that big, stinking princess dress you have in there. People are probably waiting. Let's get it over with."

"At least you make me laugh."

"Yeah, real comedian. But I just realized the sooner we get this wedding over with, the sooner we can get to the honeymoon sex. Er, we are having a honeymoon, right?"

And now I'm painfully hard.

"Yes, sweetheart. We're going on a honeymoon."

"All right, give me ten minutes."

I raise my eyebrows as she scurries out of the room, but true to her word, she's standing before me ten minutes later, and I'm having trouble breathing.

"You're perfect."

Clasping the locket around her neck, she uses her other hand to fan her face.

"I-I used to think, always be a bitch and find someone who can deal with it. It was easier to protect myself that way. B-But you make me not want to be a bitch, and I don't know how to protect myself when I'm vulnerable."

"That night in Vegas, I also told you that you didn't understand how marriage works. You do what you can, and I pick up the slack, remember? We're a team. I'll always have your back, and I'll protect you when you can't."

"Thank you for not giving up on me."

"It was never an option, Locket. You have the key to my soul."

We're interrupted by Julia's craziness. "Yes! Yes! Yes! I did it. I fucking did it. I did it, Lex! Here."

She hands Lexi a carton of eggs. "What the hell, Jules?"

One by one, the rest of my family follows the sounds of crazy until we're surrounded by everyone we love.

"That's my wedding present. I didn't think I'd do it in time, but I did. I. Did. It."

Slowly, Lexi opens the carton to reveal, gasp, eggs.

"Jules? Have you been drinking?" Lanie stage whispers across the room.

"Ugh, no," she replies, rolling her eyes.

Everyone in the room is considering having Julia committed. Everyone except Lexi.

"Sweetheart? Wh-What's the matter?"

Lexi has gone shockingly pale, and her entire body is

286

shaking in my lap. When she lifts her gaze, I'm gutted by the haunted look in her beautiful eyes.

Turning to Julia, we both stare. Julia just stands there smiling like a maniac.

"You-You-You," Lexi tries three times to get out.

"What am I missing?" I bark at Julia, who flips me off. "Julia?"

"You-You found …"

"I found your eggs," Julia finally yells. "It's taken me three damn months, but I found them at a facility in Boston."

Realization takes my breath away. Julia found Lexi's harvested eggs. I always knew Julia was a genius and on par with Ashton's computer skills, but this is something I never believed was a possibility.

Suddenly, Lexi goes limp in my arms, and I'm horrified to see she's passed out. Preston's wife comes running to the rescue. "For the last time, I'm a heart surgeon. But with this family, maybe I need to go into general practice," she jokes as she waves smelling salts under Lexi's nose.

"You travel everywhere with those things?"

"In this family, I've learned to prepare for anything." Emory smiles as Lexi comes to.

It takes her a minute to get her bearings, but when she does, the most heart-stopping smile I've ever seen graces her delicate face.

"Let's just file this under things not to do at a wedding, okay?"

Hauling her back into my lap, I kiss her head. "Best wedding ever. I love you, Locket."

"I love you, too, Beast. Always and forever."

*Want to see what happens when Julia becomes pregnant with Easton's baby? Grab the extended epilogue here! Or visit my website: www.averymaxwellbooks.com

Sneak Peek
Halton

Leaning back, I balance my chair on the back two legs with my arms crossed over my chest. I don't smile often, but I'm too fucking proud of myself right now not to be happy.

Glancing around the room at my brothers as understanding hits, I'm met with grateful eyes.

"Halt, y-you might have just s-saved GG's mountain," Easton stutters in awe.

"Not might have, East. I did, but we have to move quick."

GG is his maybe-girlfriend's grandmother, and our adoptive brother Dexter's grandmother-in-law, but I've developed a soft spot for the crazy old bird. The fact that I found a loophole to keep vultures from purchasing her mountain after Easton has been here for months makes me happy.

He can't hide his relief, and I feel good knowing I did that for him. Just because I'm destined to a miserable life alone doesn't mean that's what I want for him. Glancing around the room, I take in my family who is here, and think about the ones still in North Carolina.

We're not what you'd call a normal family by any means. For starters, we're billionaires, and on top of that, my mother has an odd habit of adopting people. It doesn't matter your age, if she decides you're family, you're subject to our chaos.

I'm the middle child of five boys. Add in four adopted brothers, spouses, and children, and Sylvie Westbrook runs an all-out circus.

Thinking about our family always leads me to the one that's no longer part of our chaos and a vicious amount of guilt sits like acid in my gut. Realizing I've tuned out the world around me again, I'm taken aback when our brother, Colton, enters the lodge, nearly taking the door off its hinges in his excitement.

It isn't until I see the object of my obsession on his arm that I lose my balance and topple to the ground.

Easton glances down at me with a 'what the fuck?' glare, but my lungs are closing in on me. I can't breathe. I can't swallow, and sweat is pooling at my spine. Rising from the ground, I find Rylan Maroney staring straight at me with a wounded expression and I lose my equilibrium.

I have to get the hell out of here, but they're blocking the entrance. If Easton notices my hands shaking or the near violent beat of my heart, he doesn't say so.

Vaguely, I hear the commotion break out around me. Everyone's happy to see her. Of course they are. She's Colton's best friend and the closest thing my brothers had to a sister until she up and left one day. Because of me and the one little lie I've regretted every day since.

"I can't be here," I mumble, thankful no one's listening.

Spinning on my heel, I barrel through the back door out into the yard where I nearly take out Lexi.

"Hey, Halt. Arrre you okay?" she drawls. "You don't look so good." Lexi is staring at me as if I'm about to keel over, and honestly, I might if I don't get out of here.

"Ash. Uh, I need to find Ash," I force out. My throat is unbearably dry, and I know I'm going to be sick. "I-I have to talk to Ash."

"Ah, okay. Do you need a ride? Are you sure you're okay?"

I nod wildly. "Yup, I'm fucking great. I just need to get out of here. See you later, Lex."

I don't wait for a response; I just take off at a dead run without caring if she thinks I'm losing my mind. I am, damnit. Rylan Maroney just crashed back into my life. The only girl I've ever loved. The only girl I've ever hurt. The only girl I can never have again because my brother is in love with her, and the one girl that will haunt my dreams because having her for one night was not nearly enough.

One night with her took my father from us. My conscience is an evil fucker.

I don't deserve her. "Colton loved her first," my father had said. "He's loved her his whole life, you can't take that from him. Your brothers always have to come first."

I should have listened to him. Maybe if I had he would still be alive, but I lied to him. Then I lied to her and crushed her heart. One little lie that broke a family just stormed back into my life and I don't know what to do.

Ashton, the true chaos coordinator, has always been my sounding board, and even though he's dealing with his own shit right now, I need him. I need him to ground me before I do something epically stupid and ruin our family forever. I've already taken our father from us, I can't risk my lie tearing Colton from us, too.

So, I run. Literally run as fast I can and hope the burning sensation in my lungs will take away the acid rot happening in my heart. By the time I reach the Wagon Wheel, every piece of my body is screaming at me and I welcome it. Anything to erase the image of Rylan's haunted gaze as I laid eyes on her for the first time in eight years.

I'm pounding on Ashton's door without caring about the other guests. When his door swings open, I burst through it.

"I-I don't know what to do, Ash. One little lie might tear our family apart, and it's all my fault."

Ashton sighs, and glances at the floor. "It wasn't your fault, Halt. Maybe what happened after, but Dad wasn't your fault."

My body heaves from the inside out and I spin on him so fast I almost fall over.

"What did you just say?"

"It wasn't your fault," he repeats even though I can tell it hurts him to speak.

"How the fuck do you know what I'm talking about, Ash? How many goddamn secrets do you keep in the name of our family?"

"Too many, Halt. Too fucking many. Sit down, I need to think."

Pre-Order One Little Lie Here!

If you loved this book please consider leaving a review. Reviews are how Indie Authors like myself succeed. Thank you!

Please leave a review here!

Avery hangs out in her reader group, the LUV Club, daily. Join her on FB to get teasers, updates, giveaways, and release dates first!
Avery Maxwell's LUV Club

ALSO BY AVERY MAXWELL

ACKNOWLEDGMENTS

It's time to acknowledge the people that help make these books possible, and I'm sure to forget someone. Sorry in advance.

First and foremost, my husband. Mr. Maxwell, you may never read this, but know that your love and support are truly what makes this possible. Thank you for being my puffin.

To my children. I know you hate that mommy works now but thank you for being the best part of every day.

Beth: My word finder, first reader, supporter, and encourager, thank you for being awesome. xoxo

Rhon: Where the hell would I be without you? Thank you for working tirelessly to get me organized and for keeping #teamavery on track.

Marie, Kia, and Leanne: Thank you for being my cheerleaders, especially when I'm doubting myself. I appreciate you all so much.

Street Team: OMFG! You guys are rock stars! Thank you for pimping me tirelessly. Your efforts have been incredible, and I don't know what I would do without you.

ARC Team: Thank you for continuing to read my stories. Your feedback is what makes me a better author.

Finally, YOU, my readers. Where would I be without you? Thank you for taking a chance on an indie author. Thank you for loving my characters and supporting me every step of the way. Thank you for asking for the next book the second you finish one. It's your enthusiasm that keeps me working tirelessly to bring you these crazy brothers. I LUV you all.

Imposter syndrome hits me hard. Every. Single. Time. It's because of you I'm able to continue, so thank you all from the bottom of my heart.

Dark City Designs: Jodi, you are amazing! Thank you for designing all the things! Your support and help with all things author-ish is appreciated more than you know. Xoxo

There For You Editing: Melissa, thank you for not tossing me overboard every time I write towards instead of toward or use an ... instead of a —. I honestly am not sure I'll ever get it, but I appreciate you fixing it. Every. Single. Time.

All my luvs,

Avery

ABOUT THE AUTHOR

A New-England girl born and raised, Avery now lives in North Carolina with her husband, their four kids, and two dogs.

A romantic at heart, Avery writes sweet and sexy Contemporary Romance and Romantic Comedy. Her stories are of friendship and trust, heartbreak, and redemption. She brings her characters to life for you and will make you feel every emotion she writes.

Avery is a fan of the happily-ever-after and the stories that make them. Her heroines have sass, her heroes have steam, and together they bring the tales you won't want to put down.

Avery writes a soulmate for us all.

Avery's Website www.AveryMaxwellBooks.com